D1436377

Justice is a Woman

ALSO BY CATHERINE COOKSON

NOVELS

Kate Hannigan
The Fifteen Streets
Colour Blind
Maggie Rowan
Rooney
The Menagerie
Slinky Jane
Fanny McBride
Fenwick Houses
Heritage of Folly
The Garment
The Fen Tiger
The Blind Miller
House of Men
Hannah Massey
The Long Corridor
The Unbaited Trap
Katie Mulholland
The Round Tower
The Nice Bloke
The Glass Virgin
The Invitation
The Dwelling Place
Feathers in the Fire
Pure as the Lily
The Mallen Streak
The Mallen Girl
The Mallen Litter
The Invisible Cord
The Gambling Man
The Tide of Life

The Slow Awakening
The Iron Façade
The Girl
The Cinder Path
Miss Martha Mary Crawford
The Man Who Cried
Tilly Trotter
Tilly Trotter Wed
Tilly Trotter Widowed
The Whip
Hamilton
The Black Velvet Gown
Goodbye Hamilton
A Dinner of Herbs
Harold
The Moth
Bill Bailey
The Parson's Daughter
Bill Bailey's Lot
The Cultured Handmaiden
Bill Bailey's Daughter
The Harrogate Secret
The Black Candle
The Wingless Bird
The Gillyvors
My Beloved Son
The Rag Nymph
The House of Women
The Maltese Angel
The Year of the Virgins
The Golden Straw

THE MARY ANN STORIES

A Grand Man
The Lord and Mary Ann
The Devil and Mary Ann
Love and Mary Ann

Life and Mary Ann
Marriage and Mary Ann
Mary Ann's Angels
Mary Ann and Bill

FOR CHILDREN

Matty Doolin
Joe and the Gladiator
The Nipper
Blue Baccy
Our John Willie
Mrs Flannagan's Trumpet

Go Tell It To Mrs Golightly
Lanky Jones
Nancy Nutall and the Mongrel
Bill and the Mary Ann
  Shaughnessy

AUTOBIOGRAPHY

Our Kate
Let Me Make Myself Plain

Catherine Cookson Country

CATHERINE COOKSON

Justice is a Woman

BCA

LONDON NEW YORK SYDNEY TORONTO

This edition published 1994
by BCA
by arrangement with Transworld Publishers Ltd

Copyright © Catherine Cookson 1994

The right of Catherine Cookson to be identified
as the author of this work has been asserted in accordance
with sections 77 and 78 of the Copyright Designs and Patents
Act 1988.

All of the characters in this book
are fictitious, and any resemblance
to actual persons, living or dead,
is purely coincidental.

This book is subject to the Standard Conditions of Sale of Net Books an
may not be re-sold in the UK below the net price fixed by the publishers
for the book.

All rights reserved. No part of this publication may
be reproduced, stored in a retrieval system, or
transmitted in any form or by any means,
electronic, mechanical, photocopying, recording,
or otherwise, without the prior permission of
the publishers.

CN5556

Printed in England by Clays Ltd, St Ives plc

Justice is a Woman

PART ONE

I

'As I see it, sir, you're a traitor to your class.'

'What is my class?'

The elderly gentleman, sitting very straight in the corner of the first-class carriage, pursed his lips and knobbled his chin before replying, 'By your manner, dress and voice, I would have said you were upper middle class, but as our conversation has proceeded so has your status decreased in my eyes.'

'And now you're forced to eject me from the middle class altogether, is that it?'

'You have said it, sir.'

The younger man sitting on the opposite side of the carriage bit hard on his lip, bowed his head for a moment, then glanced at his companion, who was sitting almost as stiffly as the gentleman opposite, and with much the same expression on her face. When she muttered under her breath, 'Joe,' he put his hand on her knee and shook it; then turning to his travelling companion again, he said, 'What your generation doesn't seem to understand, sir, is that times are changing: the war stuck spurs into the working man; he no longer considers himself so much merchandise, a means of barter, he's emerging; for the first time in generations he's seeing himself as an individual, and if he's not led properly he'll take over the reins and lead himself.'

'No working man can ever be a leader, a real leader; he's a bungler; the most he can rise to is soap-box oratory; he can excite a mob but he cannot quell a riot. The working man will always have to be led, whether in army or civilian life. It is in the order of things; it is as God and nature intended.'

As he exclaimed, 'Oh God Almighty!' Joe Remington sprang to his feet, an action which brought the elderly gentleman into an even straighter sitting position and caused Joe's wife, Elaine, to close her eyes tightly for a moment before she felt her arm grasped and herself being yanked up from the seat.

'Thank God! we're running in. Let's get out of here.'

'Joe! please.'

Joe released his hold on his wife's arm and allowed her to pass before him out of the first-class compartment into the corridor; then, almost as an afterthought, he stepped back and swung some hand luggage down from the rack before returning his travelling companion's glare of dislike and following his wife out and along the corridor to the carriage door.

When the train drew to a stop in Newcastle Central Station Elaine Remington disdained to accept her husband's assistance as she stepped on to the platform, so he turned from her and walked towards the guard's van.

He held the tickets, and so his wife had to wait for him at the barrier; and when eventually they were through and were standing under the covered way outside the station, their three large suitcases at their feet, Joe broke the silence, saying, 'I'm amazed that you are taking his side.'

10

'There are times and places for arguments, and a railway carriage, to my mind, is not one of them, and on such a subject as class.'

'It wasn't about class until *he* brought it up.'

'What would be your attitude if you were to meet him again?'

'There's little hope of that.'

'He said he was on his way to stay with Lord Menton.'

'Yes, yes, I know he did.'

'But . . . but you said Lord Menton's place was quite near; in fact, he's your neighbour.'

'Yes, I said that, but I didn't mean to imply that we are on visiting terms. Menton and my father!' He gave a mirthless laugh.

'I can understand about your father, but do you mean that you yourself are not on visiting terms with the Mentons?'

'That's just what I do mean, Elly. And look, my dear' – he turned to her fully now, his voice and manner softening – 'don't let's have a row. If we're going to have our first bust-up let it be over something important and not over an old diehard like him. Come on.' He put his arm through hers. 'Come on, smile. If you don't I'll kiss you in public long and hard and that'll cause a sensation, 'cos it isn't done, you know, kissing in public in the North.'

When she smiled faintly at him, he said, 'Ah, that's better, the sun's breaking through.' Then looking about him, he exclaimed, 'Where's David got to? I wired him; he should be here.'

'Do you always call the servants by their Christian names?'

'Christian names? David?' Joe had stepped from the kerb to the road and was gazing into the distance as he replied, 'We grew up together. Somehow, I don't look upon David as a servant.'

'Nor his wife?'

11

He turned his head in her direction and said quietly, 'No, nor Hazel.'

'But you call the butler Duffy.'

'That's only because he's always been known as Duffy from a boy, so I understand . . . And you know something, Elly?' – he stepped back on to the kerb and to her side again – 'we don't look upon Duffy as a butler; we are not in the class that has butlers. You knew that.'

'But he does buttle; he waits on table, and he acts as footman, et cetera.'

'Elly' – Joe's voice was very soft now – 'we'll have to start sending you to night-school. You're going to live on the outskirts of Fellburn, remember? You've seen the place, you've stayed at the house, you've met the people. True, it was a flying visit, but do you recall that I pointed out to you then that Fellburn . . . Newcastle and the whole Tyne area is so different from London in its outlook, even more so than Peking is to Paris; in fact, the Chinese and the French, I think, could have more in common than the Londoners – *your* Londoners, and Geordies . . . Remember the conversation we had after you had met Father?'

'Yes, yes, I remember it, Joe, very well.' Her voice was stiff.

'And what did you say then?'

She looked about her, at the mass of black-capped, dark-clothed workmen who seemed to have appeared from nowhere and were now pressing past them on their way into the station, and she muttered under her breath, 'This is neither the time nor the place.'

He was once again standing close to her, his arm linked within hers, and he bent down to her now and said, 'That's a favourite phrase of yours, isn't it? Well, not to be deflected by it I'll tell you what you said; it'll pass the time till David gets here. You said, "Darling, darling Joe, I don't care what

12

your father is, or will be, I don't mind if I have to live with him for the rest of my life as long as you have to live with him too." And if I remember rightly, Elly, you ended up by telling me that you adored me and that you would die if you didn't marry me.'

'Joe?'

'What is it, darling?'

'Shut up!'

'Yes, darling . . .' His jocularity was cut short by the honk-honk of a car horn, and he turned his head sharply and exclaimed, 'Ah, good. Here's David;' then he added immediately, with less enthusiasm, 'Good God! he has Dan with him.'

Half turning towards her, he exclaimed, 'I'm sorry about this, dear. It's David's father-in-law; he can be a bit of a trial. Sorry.'

The car that drew up slowly against the kerb was a 1912 Rolls-Royce. The back of it was cab-like; the front, although roofed, was open at the sides; and at the wheel sat a very tall man, who on first sight appeared to be black-skinned, although closer inspection showed him to be a half-caste: his skin was a deep chocolate-brown; his hair was black but not frizzy, and altogether he looked a handsome young fellow. In contrast, his father-in-law, Dan Egan, was an undersized man with a thin face, one cheek of which was scarred as if by a sword thrust.

'Hello there, David.'

'Hello there, Joe . . . Hello . . . hello, madam.' David had hesitated on the word, and Elaine, looking hard at him, merely inclined her head by way of reply.

'Did you have a good journey?'

'Yes, amazingly so, David; hardly anyone on the train.'

'They're frightened to come 'cos they won't get back; the whole bloody lot stops the night. We'll show 'em.'

13

Both Joe and David exchanged glances as Dan Egan, addressing himself solely to the windscreen, went on, 'The country's behind us, every man jack. I'll bet they'll remember the third of May, nineteen twenty-six, for years to come. We'll show 'em.'

Joe settled his wife into the back seat, then took his place beside her; and David, after stowing away the luggage, got behind the wheel again and started up the car. And all the while Dan Egan went on talking. And it was impossible not to listen to him; the only alternative would have been to close the dividing window, but Joe couldn't do that.

'Less wages and longer hours. By God! would you believe it. But we won't budge. No, not a bloody inch. Not a penny off the pay, not a minute off the day, that's Cook's law, and of every man jack of us. Baldwin, Churchill, the lot of 'em . . . somebody should put a bullet through Churchill; he calls us the enemy; the working man's the enemy of the country, he says. Aye well, by God! he'll see what enemy he's up against afore we're finished with him. The Samuel Commission. Did you ever hear owt like it?' He now turned to glare at David. 'Improve the industry, they said; amalgamation of smaller pits, they said; better working conditions, they said, such as pit-head baths. Pit-head baths, I ask you! Longer hours and less pay they're offering us, but they'll go to the expense of pit-head baths. They talk like bloody maniacs, the lot of 'em, bloody maniacs. Baths . . . clean their arses . . .'

'Dan!' Joe was leaning forward now, tapping him on the shoulder. 'You know what they say in the club; ladies present.'

Dan Egan glanced over his shoulder and met the cold gaze of Elaine, and his head made the slightest movement of acknowledgement as he said, 'Aye, well, I'm a bit het-up, you see. Sorry.' Then looking full at Joe, he added, 'I suppose you think I'm taking a liberty ridin' in your car; well, I never

14

asked to. I was on me way back on me feet when David here spotted me and he said you wouldn't mind.'

'No, no, of course we don't mind. And we understand it's a very testing time.'

'Testin'!' The head was turned away now, the gaze and the voice directed towards the windscreen once more. 'Testin', that's puttin' it mildly, lad; there'll be skull and hair flyin' afore this is over, you mark my words. At midnight a national strike starts: transport and railway workers, heavy industry, gas, electricity, the whole blo . . . lot. The whole country's behind us.'

Squeezing Elaine's hand, Joe looked at her helplessly as Dan continued to talk while the car sped over the bridge into Gateshead and through the town and on into Fellburn; and there it skirted the docks and Bog's End, ran by the park and up Brampton Hill, past the large residential houses standing in their own grounds, and on through the new suburbs which were built on yet another hill, from which could be seen the headings of the Beulah pit and the pit village in the distance; then past the walled estate of Lord Menton, which gave way to a stretch of open country that rose slowly upwards to Joe Remington's home, the house known as Fell Rise.

You couldn't see anything of the house until you topped the Rise and there, in the distance, you saw what looked like a miniature church spire. Not until you were well past the belt of trees, past a large paddock and had turned in through the iron gates and up a drive bordered by larches, did you realise that the spire was the roof of what appeared to be a glass observatory.

This part of the square tower rose above a number of red-tiled roofs and was enclosed in glass from where the whole surrounding countryside could be viewed. One could imagine too that each room on the second floor of the house had its own separate roof for there were four lead-lined gutters running into pipes down the front of the house. Below the deep eaves the walls were covered to almost the ground-floor windows with wooden scrolling. All the woodwork was painted red, as was the main door, from which four shallow steps led down to the shingled drive.

To the left of the drive the shingle gave way to a paved courtyard, one side bordered by outhouses and stables, the latter now used as a garage. At right angles to this were the kitchen quarters; and set deep into the wall of the third side of the patio, in the main house, was a huge stained-glass window.

To the right of the drive the house was bordered by a narrow terrace from which two sets of steps led down to a wide lawn. This itself was edged by the netting of a tennis court; and around the whole area were well tended flower beds. The remainder of the seven acres of grounds lay at the back of the house: there was a kitchen garden, at the end of which were four long greenhouses, and a formal rose garden; then a small lake and woodland.

As David drew the car to a stop in front of the main door, Joe jumped out, then held out his two hands to Elaine, saying, 'Well, here we are! You're home, Mrs Remington.' He assisted her from the car, took her arm and escorted her to the foot of the steps; but there he pulled her to a momentary halt and called over his shoulder, 'Be seeing you, Dan. Thanks, David.'

There was no reply from Mr Egan, nor one from David, except that David inclined his head towards him, smiled and nodded.

'Must you, darling?'

'Must I what?'

They were at the top of the steps now and Elaine, smiling faintly, said, 'Oh, it doesn't matter; I suppose it's you.'

'Oh, you mean saying goodbye to old Dan?'

'Yes, I suppose that's what I mean.'

'Well—' There was a slight alteration in the expression on Joe's face: the buoyant breeziness faded for a moment and his broad features became set as he stared at her before saying, and with no lightness in his tone now, 'You don't understand them yet; but then, you've got a lifetime for that.'

As he went to open the door it was almost pulled out of his hands, and they were confronted by a small stout woman, and when she exclaimed, 'Well! well! I was up with himself and didn't hear you,' he replied jovially, 'Hello there, Mary. Well, here we are then.'

'And only just in time, I'd say; another day and you wouldn't have got back.'

Mary Duffy was speaking to Joe but she was looking at her new mistress, and to her she now added politely, 'I hope I see you well, ma'am, and you enjoyed your honeymoon.'

'Yes . . . yes, Mrs Duffy; thank you. Although naturally I was sorry it had to be cut short.'

'Well, there'll be more than that cut short afore this is over, I'm thinkin' . . . I'm glad you're back.' She was looking at Joe again. 'Himself is still away up there; his legs are givin' him gyp, an' don't I know it: he must have sharpened his temper at the same time he was stropping his razor this mornin' 'cos he hasn't got a civil tongue in his head, not even for the cat.'

'Well' – Joe pushed the old woman gently in the shoulder – 'don't tell me you can't deal with his temper, you've had plenty of practice. The day you let him off with anything I'll know you're slipping.'

He turned now and looked to where his wife was ascending the stairs; then, bending swiftly to Mary, he said, 'A nice tea, China, in about twenty minutes. And I hope there's plenty of hot water.'

'It's as usual.'

Mary Duffy watched young Joe, as she thought of him, running up the stairs after his wife, and when he had disappeared from view she did not immediately return to the kitchen quarters but remained perfectly still, for in her mind's eye she was picturing a little boy descending the stairs for the first time on his own, one small hand trying to encompass the stout rails of the balustrade, while the other pushed off the hand that would have assisted him.

The picture in her mind moved on, and she saw the boy at the age of seven standing practically on the spot where she was standing now, his eyes and throat full of tears, and endeavouring not to let them flow while he waited for his mama to come down the stairs and escort him to the boarding-school for young gentlemen. That had been the end of one long fight and Mama had had the final word. 'Justice is a woman,' she had been fond of saying. Aye, and she was right, justice was a woman, and she had passed sentence on himself; she had made him pay for his misdeeds, more so than if he had stood before the final judge.

And now it was as if the years had slipped away and the past was the present, for that bit of short-skirted humanity who had just gone up those stairs was as like his mam in face and manner as if she had been born again. It was strange, very strange that he should choose one like that . . .

Still, things were more even now. Young Joe might be like his father in lots of ways, stubborn, self-willed, and vulnerable, aye, vulnerable, but he had one up on his father: he'd had education and he could use his tongue; he wouldn't have to resort to bloodies and buggers and blasts and sods to get over what he meant, and in doing so scorch the sensitive ears of his lady wife. No, young Joe could sieve the thoughts in his head through his teeth, and when they hit you they stuck in like splinters. No, that young madam wouldn't have it all her own way as his mother had had, and she thanked God for it. But as yet he was running like hot butter all over her.

Tea, he said, in twenty minutes, China. She swung her heavy body around and walked slowly towards her kitchen.

Elaine had removed her outer clothes and was now taking in the sitting-room that adjoined the bedroom, the room Joe had said was once known as the boudoir. It still had traces of that boudoir about it, which Elaine had already decided in her mind she would eliminate as soon as possible, for the betasselled velvet pelmets cut down the light from the two windows, one at the front of the house looking south, the other set in the west wall, giving a view over the gardens. Then there was the Louis XV suite: a very nice framework, but the tapestry had lost all its original colour and was threadbare in parts. Well, she would alter than too.

'What were you saying?' She looked up at Joe as he bent down towards her and repeated, 'I was saying, Mrs Daydreamer, how would you like to accompany me to the floor above and say hello to your father-in-law?'

'Oh, Joe!' She gave a little impatient movement of her head, even while smiling at him. 'I want a bath and a change of clothes, and more than anything I want a drink.'

'Well, as I told you, tea should be up at any minute now. No; I said twenty minutes.' He looked at his watch. 'Another ten minutes. But it isn't tea you want, is it?' He poked his face down towards her, and when she smiled at him with compressed lips he kissed them before straightening up, pointing his finger at her and saying, 'No drink before dinner.'

'Don't bully me.'

Again he was bending over her; again his lips were on hers; then, holding her face gently between his hands, he said, 'Who could ever have the heart to bully you? Persuade, coerce, flatter, beg, but not bully.'

19

Gently she pressed herself from him and laid her head against the back of the couch, and, smiling at him softly, she said, 'Go and see your father. Tell him I'll be up as soon as I've had a bath and changed and had . . . a sup of tea.' She mouthed the last words in an imitation of the Northern dialect.

Joe smiled happily as he left the room, hurried across the wide square landing and ran up the stairs to the second floor, where his father had spent most of his time for the past three years.

Why a man who was suffering from severe arthritis in most of his joints should want to spend his time in this part of the house, where the four large rooms were partly attics, was puzzling until you actually entered the rooms; then the views from the windows provided one answer. But the main reason that kept Mike Remington up here most of his time was that two of the rooms were used as his workshops.

Mike had been an engineer before he became a business-man; now incapacitated, he had returned to his original trade. In a small way, it could be said, for he worked in wire and wood. Slowly and painfully he created churches, houses and ships. However rough he might be with words and towards people, he was, and always had been, tender with wood.

The last but not the least of the attractions of the second floor was that if you had the agility to climb the steep staircase, you had a view from an observatory that was second to none in the county, for on a clear day you could see beyond Fellburn to the bridges that spanned the river at Newcastle; and in the opposite direction, away over the pit-heads, you could see the upper outline of the mighty cathedral at Durham.

When Joe pushed open the first door on the landing he was

surprised to see his father sitting by the
looked the drive, his gnarled, twisted finge

When the head was turned towards him,)
'Hello, there. What's the matter? Have you ͼ
on strike before the others? You can be blacklisͳ
you know.'

He was now standing in front of the man whose sı.   ͻ
covered the back of the chair and still gave off the impͳ ͻsion
of strength, as did the big iron-grey-haired head above them.
Although the flesh on the face was sagging, particularly
around the eye sockets, his father was still handsome. But
it was the clear steely blue of the eyes that gave power to the
face, and now they were directed on his son, and what they
saw made some part of him ache, for it was as though he were
looking inwards at himself when his body had been vital, his
back straight and his joints moving freely in their sockets.

'You've been in the house fifteen minutes,' he said
accusingly.

'Have I?' Joe looked at his watch. 'Yes, you're right; fifteen
minutes. What did you expect me to do? Bound up the stairs
and leave my wife, my new wife, to find her way around?'

'Summat like that.' There was a quirk on Mike's lips now
which gave way to a smile, then a chuckle, in which Joe
joined.

'Well, how did it go?'

'Like any other honeymoon.'

'That's not sayin' much.'

Joe now turned and, pulling a chair forward, sat down,
saying, 'Everything's fine, except that we could have done
with another week. I cursed the strike.'

'You wouldn't be the only one; there's going to be hell
to pay afore this lot's over. Just imagine it: the whole
bloody country coming out; everything at a standstill; it's
unbelievable.'

..ow about our lot?'

'Oh, our lot.' Mike scratched his ear. 'Well, you've got something on your hands there, lad, I can tell you.'

'But more than half of ours aren't union men.'

'No, that's true, but a good third of them are. And if sympathy doesn't get the rest to join, the name blackleg hurled at them often enough, or being dragged up an alley and the guts beaten out of them, might help to change their minds.'

'Aw, I don't think it'll get that far.'

'Lad, you know nowt about it; so far in your life you haven't seen men really hungry. And that's not the worst. They can go without it themselves, but when their wives and bairns have cramps in their bellies for want of a bite, then I say, look out!'

'What does Geordie think? He's in charge, he should know the feeling.'

'Aye, he does, 'cos like me he's seen this happen afore. Oh aye, he knows the feeling all right; he's got reason to. He remembers being punched silly by some bloke from Birtley. He was in the pits then, just a young lad. His father had died and was buried down below – they never found him – and he had to support his mother and four young 'uns, an' so he went back, along with some Irish the owners had brought in. He said never again, never again. There was no room in the pits for him after that, and that's when he came to me. Oh, Geordie knows the feeling all right. He's particularly mad at this minute 'cos of the order that's just come in.'

'What order?'

'Well, what were you after afore you went away.'

'Oh, you mean the wireless cabinets. It's clinched?'

'Aye it's clinched.'

'Oh, that's splendid.'

'Splendid? Yes, as you say, splendid, if you're able to make them, but if they come out, what about it?'

22

'Well, it'll certainly hold things up, but I can't see them being out for more than a couple of weeks or so; the country wouldn't stand it.'

'You'd be surprised, lad, what the country'll stand. An' you'll be surprised at what those bloody miners'll stand to get a fair deal. Mind, I'm not for them' – he stabbed his finger at his son – 'but at the same time I'm not agin them, for God knows only starvin' men and bloody madmen would go down a pit anyway.'

'Some like it.'

'What?'

'I said some like it working down the pit. It's a way of life. You know it is.'

'I know no such bloody thing. They go down because there's no other way for them to get their bread. Anyway, after you've had a bite I think you'd better get along there and have a crack with Geordie. You won't see any of the men, they'll likely be gone by then, but try an' find out what that Barry Smith and Bill James is up to, because they're two bloody red Russians, and they're the ringleaders, if I know anything. I should 'ave given them the push years ago.'

Joe stood for a moment looking down at his father, whose eyes were now directed to his knees, each cupped by a gnarled hand, and he asked quietly, 'What have you been doing while I've been away? Did you finish the ship?'

'The ship?' Mike's head came up. Then he shook it. 'Somehow, I hauled myself up to the glasshouse' – he jerked his head towards the steep open staircase that rose from the end of the room – 'and did a lot of gazing about me 'an quite a bit of thinkin'.' He nodded slowly as he stared into Joe's eyes and repeated, 'Aye, quite a bit of thinkin'.'

'What about, may I ask?'

'You.'

'Me?'

23

'Aye; I said you. You and your marriage and your future. Look at me.'

'I'm looking.'

'I mean, look at me an' me life: what have I done with it? Where's it landed me? Fifty years of age. I should be at the height of me power, but here I am, a prisoner of me bones.'

'You could be helped.' Joe's voice was soft. 'I've told you, there are spas and places . . .'

'And I've told you, lad, I'm goin' to no bloody spas, sittin' with me belly hangin' over me pants and seeing meself pictured in dozens of other bellies around me, and havin' nurses, young 'uns at that, seeing to you as if you were senile. No, it's not for me. What I've got I'll put up with. As Graham says, I'm me own worst enemy because I've voted for a slow death. The latest is, he's talking of putting pins in me hips. By the way, we've never talked of the person in question. Where is she?'

'She's having a bath and a cup of tea. She told me to tell you she'll be up very shortly.'

'Oh, I'm thrilled.'

'Father!'

'All right, all right, I'll behave myself. I promise I'll come out with nothing worse than bloody in her hearing.'

'Do you like her?'

'I don't know yet, lad. What have I seen of her in order to answer that question? You met her three months ago on that trip to London when you went about the Bakelite for that order. Then she came down here once for a week-end, during which time I spoke to her twice; no, no, I'm tellin' a lie, three times. Then what do you do? You spring it on me you're going to be married by special licence in London and take your honeymoon on your holiday. And now you ask me, do I like her? . . . Do *you* like her?'

24

'What!' The word came out on a laugh.

'Just what I said, do you like her?'

'Oh, Father, don't be silly. Why ask such a damn fool question?'

'That isn't a damn fool question. And you're no damn fool; you know what I mean all right. There's all the difference in the world atween likin' and lovin'. Oh, you love her, I've no doubt about that. She's got into your blood. I saw that straightaway. But now the question you've got to ask yourself is, do you like her? 'Cos let me tell you this, lad, liking's much more important in marriage than love, and you'll find that out. But' – he sighed deeply – 'what the hell am I goin' on about. What we should be putting our minds to at the present moment is not liking or loving but how we're going to keep the shops going if they start getting at our blokes; so go on, get yourself off and down to see Geordie.'

Joe turned and made his way towards the door, saying on a laugh now, 'All right, I'll go straight down, but you'll have to look after my wife.'

He had opened the door and had one foot on the landing when his father spoke again, but softly: 'Joe.'

'Yes?'

'Don't make the same mistakes I did, lad. No matter what happens, don't do it.'

They stared at each other for a moment across the space before Joe closed the door and walked to the top of the attic stairs. Before descending them he stood with his head bent, his teeth biting the side of his lip as he looked down them. Don't make the same mistakes I did, his father had said. By God! no. Oh no, he wouldn't do that. No matter what happened, he wouldn't do that.

2

'All right, darling; but promise me, now promise me faith-fully you will take me into Newcastle tomorrow night and do a show and perhaps dance. Oh yes, let's dance.' Elly put her hand across the dining-room table and caught his.

'All right, I promise, a show or a dance, perhaps both, that's if you behave yourself tonight and be very tactful and don't turn your nose up at anything you might see or hear.'

'As if I would.'

'Yes, as if you would. All right then, I'll put you to the test: we'll call in at Dan Egan's house before we go to the meeting.'

'That's the man who never stops talking; Brooks's father-in-law?'

'David's father-in-law.' He held up a finger as if chastising her.

'Oh Joe!' She shook her head at him now. 'I can't get used to calling the servants by their Christian names. And there's something else, we really must do something about Ella.' She was bending forward, whispering now: 'She can't be called Ella when you will insist on calling me Elly. Why, this

26

morning when you called across the hall, she came running from the kitchen. I've told you, it won't do; she must answer to something entirely different, such as Annie or Jane.'

'Well, you'll have to tell her, won't you?' He cut into a piece of Stilton, placed it on a dry biscuit, then bit on it before adding, 'But I know what her reactions will be. Eeh! ma'am, what! change me name? I've always been called Ella. I don't see why I should change it. No, no; I don't see why I should.'

'She wouldn't dare.'

He stopped chewing and looked at his wife. His expression was straight, rather stiff now, and all banter had gone from his voice as he said, 'She *would* dare. I've told you, Elly, these people are individuals.'

'They're servants.'

'Yes, they might be, as we're all servants one way or another, but they're not the bowing and scraping kind you're used to. I warned you, I told you.'

Reaching out towards the cheese tray, she took up a small piece of Cheshire and almost slapped it on to her plate as she said, 'As I see it, when you're paying people they should be made to conform to set standards.'

'This isn't London or Huntingdon, this is the North East of England.'

'Yes, yes, I know.' She was nodding her head briskly now. 'You've told me that so often in the past week that I've no doubt about it at all now. Definitely it is the North East of England, and it's more foreign, I might tell you, than a foreign country; they even speak a different language.'

Now he was laughing, his head bent, his chin gripped in his fist, and he nodded as he said, 'You're right there, but if you study hard you'll soon learn it; they'll be only too eager to help you, all of them.'

'Oh, don't be facetious.'

27

His head came up, the smile left his face again and he stared at her for a moment before he muttered, 'It's about time we were going; that is, if you're still coming with me?'

She looked up at him, unblinking. 'Yes, I'll come with you . . . in a moment,' she said and rang the small bell that was to her hand on the table. When the door opened and Duffy entered, his tall, lean body seeming to act as merely a peg for his dark suit, she turned her head slightly towards him and said, 'Send . . . Ella in to me, will you please?'

Duffy did not answer, 'Yes, ma'am', but stared at her for a second before turning about and going out.

'Oh my God!' exclaimed Joe.

'What?' As she spoke the door opened and Ella entered.

Ella took after her Aunty Mary in many ways, the most obvious being her smallness and inclination to plumpness. She was also pretty. She came right up to the edge of the table and, looking at her mistress, she said, 'You wanted me, ma'am?'

'Yes.' Elaine's voice was smooth, even sweet. 'It's . . . it's about your name.'

'Me name, ma'am?'

'Yes, your name. You see it's all very confusing, because my husband' – she glanced towards Joe – 'insists on abbreviating my own name which, I'm sure you have noticed, sounds similar to yours, and so in future we will call you by another name. Which would you like? Jane, Mary, Annie?'

Ella had moved one step away from the table. She now glanced towards the young master, who was standing at the sideboard with his back to her; then she looked at her new mistress again, and her face no longer looked pretty but pugnacious as she said, 'Me name's Ella, ma'am. I've always been Ella and I don't fancy being called Mary or Jane or Annie, but if it's got to be, then himself will have to tell me. But I doubt if he will, as he always calls me Ella.'

The mistress and the maid stared at each other and it was evident that the mistress could hardly believe her ears. She turned now and looked towards her husband and Joe said grimly, 'Leave it.'

There was a full minute's silence in the room before Ella turned about and marched away, and the door had hardly closed behind her before Joe burst out, 'I told you! I warned you! You're getting off on the wrong foot: it's no good trying to get your own way with a silver tongue; they can see through it; and once you get their backs up you won't be able to get near them; the Roman Wall will be easier to get through, I keep telling you.'

'Yes, you keep telling me. We've been married just over three weeks and all you have done is tell me what I must do in order to survive here. Now *you* can tell *me* something. Who's master in this house, and who is to be mistress of it? Or, if there is to be no mistress, just a master, again I ask you, who is it?'

There was another long pause before Joe said gruffly, 'As long as my father's alive he's the master here: he built this house, he loves the place, even if it has turned into his prison. Does that answer your question?'

'And what is *your* position?'

He thrust his jaw forward and brought his teeth together, slanting his gaze at her before saying, 'Just the son, and the manager of the works, and it's likely to stay that way for a very long time because arthritis kills slowly. And that's how I would want it.'

He moved towards her now and gently drew her to her feet, and when they were face to face, his deep brown eyes looking into her clear grey ones, and his tone once again soft and placating, he said, 'But there's no question as to who's mistress.' His arms went about her and his lips brushed themselves backwards and forwards over her brow as he

29

murmured, 'Play it softly, dearest. Try to play it softly.'

Looking into her eyes again, he said brightly, 'Come on; let's go over to David's. You've never seen his house; nor have you met Hazel. She came back from visiting her mother's last night. Come on now, and let them see you as I see you. Let them all see you as I see you and then they'll love you; they won't be able to help themselves.'

He pressed her tightly to him, and after a moment she responded and they kissed and made up for the second time since she had come into the house five days ago.

The Cottage, as it was called, was situated to the side of the entrance gates. It was actually the original house that had been built two hundred years previously and had taken its name from the land known as Fell Rise, but when Mike Remington created his dream twenty-five years before, he had transferred the name to his house and the original Fell Rise had been renamed The Cottage.

It was a pretty place, both inside and out. Black timbers patterned the outside, and inside, the thick beams that ran down the middle of the living-room ceiling were still in excellent condition, with hardly a trace of worm in them. And the furniture, too, was in keeping, being mostly of black oak, with upholstery of chintz.

Hazel Egan had married David Brooks a year before when they were both twenty-three years old. That Hazel, a good-looking, tall, brown-haired, brown-eyed girl should marry a half-caste, be he ever such a decent chap, was regarded with disapproval, not only in the Beulah pit village but over most of Fellburn too; and it was said that she wouldn't have been driven to it if she hadn't got herself into the family way. Yet, as the months went by, it became clear that she had not married David for that reason, for as yet there was no sign of a pregnancy.

Their courtship had been long and furtive. In their early childhood days they had gone to the same school, and then to the surprise of many, and condemnation of not a few, David had passed for the Grammar School, and their ways had divided. But only for a time. Ever since they were both fifteen years old they knew that they loved each other, and when they were twenty they knew that because of David's father's objection, and the strong objection, not only of her own parents, but of her elder brothers, they might never be able to marry. Yet they still went on loving and hoping.

In 1924, when David's father died, one big obstacle was removed, and it was then that Hazel took it into her own hands to remove the rest, and so early in 1925 they were married in a registry office, which in itself added to the disgrace of marrying a coloured man. But what did it matter? As Hazel said to her mother, when you turn out the light, all men are black.

She now stood encircled in David's arm to the side of the window from which they could see to the far end of the drive, and without taking her gaze from the window, she said, 'What makes you think I won't like her?'

'She's uppish.'

'Is that why you don't like her?'

'No. I don't like her because she doesn't like me; she sees me as a black man.'

'Don't be silly.' She pressed closer to him. 'Anyway, you're not a black man, you're a nice brown man, and it wouldn't matter to me if you were as black as Cherry Blossom boot polish, although they do make a nice brown one, you know.'

As she giggled he turned his head and looked at her. There was no smile on his face but his voice was deeply tender as he murmured, 'Why should I be so lucky, while he lands up with her?'

'What are you going on about, what do you mean? She likely suits him.'

'Wait till you see her . . . Ah, here they come. He said they'd drop in, but I didn't think he'd bring it off.' He now sprang back from the window, pulling her with him and, pointing to the chintz-covered couch set at an angle to the side of the fireplace, he hissed, 'I'm sitting there reading the paper and when the knock comes on the door I'll call casually, "Come in," and make out I'm very surprised to see them. And you are in the kitchen making a pot of tea, and you put your head round the door and you're very surprised to see them an' all.'

For a moment they leant against each other and smothered their laughter; then David took up his position on the couch and Hazel ran into the kitchen.

When the knock came on the door, David called casually, 'Come in,' and when it opened and he saw Joe stand aside to allow his wife to enter, he sprang up from the couch with well feigned surprise, saying, 'Oh. Oh, I didn't expect you, ma'am. But come in; you're welcome.' Then turning his head to the side, he called, 'Hazel!' and Hazel answered him from the kitchen, saying, 'Just a minute, I'm mashing the tea.'

'Oh!' Hazel appeared in the doorway to the sitting-room; then coming slowly forward, she looked at the wife of her husband's employer, the employer who was also his lifelong friend, and she saw immediately what David meant.

'This is Hazel, my wife, ma'am.'

'How do you do?'

'How do you do, ma'am? Won't you sit down?'

'Thank you.'

There was a moment's silence while they all became seated. Then Joe, looking at David, said, 'Before going to the meeting in the Lodge I thought I'd like to have a word with Dan.' He now turned his gaze towards Hazel and said,

'Your father knows how the land lies better than any man. Our men have a proposal to make, but I doubt if it will be acceptable as they're not in the miners' good books and, of course, it's to be understood, so I thought we'd call round at your home and discuss . . .'

'Oh!' Hazel was flapping her hand in Joe's direction now and laughing as she said, 'On Friday night! Oh, you know what our house is like on a Friday night; it's the gathering of the clans before they go to the club.' She turned now and looked towards Elaine, explaining, 'You see, ma'am, there are eleven of us and as yet there are only three married, including myself, but the other two, my married brothers, they always come home on a Friday night with their wives and children. There are five grandchildren and it's like bedlam. You won't be able to get in.'

'Oh, I'm not that big; I'm sure I'll be able to squeeze in somewhere,' said Elaine.

As they laughed they looked towards the seated figure, her grey skirt riding well above her knees, the short matching coat lying flat on her chest like a schoolgirl's blazer, and the red toque-shaped straw hat pulled well down over her pale brow and ears. The shape of her face seemed to exaggerate the height of the hat, for in itself it was long; the skin was clear and very delicately tinted near the cheekbones but showed no tinge of red because that was unfashionable; the nose was small for the length of the face, and straight, the nostrils thin. It was the mouth that was the most striking; it was beautifully shaped and when she spoke both her bottom and upper lips spread wide to show in a complete oval her perfect white even teeth.

The picture that Elaine should have presented was of a beautiful twenty-two-year-old young lady and, because of her colouring and slight figure, appearing much younger than her years, but the impression that she actually created was of someone much older, someone who was entirely in command of herself: in short, a sophisticated woman. The look that she now turned on her husband could have been taken merely as one of interest, but behind it was hidden her sheer amazement at how he was addressing the chauffeur-gardener, for he was saying, 'I'm sorry, David, to drag you out after tea, but if I leave the old lady outside the Lodge for any length of time those little beggars will have all her clothes off.'

And she was equally astonished at the chauffeur's answer, 'Oh, that's all right, J . . . sir. You know I don't need an excuse to drive her at any time.'

The man had been about to call him Joe again! Really! What next? Play it softly, he had said. And this house, this kind of house for a chauffeur was entirely out of his class. Why, it was as big as the house her cousin Kathryn lived in . . . had been reduced to living in, and she was a titled lady. The world had turned topsy-turvy; at least this quarter of it had.

She had been here a week now and as yet she had met no-one of any note, either young or old, nor had she spoken to one intelligent human being. All people could talk about was the strike. Why did they take any notice of such people as miners? That's what she would like to know. They were always causing trouble, and now they had brought the whole country to a standstill. They were barbarians, ignorant, uncouth barbarians, and Joe was seemingly taking great pleasure in the fact that he was intending to thrust her among them.

Eleven people, this girl said, were in her family! That was likely why she had jumped at the chance to get away; and, of course, there had been the added incentive of occupying a house such as this, even though she'd had to risk social ostracism to get it. She didn't like the girl. She looked cheap, and of course she must be to have taken the step she did, marrying a coloured man. Huh! Moreover, she was much too free, much too pert. She was another one like . . . Ella, or Jane, as she would be called if she got her way, and she *would* get her way.

'It's a lovely room, isn't it?' Joe brought her wandering mind back to him and she said, 'Yes; yes, it is, most fascinating. It puts me in mind of my cousin's house.' She now turned to Hazel. 'My cousin is Lady Kathryn Fowley; she lived at one time in Pelton Towers, but then because of reduced circumstances she had to take a smaller house, and it's very like this one, but' – she smiled at Hazel now – 'nothing like as prettily furnished.'

'Well, I can't take credit for that,' Hazel replied without smiling. 'It was himself . . . I mean the master who had it all set out in the first place.'

'Oh. Oh, I see.'

'Well, are we going?' Joe had risen to his feet, as also had David, and as David went to get his coat, he said, 'What about you coming along, Hazel?' He turned and glanced in Elaine's direction before adding, 'You might help to soften the blow for ma'am.'

'No. If you don't mind I'll stay put; I've lots of things to see to. And anyway, I don't think anything or anybody could soften the sight of our house on a Friday night; it's something once seen never forgotten.' And straightaway she added, 'Goodbye, ma'am, and thank you for visiting me.'

'It's been a pleasure. Goodbye.'

David opened the door, and Elaine stepped out onto the narrow brick terrace, but she turned her head quickly and looked back into the room and at Joe, who had taken hold of Hazel's hand and was whispering something that she couldn't catch. What she did hear was his last words which were, 'Be seeing you, then.'

35

As she turned about again and stepped on to the grass drive her thoughts were of how incredible the whole situation in the household was.

It was certainly true what that girl had said; nothing could soften the sight of the Egan family on a Friday night. Elaine stood just inside the doorway of the small room, which was crowded with men, women, youths, and girls, and seemingly numerous children of all ages; however, the word she used to describe the scene to herself was not crowded but infested.

Joe had said, 'Hello, Mrs Egan. How are you? May I introduce my wife?' and a small, undersized and aged woman had thrust herself forward through the throng of her family, wiping her hands on her apron and in a voice that hardly seemed possible could come from her mouth, so much was it like a man's, loud and hearty, saying, 'Well! this is a pleasure. A pleasure indeed! How do you do, ma'am?'

Elaine took the hand that was now extended to her and forced herself to smile and say, 'Very well, thank you. And you?'

'Oh me. Well, I ask you, how could anyone be other than near death's door with this crowd around them?' She now swept her short thick arm in a wide circle, and when it came in contact with the shoulder of one of her sons he broke the silence that had fallen on the rest of the family by crying, 'Watch it, Mam! No hittin' below the neck,' which caused a chorus of smothered splutters to spread through the room.

'Listen to them, ma'am. Listen to them. No respect. That's what it's like the day. Can I offer you a seat?' She was looking at Joe now.

'No, thank you, Mrs Egan. We . . . we shan't be staying; we're due at a meeting at the Lodge.'

'Oh aye, the Lodge.' The little woman was now nodding towards Joe. 'It's Dan you'd have been wantin' to see then.

Well, he's been gone this half hour or more. Couldn't wait to get up on that platform an' talk himself blue in the face. That's Dan. But as I said to him, less talk with the tongue an' let the pick and shovel speak for itself, an' we'd all be better off. But there, I better not start 'cos they're all in the same boat.' She jerked her head to the men standing near a far door and two others seated at a table, one with a child on his lap, and she added, 'They're all in it. And after all, it is a bit thick, isn't it, to ask them to go down for less. But what is less, 'cos me, I've never seen the inside of his pay packet since the day I married him. I get me due an' that's all. Two bairns or ten, 'twas the same amount.' Then looking straight into Elaine's face she said in a less strident tone, 'I suppose you find this all very strange, ma'am, comin' from London as you do? We're a rough lot, 'tis well known we are, but it's well known that our hearts are in the right place. One thing that can be said for us, an' not only in this pit village but in every one the breadth of the country, we keep faith with them that keeps faith with us. Isn't that right, Mr Joe?'

'Yes, it's right, Mrs Egan, quite right.'

'If you know that's quite right, why aren't you on our side, then, Mr Remington?' was the question immediately posed to Joe by one of the men standing near the door, and Joe drew in a long breath and remained quiet for a moment under the cold gaze of the young fellow's eyes, before he replied, 'Now you know as well as I do that most of my men are not affiliated to any union. Perhaps there's a good reason for it, perhaps they haven't had to struggle as hard as you fellows, and right back down the ages. But still, there it is, and that's the way I want it. And that's the way my father wanted it. We believe that men should be allowed to make up their own minds whether they want to be free or be led.'

'Bugger that! we're not sheep. 'Tisn't a case of being led, it's a case of gathering strength. Even the bloody Bible says that: where one or two are gathered in My name . . . an' the name of our strength is the union. Individuals can do nowt . . . *nowt.*'

Now the other three male adults took it up, saying, 'Aye, that's right, nowt, nowt.'

Then the man who appeared to be the eldest among them, yet was the smallest, being thin and wiry and undersized, said, 'Your lot, Mr Remington, is the only ones that are workin' in the town. And we won't forget it. We've got long memories, an' some of 'em will have their canisters sorted afore this's over, if I know owt. An' who's to blame them that does it?'

'I wouldn't advocate taking that line if I were you.' Joe's voice was grim now. 'You might find you've bitten off more than you can chew. I came here to see your father, to tell him that George Bailey has a proposal to put to his meeting from my lot of sheep, as you call them. I doubt very much, if the tables were turned and you were in their places, you would consider giving up a day's pay each week for a month to help their cause. Alternatively, they propose to have a token strike for a week to show that they're in sympathy with you. And I can tell you here and now that I'm dead against the latter.'

The four men were silent; in fact, the only sound in the kitchen now was the crackling of the blazing fire and the discordant breathing of the occupants.

Joe turned to Mrs Egan and said, 'Good-night, Mrs Egan,' and nodded briefly at her; then taking Elaine by the arm, he added, 'Come along.'

They left the hot and now quiet kitchen and emerged into the cooler atmosphere of the street. They had left David with the car on some waste ground that bordered the rows of cottages. The street was cobbled, which Elaine found difficulty in negotiating with her high-heeled shoes. Joe still had hold of her arm and his grip was tight. He looked angry, and she considered he had every right to be angry. She hoped that the scene she had just witnessed in that appalling room, full of those uncouth, ignorant individuals, would have shown him finally that his sympathy was wasted.

From the conversations she had overheard between Joe and his father, she had guessed that their sympathies lay, perhaps reluctantly, with the mining community. She might have been able to understand it more if the old man, as she had come to think of her father-in-law, had come from a mining family, but apparently four generations of them had been carpenters, and before that wheelwrights.

Yet now, when their way of life was middle-class, they were in it but not of it, for they knew no-one of any importance whatever, not even in the business world. Their only friends, apparently, were a family called Levey. Marcus, the husband, had a wife, Lena, and a daughter, Doris. He was a solicitor in Fellburn, and at the present moment was in Devon attending the funeral of his father. But what was a solicitor? There was the doctor, too, of course; but he was just an ordinary practitioner after all.

As they reached the end of the row of cottages, what seemed to her to be a horde of savages came at them and almost upset them both.

Five boys were kicking a tin can, and when it landed at Joe's feet he kicked it back to them, but there was no smile on his face as there would have been another time.

There were a number of children around the car and they became silent on their approach, until David started up the engine. Then one of them yelled, 'Stingy darkie, wouldn't gi' us a ride in the old tin can!' As the car drew away, the rest of the children took up the chant, 'Stingy darkie, wouldn't gi' us a ride in the old tin can!'

As if he hadn't heard them, David put his head back and asked, 'Is it still the Lodge?' He made no comment about

39

their visit, having gauged enough from Joe's expression to give him an idea of what had transpired in his father-in-law's house.

'Yes.' The answer was brief . . .

The Lodge was an ugly, brick building. It had originally been a chapel, but this had been allowed to go to ruin when a larger and even more ugly building had been erected in a suburb of the town itself.

As the car drew up outside the Lodge, George Bailey ran down the steps towards it, and as he opened the car door, Joe said, 'I'm sorry I'm late, Geordie.'

'Aw, I think it's just as well, sir.'

'What's happened?'

As Joe extended his hand to help Elaine from the car his manager said, 'I wouldn't let your lady come in if I were you, sir; things could get ugly. Egan's on his feet now and he only wants a match to set him alight; he's a firebrand, that man.'

'Did you speak to him?'

'Aye, I did. I told him what was proposed and his response was: Why offer skimmed milk? As for comin' out, we should come out now and stay out with all the rest, he says. To the offer of a day's pay a week for a month, he said that was "Live like a horse and you'll get grass", and that we were betting on a cert, for they'd have won afore the month was up . . . And I heard another thing, sir. I was talkin' to Bembow, district secretary, you know, of Hammond's, and he says there's talk of them all going back, transport, railway workers, heavy industry, the lot. You see, they never expected such a flood of volunteers: one-time officers driving milk trains, an' university students on lorries; it's as if the upper crust was out to prove that there was nothing in this business of work, the workin' man's work, and he says that given half a chance there'd be scores ready to go down the pits, such is the feeling against the miners.'

'Has Egan put our proposal to the meeting yet?'

'Aye, he did, sir, but in such a way that he got the answer from them that he wanted, the same as he gave to me; skimmed milk.'

'Stay where you are.' Joe now pressed Elaine back into the car then added, 'Stay put, David. If they come flooding out of there and things look ugly, drive home; I'll make my own way back.'

'No, I'd rather come with you.'

'Stay where you are.'

It was an abrupt, curt order, and she sat back in the seat bristling with indignation and wondering what she could say to this dark-skinned individual sitting in front of her. Well, she would say nothing; she wasn't obliged to hold a conversation with him . . .

Joe entered the hall with his manager but could get no further than to the side of the door. The place was crowded and smelt of sweat and stale clothes. Dan Egan was standing at the front of the platform, his whole body looking as if each limb was separately being worked by springs, for as he talked he stepped first to the right, then to the left, then a little forward, then backwards, his arm and his head jerking all the while. His voice was thin but high and piercing and he was crying now, 'Miners' blood is cheap, man, 'cos it isn't red like ordinary blood; no, when it comes out it's black and blue, black from the dust and blue from all the bloody knocks its poor old veins have had.'

The ripple of appreciation that swept over the hall at his cynicism sounded like a wave washing over a pebbled beach.

'And you know what we should stand out for besides livin' wage? We should make it a point that every man

41

jack in the government an' in the House of Lords should do a shift down below, an' their wives should spend a day in wor kitchens, gettin' up at three in the mornin' like our missises do, washin', cookin', scrubbin', bangin' the pit clothes . . . scrubbin' wor backs.' He now thrust his hand down in the direction of a big miner sitting in a front seat and he yelled, 'How would you like Lady Golightly wielding a flannel up and down your spine, Peter?'

There was a great roar of laughter at this, but it died away when Dan Egan, raising his hand high, cried, 'Aye, we can laugh, but, lads, it's grim laughter and it'll likely get grimmer as the days go on. And, lads, hear this, an' I'm only repeatin' what's in the heart of every one of you, we're seein' this through, even if the skins of our bellies get stuck to our backbones.'

'Hear! hear!'

'Hear! hear! Hear! hear!'

The hall rang to the sound.

Again his hand was held up and now he was stubbing his finger forward: 'An' don't let us delude ourselves at this stage, don't let's think that the others are going with us all the way. To my mind they're makin' a token show, although we're grateful for it and we won't forget them. Nor will we forget—' Now his voice sank deep in his throat and he repeated, 'Nor will we forget them that stood on the sidelines. I have it in me heart to forgive the volunteers, and the polis, and even the bloody army if they turn it on us, but never those workmen-like worsels who stayed in. Blackleg is a dirty word; to me it's blacker than black, it's pitch, and it stinks in the nostrils of every decent working man. When I pass one such individual I look him in the eye, I sniff hard, then I turn me head away and blow the snots out.'

42

Joe turned abruptly and went from the hall, and George Bailey followed him, and they paused for a moment outside and looked at each other.

'It was a wasted effort.'

'Aye, Mr Joe, I think you're right. To my way of thinking, men like Egan do more harm than good.'

'Yes, and to mine too. But I suppose as he sees it he's fighting for his life and that of all the others, and I fully understand that. But when I hear him rant on like that it makes me wild. And his sons are as bad; they've erected a barrier: they're on one side and we're on the other; everybody on their side is reasonable; on the other, to their way of looking at it, there are only mine owners, politicians, and non-unionists.'

They both turned and walked away from the Lodge. Neither of them mentioned the fact that the car had gone until they reached the end of the road, when George Bailey said, 'You're going to have a long walk ahead of you, sir.'

'Oh, I don't mind that; it's a nice evening.'

He looked up into the sky. The sun had long since set, and the soft greyness of the long twilight had fallen over the town. There was no sound at the moment: the whole town, its pits, factories and docks, all seemed to be sleeping. He was still gazing at the sky as he said, 'You can feel everything has stopped, even at this time of night. Away up in the house of an evening I've often opened the windows of the observatory to hear the hum. It was, in a way, like pulling back the bed covers from over a face to make sure that the person was breathing; but now the breathing has stopped, the town's dead. Ah well' – he sighed – 'I fear a lot of things are going to happen before that hum starts again. What do you say, Geordie?'

'I fear it too, Mr Joe. I also fear for our chaps.'

43

'Oh' – Joe's face took on a grimness now – 'let them start anything in that quarter and they'll find out their mistake, for I wouldn't hesitate to ask for police protection for every man jack in the factory. Anyway, I hope it doesn't come to that.'

'Aye, I do an' all, sir. And given a fair chance, man to man, our chaps can take care of themselves; only at times like this it's often four to one or more.'

'Yes, you're right there. Well, we'll have to hope it won't happen. Now I must be off. See you in the morning, Geordie. Good-night.'

'Good-night, Mr Joe. Give my respects to himself. How is he, by the way?'

'Much the same.'

'Pity, pity. Good-night, sir.'

'Good-night.'

They separated, going in opposite directions. Joe, cutting across a field, jumped a low dry-stone wall, climbed a hill, dropped down the other side and so reached the main road that led from the town.

Once on the road his step took up a slow rhythm. He was worried, and about a number of things, and the most important one rose to the top of his mind. She had found the Egans and their way of living, everything, repulsive. She was of another world, and she wasn't going to take to this one, which in the long run was bound to prove awkward, to say the least.

Why did he love her? He had asked himself this question since the first time he had set eyes on her. He couldn't pinpoint exactly what it was about her that attracted him, but attract him she did; and she would likely go on holding that attraction for him until the day he died. Was it her face, her mouth, her eyes . . . or that hoity-toity manner of hers? He had been amused by that, and still could be if it was directed towards himself alone, but when she imposed it on others and he saw its effect on them he was upset by it. At her uncle's home in London and her cousin's in Huntingdonshire her manner hadn't stood out; all her people seemed to have that air about them, although he guessed they hadn't one penny to rub against the other; and he imagined that her uncle, Turnbull Hughes-Burton as he was called, didn't eat as well or didn't have as much in his pocket as some of the men in the factory here, but he, like the rest of them, put a face on their situation and pretended nothing had changed in their way of living during the past ten years.

Lady Kathryn Fowley was the only one among them who seemed to face facts. She helped herself by growing quite a lot of her own food.

And then there was Betty, his new sister-in-law. But then Betty didn't seem as if she really belonged to that family. He could never imagine her being Elly's sister. It wasn't only the six years' difference in their ages, it was the whole overall look of her. She was a different type altogether. He had the idea that Elly had made use of her over the years, but then she was the kind of person who let herself be made use of. She seemed to like it; she was a cheery individual. She had told him she had worked in munitions during the war and had also driven an army truck, and he could well imagine it.

When the thought passed through his mind that it was a pity that some of Betty's robustness hadn't rubbed off on to Elly, he had a feeling of guilt and he told himself hastily that it was because Elly was who she was that he had fallen in love with her; he could never have fallen in love with Betty. The very thought brought a smile to his lips. Poor Betty.

He had covered half the journey home when, passing the end of the Menton estate, he saw the unmistakable shape of the old Rolls. David had come back for him.

'Hello, David. You shouldn't have turned out again.'

45

'I thought you might get molested on the road; you never know what happens on a dark night.'

They both laughed as Joe took his seat and banged the door closed.

'Did you have any trouble back there?' Joe was watching David as he backed the car on to the grass verge, pulling hard on the wheel as he said, 'No; no trouble; but madam, your wife, said she wanted to be taken home.' He swung the wheel round again, the car straightened out, and it had gone some distance down the road before Joe said, 'You haven't taken to her, have you?'

'Well now' – David's gaze was still directed ahead – 'that's neither here nor there. Whether I've taken to her or not is no matter. The fact is she hasn't taken to me. She dislikes me intensely.'

'Nonsense!'

David's head jerked round now towards Joe and he said flatly, 'It isn't nonsense, and you know it isn't. She sees me as a black man and, what is even worse, married to a white woman; and, added to that, living in a decent house; and what is even worse still, not to mention incomprehensible, is that my master treats *me* as an equal. He speaks to me as if I were a human being and, of course, one shouldn't treat servants like that; it isn't done in good-class society.'

'Stop it, David.'

For answer, David brought the car to a grinding halt and, his hands gripping the wheel, he bent over it and with his head down, he said, 'This thing's got to be faced, Joe. We're all in a new situation. You yourself are responsible for it. And she's not really to blame for her attitude; you can't expect her to understand. If you want peace you have to face up to the fact that I am the chauffeur-gardener and you are the master; and in future you'll have to add a slight air of condescension to your manner when dealing with me.'

'Don't talk such bloody rot! Even if I could bring myself to do it, I wouldn't, not for her or anyone else, you know that.'

David drew himself upright now from the wheel and lay back against the seat, his hands lying limp on his thighs. Joe sat in a similar position.

'We're stuck, aren't we?'

Joe nodded his head twice before repeating, 'Yes, we're stuck. As it was in the beginning is now and ever shall be.'

'You're going to have a rough time of it, then.'

'I'll manage that side of the business, never fear.'

'What does himself think of her?' The question came low, muttered.

'I don't really know, but he talks to her and she to him; in fact, she seems to like going up there.'

'Well, that augurs good, I should say, although it's a bit surprising.'

'Don't take that attitude, David.'

'I'm sorry.' David now twisted around in the seat and, putting his hand on Joe's knee, he gripped it and shook it as he said, 'I won't make things difficult; I'll work in.'

They now looked at each other through the fading light and they both grinned weakly, before David turned to the wheel again and, starting up the car, drove towards the house.

3

On 12 May 1926 the General Council called off the national strike. For nine days the country, the working part of the country, had supported the miners, but now the latter were on their own, and so they were to remain as the weeks grew into months. And that's what Mary Duffy said to Ella as she stood sullenly by the kitchen table: 'They're on their own and likely to remain that way even for a long time yet, so be thankful you've got a full belly, miss; you would have something to grumble about if you were like most of them back in the town there; there's hardly a fat woman left. You're Jane to her, an' that's all there is about it. You should be used to it now. You've got to take it as one of the things the likes of us have got to put up with.'

'Me name's Ella.'

'Aye, we all know it is, lass, but himself has agreed to it. Don't forget that.'

'She's got him turned soft.'

'Don't you believe it. He knows what he's doin'. He's out to keep the peace, an' if by allowin' you to be called Jane he can manage it, then I'm with him.'

'I could spit in her eye every time she calls me Jane.'

'Now, now.' Mary turned heavily around from the stove and placed one foot firmly before the other as she slowly advanced to the table and, bending across it, thrust her finger out towards her niece as she said, 'Listen to me, miss. We'll have none of that talk. No matter what you think about her, you'd be wise to keep it to yourself, an' the fact that you want to spit in her eye will soon become clear to her if it isn't already, so use your head, girl, and keep your tongue civil 'cos, mind, I'm tellin' you this: Master Joe might appear easy but let him find out you've been rude to her in any way an' by God! you'll wonder which cuddy kicked you. He closes his eyes to lots of things but I wouldn't answer for your chances to be kept on here if he found you openly cheeked her.'

'He stood up for me about me name that time, I heard him.'

'Aye, you've said that afore; well, I wouldn't push your luck. The trouble with you is you don't know you're born yet; you've never wanted for anything, you've had life served up to you on a plate. And remember your place, we're servants here.'

'Oh, you'll never let me forget that, Aunty Mary. Servants.' Now Ella poked her face towards her aunt and hissed, 'That's all you hear: mind your place, you're a servant. Well, let me tell you, Aunty Mary, I hate being a servant. And who are they after all? Me da said me granda worked with his granda and himself an' all; and himself started at the bench an' called himself an engineer. Labourer he was, with hardly any schooling. But if all tales are true there were some things he didn't need schoolin' for, an' you haven't to go more than a few yards to prove it. And if he hadn't any money at the time . . .'

'*Shut your mouth! Shut your mouth this minute, girl!* And if I hear you open it again in that direction I'll go up to the missis meself. It's a great pity, I'll say to her, but your mother's sick and she needs you at home. Now I'm warnin' you. You say you hate being a servant, but there's something you hate more, an' I know it, an' that's being one of four in a bed. Now go on and pick up those silks' – she pointed to the small pile of black silk lingerie that was lying on a side table – 'and get them washed, and carefully, an' towel-dry 'em and iron 'em, *and* be quick about it. And if I hear another word out of you this day I'll take me hand and I'll wring your ear.'

The look on Ella's face said plainly, 'You try it,' but her lips remained tight as she floundered around and, grabbing up the silk underwear, strode across the kitchen, through the door which she banged after her, and to the wash-house across the yard.

Mary stood supporting herself against the back of a chair as she drew in one deep breath after another, and when the door leading to the hall opened and her husband appeared she said to him straightaway, 'That one's playin' up again. She'll say something one of these days and that'll be the end of her. There's always something to worry the life out of you.'

'Well, I can give you something more.' Duffy placed the tea tray, with the silver tea service on it, carefully on the table before he went on, 'In fact, two things more. Firstly, she wants the bills presented to her every Friday mornin'.'

'But she gets the accounts book.'

'Aye, she gets the accounts book, but she says she wants the things i-tem-ised. That's the word she used, i . . . tem . . . ised. Aye, everything we order has got to be put down in black and white. She's got wind of something; she must have seen the bairns leavin' with the bags.'

'Oh, my God! But anyway' – Mary now bristled – 'himself wouldn't mind; as for Master Joe he wouldn't give a damn, he'd give them the stuff.'

50

'Aye, Master Joe might, at one time, but don't forget he's married now, an' that makes a difference.'

'As if I could.' Mary's attitude was now quite different from that which she had presented to Ella when speaking of her mistress. 'There's never been a moment's peace since she came into the place. But the other thing?'

'She caught David handing out tomatoes and taties to Dan Egan and another fellow, an' by the sound of it she not only put a stop to it but she put David in his place; at least, she tried to, and they're going at it hell for leather up there now about it.'

'Master Joe and her!'

'Aye.'

'Do you think she'll get the better of him?'

'That remains to be seen. He's in an awkward position is Master Joe, atween the devil and the deep sea, you could say.'

And that's just what Joe was thinking as he sat holding his wife's hands in the sitting-room upstairs. He could see that she had a point. As she said, if she was mistress of the house the expenditure was her business. What was more, she had been used to seeing to household books since she was eighteen. Accounts were the one thing she was good at and the accounts in this house, she felt, when gone into would prove that they were being robbed, and not only inside but outside too. She had emphasised the latter.

He stroked her fingers gently now as he said, 'Why worry your head about such trifles? I know they order more than they should but, as I see it at present, it's for a very good cause. You know, dear, some of them down in the village are near starvation, the women in particular; they won't eat themselves in order that the children can get a better share.'

'That's all very well, Joe, but it really isn't your concern. The authorities and the Poor Law are taking care

51

of them and they won't starve; there's soup kitchens and . . .'

She was almost thrust from him now as he rose abruptly before going to the window to look out on to grounds that were parched in the mid-day heat.

It was impossible to hose all the lawns and the sun was shrivelling the grass. It was a glorious summer. The weather had brought on the fruit and vegetables apace: the greenhouses were bursting with tomatoes; the apple and pear boughs were bending towards the ground with the weight of their fruit; they'd had loads of strawberries, gooseberries, raspberries and blackcurrants; the cellar had shelves full of preserves and jams, and in the house they'd eaten their own fruit every day for weeks, besides which they took for granted a three-course lunch and a four-course dinner every day.

Sometimes, as they sat eating their fill, he would find it difficult to keep his mind off Fellburn and the villagers; yet she had just said they wouldn't starve down there. Would she ever understand them? Would she ever fit in?

Yet she seemed to fit in upstairs well enough with his father, and with Marcus and Lena Levey too. Marcus thought she was great fun, and Lena had said she was beautiful, while Doris, their daughter, had a schoolgirl crush on her. It was strange, but it seemed to be only in the kitchen quarter of the house where she didn't fit in; and, of course at The Cottage, for she had taken a strong dislike towards David and Hazel, most openly towards David. It wouldn't have been so bad, he thought, had she detested all the rest of them, even his father, if only she had taken to David.

Still with his back to Elaine, he spoke David's name now: saying stiffly, 'David has my permission to give all the surplus vegetables and fruit to the miners. I've told you this before; and you've no right to interfere with that arrangement.'

He sensed she was on her feet now and he could gauge

52

the expression on her face from the tone of her voice: 'And I told *you* I didn't agree with it, at least not in the quantity he gives away, and always to that man Egan, who'll likely go and sell it and drink the proceeds.'

Swinging round to face her now and his voice loud, almost on the verge of a shout, he cried at her, 'For your information, Dan Egan doesn't drink. This might seem strange to you, but he's a man of high morals. He's got a big mouth and he uses it, but he uses it for a cause. Everything Dan Egan gets from my garden is taken to the club house and shared out.'

'You should have been a miner.'

'Yes, perhaps I should.'

'That gentleman in the railway carriage was right: you're in one class but you belong to another.'

'Be careful, Elly; I don't want to fight with you.'

'It appears to me we have done little else for weeks. You thwart me at every turn. You should allow me my place in this house. Your father respects my wishes more than you do: you would never have allowed me to change that girl's name, but he did; he understood the situation. He doesn't kow-tow to the kitchen; you, I am sorry to say, have no sense of the fitness of things and your place in society, nor do you understand people. You have never given me credit for having a brain. You saw me at Polly Rawlston's dance as a gay, bobbed-haired, Charleston-swinger with just enough brains to enable me to chatter entertainingly, to tinkle on the piano, to dribble French in restaurants and . . .'

'I've told you to be quiet, Elly; you're going too far.'

'There, you see, when I bring up something of importance, such as my ability to think, you tell me to be quiet, that I am going too far. I understand that the men in the village and town down there still treat their wives like serfs; they don't seem to know that women have the vote. There's one life for the master of the house, which includes his freedom to do as he wishes and go where he likes without question, and another for his wife, whose duty appears to be to rear children by the dozen, such as happens in Egan's house, and to cook and slave for her lord and master.'

She stopped abruptly and her face stretched in surprise as Joe turned from her and threw his head back and laughed loudly. When he put his hands on the head of the couch and leant over it, she cried at him, 'I'm glad to see that I amuse you, although myself I see no humour in what I have said.'

'No?' He rubbed each eye with his finger; then approached her again and, taking her gently by the shoulders, shook her, saying, 'It's wonderful, marvellous: you're for them, at least the women; you're on their side.'

She stared back at him coldly for a moment before she replied, 'You have misinterpreted my words; you see things as you want to see them. I was merely stating a social fact. And for your information, I despise them because they haven't got the gumption to alter their way of living. The women must know what they're in for before they marry such men.'

His hands slid slowly from her shoulders, all traces of laughter and amusement drained from his face, although his voice sounded level and ordinary as he asked her a question: 'You would never have married a poor man, would you, Elly?'

The question brought the colour sliding up over her pale skin. For the moment she seemed lost for an answer, and she swallowed deeply before she said, 'I . . . I didn't marry you for your money. And anyway, you're not rich as rich men go.'

'No, as rich men go, I'm not a rich man, but I'm what you call comfortably off, comfortable enough to give away the fruit and vegetables from the garden. And in future I'll thank you, Elly, not to interfere with David's work; outside is beyond your province.'

Her face had shown her keen displeasure before, but now it expressed raw anger as she cried at him. 'David! David! I'm sick of that man's name; he has caused nothing but dissension between us. Why don't you get rid of him? Yes, any other man would. If a servant, particularly a half-caste, was annoying his wife he would get rid of him, but what do you do? You take his part at every turn. Who is he anyway that you should consider him so much? I know what I'll do.' She half turned and gripped at the handle of the door before ending, 'I'll go upstairs and see your father. As you said, he's still master of this house and he'll understand my side of it as he did about the girl downstairs. We'll see if Mr David Brooks is to be put before me!'

She was too shocked even to cry out when she felt herself being carried, half dragged across the room and flung down onto the couch. And then he was standing over her, glaring down into her face, and his lips were trembling as he said, 'Don't you ever dare go up there and ask for David to be dismissed; in fact, don't you dare mention his name. Do you hear me?' When he gripped the front of her dress her hands clutched at his wrists and she gazed at him in fear for a moment, her eyes stretched wide, her lips apart, her tongue moving up and down between her teeth; and her face seemed to stretch even longer in her shock and amazement as he went on, 'My father suffered hell for years through one woman, my mother. And at this stage of his life and condition of his health I'll not allow you or anybody else to disturb him. He's . . . he's fond of David, as . . . as we all are. You go up there and talk about having him dismissed and it'll—' He gulped in his throat as he swallowed a mouthful of spittle, then closed his eyes for a moment, after which he released his hold on her, straightened his back, and then, after a long pause while they stared at each other, he said softly, 'I'm sorry.' And on this he turned from her and walked hastily out of the room while she lay still, staring towards the door.. . .

He had been to the bathroom and sluiced his face in cold water, and now, as he stood on the second landing, he passed both hands over his damp hair, after which he inserted his finger around the inside of his shirt collar before opening the door and entering his father's room.

Mike was just emerging from the workroom. His back was slightly bent and he walked slowly and with a shambling gait. He reached his chair by the window before he spoke; then, turning his head to the side, he asked quietly, 'What was all that about?'

'What do you mean?'

'Aw, lad' – his tone was gruff – 'I'm not deaf. Remember your rooms are just below.' He pointed a misshapen finger down towards the floor.

'We had a disagreement.'

'That's a bloody understatement, if ever I heard one. What's up atween you?' The question was asked quietly and with concern.

Joe now walked to the window, then lowering himself slowly onto the broad sill, he leaned forward and gazed out over the gardens before he replied, 'I could say it was the heat.'

'But you won't.'

'No, no, I won't.'

'Things going wrong?'

Joe now turned and looked at his father. 'We don't seem to be speaking the same language,' he said.

'Huh! Well, damn it all! you didn't really expect to, did you? You know what I said to you a while ago: don't make the same mistake as me. That should have told you to start the way you mean to go on.'

'That's what I thought I had done.'

'And she's not having it?'

'It would appear not.'

'What was it about this time?'

'Oh, everything and nothing.'

Mike slowly edged himself forward in the leather chair; then twisting his body to the right, he pressed himself upwards until he was standing as straight as he was able to, then turned from the window and walked slowly towards the cabinet at the far end of the room. He took out a bottle and two glasses, and as he poured out the drinks, in a tone that was scarcely above a mutter, he asked, 'Have you put her in the picture?'

'No, of course, I haven't; nor have I any intention of doing so.'

'What if somebody else should?'

'That's impossible. Who could, anyway? It would only be hearsay.'

'Aye. Aye, hearsay.' Mike turned now and said, 'Come and get this; I think you need it.'

When Joe reached his side, Mike handed him the glass of neat whisky and, lifting up the other one, he gazed at it before putting it to his lips, and in one gulp he threw it off and shuddered. Then he put the glass down and turned away, saying, 'It was a damn silly thing to ask.'

'Then you shouldn't have asked it.'

He reached his chair and sat down before he spoke again. 'You know what she told me the other day?' he said.

'What did she tell you?'

'Well, I asked her what she thought about startin' a family and she told me you had both agreed that such annoying trivialities – and those are the very words she used, although she laughed when she said them – weren't going to interrupt your life for the next two or three years. So what do you have to say about that? Is it true?'

'No.'

Mike looked at Joe, who was draining his glass, and he repeated, 'No?'

'That's what I said, no.'

'How do you mean?'

'Well, I think that what she needs is some responsibility; she wants to run something, rule someone. She's finding me difficult, so I thought the best thing' – he paused now, thrust out his lips, nodded his head slowly and ended – 'was to start a small army for her and as soon as possible.'

The laughter that erupted from Mike sounded as if it was coming from a great robust healthy body. His head was back and hanging to the side, one hand was pressing against his ribs. And Joe, looking at him, laughed too, but his laughter was more in the nature of a deep chuckle and the essence of it was not caused by the admission of his own deviousness but by the sight of his father's enjoyment.

Mike now sat rubbing his face with a large mottled silk handkerchief and the laughter was still bubbling in him as he said, 'Aye well, I've got to hand it to you. Talk about a cunning young bugger. Has it taken?'

'I don't know yet; time's young.'

'Well, well, there's one thing sure, you've got your head screwed on the right way, lad.'

As Joe looked at his father he knew that his admission of tricking his wife into conceiving, if such should happen, had pleased him more than if he had come up in a straightforward way and said that Elly was going to have a baby; and it proved one thing conclusively to him: his father didn't like her any more than those in the kitchen did, or those in the cottage.

'Well, I've got to go,' he said. 'Oh, and by the way, I'd almost forgotten to tell you, the London visit has borne fruit at last: we got an order this morning for a thousand cases, a third of them with fancy beading.'

'Good! Good!'

'Be seeing you.'

'Be seeing you, lad.'

As Joe reached the door, Mike twisted around in his chair and said softly, 'I think I'd better have a thicker carpet put in here' – he motioned towards the floor – 'against the day when she finds out you've done it on her.'

Joe's only answer to this was a jerk of the chin, and as he went down the stairs and made for his wife's sitting-room again, he was thinking it would take more than a carpet to smother her reactions if his trickery were to work out as he hoped it would.

4

But Elaine did not even raise her voice when she discovered she was pregnant; she was too shocked and dumbfounded, and at first she would not accept the evidence her body was presenting to her. Her monthly cycle had always been irregular but it had never caused her distress, being merely an inconvenience.

Her first bout of morning sickness took place on a Sunday, and she put it down to the roast duck she'd eaten at the dinner-dance in Newcastle the previous evening. This, together with a number of cocktails, must, she thought, be the cause of the upset. She lay in bed until noon, and Joe sat by her side for quite some time holding her hand and stroking her damp forehead while she talked intermittently about the future, the near future, the autumn.

Couldn't they go up to town and spend a few weeks with her Uncle Turnbull? He'd be so glad to have them because they would be like paying guests. It was very embarrassing for her uncle to be reduced to that state, but there it was, he couldn't afford to entertain any other way now. There was so much on in town in the autumn and if they could get Cousin Kathryn up out of the depths of the country, her name was a key that fitted so many doors they would be invited to all kinds of functions.

She placed her fingers around his bony wrist as she ended this statement: 'You could be gay, you know, Joe, if you'd only let yourself go. Why, last night at the table you had everyone rocking. You were very witty. Do you know that? Not just humorous, but really witty.'

'Was I?' His reply sounded inane. 'I didn't know there was any difference.'

She slapped his arm. 'Don't be silly,' she said. 'But what about it, going up to town, I mean?'

'We'll see.' When he rose from the bed she pulled herself upwards against the pillows and coaxed further: 'Joe! Joe, I want an answer.'

'And you want it to be yes?'

'Please.'

'I'm . . . I'm sorry, Elly; it's no good making a promise that I might have to break. I've got a business to see to, and things are precarious; you know they are. Our men are being subjected to all kinds of insults, and assaults too. I've told you about the ugly scenes in the town, all because they didn't come out in sympathy in the beginning. They've forgotten that some of the men gave up a day's pay to them for weeks.'

'But you've got a manager and staff to see to things.'

'Yes, they're all very well in their place, but it's my responsibility, and I must be here.'

'And I must be here too?' Now she was sitting bolt upright in the bed, and she tossed her head so sharply that her cap of short, shining hair seemed to spring away from her scalp for a moment. 'I'm fed up,' she said. 'Do you hear me? I'm fed up! I haven't a soul to talk to.'

'Don't be silly.'

'Don't tell me I'm silly. You tell me one intelligent person with whom I can converse.'

He stopped by the dressing-table and, bending down, picked up a comb and ran it through his hair, and he looked at her reflection in the mirror as he said, 'My father mightn't have the kind of accent you're used to, but you'll go a long way before you'll find a more intelligent man. What you don't seem to have discovered is that he's widely read.'

'All right! All right! All right! But you are missing the point. Your father is an old man, I want someone of my own age and cla . . .'

He straightened himself up, turned slowly and looked at her; then, as slowly, he walked towards the bed and gazed down on her bent head. She was apparently examining her painted nails and she was no doubt expecting him to come back with a tirade on class, but he brought her head upwards and her eyes wide as he said, 'Then why don't you invite one of your friends to stay with you for a time?'

'You mean that?' Her face was moving into a slow smile.

'Of course. Why shouldn't I?'

'But . . . but your father, wouldn't he mind?'

'Not in the least; he'd enjoy seeing a new face. What about your uncle?'

'Oh, Uncle Turnbull.' She shook her head, then laughed as she added, 'Don't forget it's someone I want for company; Uncle can be a bore.'

'What about Lady Kathryn?'

'Oh, I don't know. She's good company when you can keep her in one place, but if I know Kathryn she'd want to spend all her time in the garden.'

'Your school friends?'

'Oh' – she shrugged now – 'most of them are married. My best friend Anna got herself married to an American rancher last year and she's only written once and that seemed to be from the back of a horse.'

He began to laugh and she laughed with him, then said, 'Of course, there's Betty.'

'Oh yes, Betty. I forgot about Betty. But she's working somewhere, isn't she?'

'Yes, but she would come if she thought I needed her. Betty is the type of person who loves to be needed. I told her once she was born to be an old lady's companion, cheerful, willing and wanted. She used to make me feel frightfully inferior at one time, until I recognised that all her good points had been given her in compensation for her face.'

'That's cruel. I think she has a nice face. She seemed to be a nice person altogether.'

'She is, she is, but you can't get over the fact that she's a great lumbering lump of a woman.'

'Compared with you she may be, but she didn't seem extraordinarily large to me.'

'Oh, it isn't her build. Anyway, Joe, you haven't lived with her, you don't know: she's clumsy, she has a habit of breaking things.'

'Oh, well, if that's her only drawback she won't do much damage here: we've only got two valuable pieces of porcelain in the house, and the Sunderland glass we can put in the cabinet, and then give her her head.'

They were laughing again and he said, 'Go on, why don't you write to her?'

She sank back now into her pillows and looked up at him as she said, 'Oh, I don't know. She can be heavy going. I'll wait; I'll put up with you for a while longer. But I'm going to tell you something.' She grabbed again at his hand. 'If you don't take a break in the autumn I'll go up to London on my own, because I just couldn't stand the sameness of a whole winter here. I'm telling you.'

'All right, all right.' He nodded at her. 'Do that; go up and enjoy yourself.'

She dropped his hand and gazed at him; then she watched him grin at her before turning away and leaving the room. She lay back in her pillows, and immediately stretched her eyes wide, pursed her lips, turned her head first to the right and then to the left and exclaimed aloud, 'Well! Well!'

When the nausea occurred again on the Monday morning, Elaine groaned, 'No, no; it can't be. It can't be. Impossible. He didn't. He wouldn't.'

But after an early visit to the bathroom on the Tuesday morning as well, she returned to the bedroom and stood by the bed and waited for Joe to come from the small dressing-room that adjoined the bedroom, and when he did, such was the expression on her face that he stopped in the act of buttoning his waistcoat and asked quietly, 'What's the matter?'

'You're a swine.' The words were low, scarcely audible.

'What did you say?' He was approaching her slowly now.

'You heard what I said. You know what you've done, you do. You do. And you promised.' The effort to speak was so great that her chin came forward on to her bare chest and she gulped twice before bringing her head up again and accusing him, but still softly, 'You did it on purpose.'

'What are you talking about?'

'You know, you know very well what I'm talking about. You have made me pregnant.'

She watched his face crinkle into a smile as he whispered, 'Pregnant?' Then his whole expression changing, he waved his hand in front of his face as if brushing off a fly, and said, 'Don't be silly.'

'I hope I am being silly, but I know I'm not. I wouldn't mind so much, but you promised on your oath you . . .'

'And I kept my promise; you know I did.' He turned

64

from her now and walked across the room. 'I . . . I don't know when it could have happened, unless it was that night we came back from the Leveys; we'd both had more than enough that night . . .'

'Yes, yes, I remember; we both had more than enough' – she was hissing at his back now – 'but I wasn't so tight that I don't remember you going into the bathroom. You! you've tricked me, and I hate you. Do you hear? I hate you. And what's more, I won't have it; I'll have it taken away.'

'You'll what?' He had swung round and moved towards her so quickly that she flopped back on the bed in not a little fear at the sight he presented, for his lower jaw was thrust out and his whole attitude overall was aggressive. 'Don't you ever say that again!'

She hitched herself along the bed away from him, and now her chin went up as she said, 'I will say it, and I mean it; I'm not going to be tied down at this stage. I . . . I told you before we were married, we talked it all out, and what did you say? All you wanted was me.'

'I know what I said, but this has happened and now it stays. The child will be part of you.'

'Not if I can help it.'

'Listen.' He was bending over her now, where she lay half on the bed, her feet still on the floor, and as if the words pained him, he said, 'I don't want to lose my temper with you, not at this moment when we should be all in all to each other, but if you attempt to carry out your threat you'll never get back into this house again. And I mean that. I'll throw you off even if I have to take you to court. You'll have the child. Whether you like it or not, you'll have it. My God!' He pulled himself up straight and, gazing down at her, he shook his head slowly as he added, 'I wouldn't have believed it. Now, since I know how you feel, I'll tell you how I feel. Yes, I tricked you; I wanted a child so badly I tricked you. But

I wasn't thinking only of myself when I did it, I was thinking of you, hoping it might make a woman of you, alter your outlook, your silly, selfish, middle-class outlook. I thought, in my ignorance, that after a small protest you would throw your arms about me and say, "Isn't it wonderful!" But not you. Well, we both know where we stand: you said you hated me; well, at this moment I can return the compliment, and I only hope for your sake it's a passing phase.'

He now turned away from her and his step, as he walked towards the dressing-room again, was slow and heavy. It had lost its spring; he walked like a man well on in years and heavily burdened.

PART TWO

I

Beatrice Hughes-Burton joined the Remington household at the beginning of November. Elaine was now four months pregnant and apparently had accepted her condition, if not joyfully, then at least without any outward show of hostility.

From that particular Tuesday morning when Joe had frightened her – and she had admitted to herself that she had been frightened, not so much by what he might do to her person, but by his threat that he would throw her off; she knew him well enough by now to realise that he had an aggressive side to him and against all his personal feelings he would have carried out his threat if she'd had an abortion – from that morning she had done a lot of thinking, and all centring around herself and her needs. She knew the one thing she couldn't face was life without certain of its comforts, and the thought of being on the open market again, with the stigma of separation attached to her this time, was not to be borne; that particular market was flooded with a great many women of her class, young widows and disappointed brides, the residue of dead young officers. Those men who had escaped had nothing to offer in marriage except love, and as she had witnessed, that love brought little comfort in a third-floor flat in Bloomsbury. So she had allowed Joe to bring her round to accepting the disaster that had befallen her.

And she also deemed it expedient to change her tactics insofar as expressing her opinion of the people in whose midst she had found herself, for she was being forced to recognise that her husband was the son of his father and that they both stemmed from the working class; in fact, they had never left it, and in a way this was a matter of pride with them both. Even Joe's education, she was finding, was but a thin veneer, and there were times when he took no pains to hide it, when he seemed to take pride in stripping it off by resorting to the idiom of the area. What it all amounted to, in his case, she had concluded, was a deep feeling of inferiority; you had to be born of the middle class, or the upper class, you couldn't be born into it. Even though his mother had been a lady, so she had been given to understand, he himself in no way showed evidence of it; on the contrary, he seemed to take a delight in hob-nobbing with menials. That objectionable being who lived in The Cottage, for instance. Oh, how she disliked that man; it put her teeth on edge every time she saw him with Joe. If the man had been white, Joe's attitude towards him would still not have been natural, ordinary, for he seemed to go out of his way to placate the fellow. It wasn't as if he was afraid of him, no, not that, but as if he held him in high esteem, as one would a very close and well loved friend.

And then there was the man's wife. That creature, Egan's daughter. She was much too familiar with Joe, and Joe with her. Yesterday she had seen him put a hand on her shoulder.

She had walked down the drive to meet the car. She was finding she had to do such ordinary mundane things to fill in her time and stem the feeling of utter boredom. She had just turned the bend in the drive when she saw the car inside the gate, and there was Joe going into the cottage with the girl, and they were laughing together, quite loudly. The girl was in her outdoor clothes and it was apparent that she had ridden with Joe in the car.

She had turned on her heel and marched back to the house, determined she would have something to say to him when he came in. Yet before reaching the front door she had asked herself what she would say, and how she would say it; after all, he had probably merely given the girl a lift back from the town. Yes, but why had he to escort her into the cottage? Well, his answer could be: 'Why not? I couldn't leave her to find her way in alone, could I?' Such a flippant attitude on his part had shown itself of late; it was his idea of humour.

Before she heard him come whistling into the house she had decided to adopt the adage regarding discretion being the better part of valour . . .

But today she gave no thought to the girl or her coloured husband. Today she was feeling happy, even excited, for today Betty would be here; and oh, how she longed to see her and to have someone of her own class to talk to.

It was strange, but until now she had never really thought of her sister as being of her own class, nor even of her generation; there was six years between them, and Betty's war service had seemed to coarsen her and make her more voluble. Nevertheless, she was her sister and her volubility was spoken with a recognisable accent; and they both knew the same kind of people. Moreover, Betty was wonderful at nursing and so sympathetic. Oh, she was glad she was coming.

Suddenly she put her hands on the dressing-table, bowed her head and laughed softly to herself as she thought, Good Lord! I'll have her growing wings in a moment; I really must be bored. After all she's still Betty, as she was in the beginning, is now, and ever shall be . . .

'Are you ready?'

She looked through the mirror towards the door where Joe was standing, and adjusting her hat she nodded at him, saying, 'Yes, I've just got to put my coat on.'

When she picked up her coat from the chair he helped her into it, then tucked the fur collar close under her chin, saying, 'Keep warm, the wind's enough to cut you in two.' Then, bending his face to hers, he kissed her slowly on the mouth, and as he traced his finger around her lips he said, 'You've got the most beautiful mouth I've seen on a woman.'

'Is that the only beautiful part of me?' She looked at him coyly.

'The only beautiful part?' He put his head to the side as if thinking. 'No; but it's the best bit of you, apart, perhaps, from that.' He gave her stomach a sharp tap, and she turned from him, saying, 'Oh you!' and he laughed as he followed her out of the room, saying, 'And you, and it – or them.'

As they crossed the landing he put his arm around her shoulders and hugged her to him and muttered under his breath, 'Wouldn't it be marvellous if it was them; two, or three of them?' And when, almost violently, she pushed him away he let out a deep throaty laugh that resounded through the house, right down to the kitchen and up to the top floor, where Mike, hearing it, nodded slowly to himself as he said aloud, 'That's good.'

When they reached the station the train had already arrived and they espied Betty at the far end of the platform talking to someone, which caused Elaine to move her head impatiently even while she laughed gently, saying, 'Trust Betty to pick up somebody on the journey.'

72

Beatrice Burton had her back to them, and she turned a delighted and wide-lipped smile on them when they appeared at her side, saying, 'Oh, hello, Joe. Hello, Elaine.' She bent forward impulsively and kissed Elaine; then she held out her hand to Joe, saying, 'Nice to see you again, Joe. Oh, by the way' – she turned to the person to whom she had been speaking – 'This is Mrs Ambers.'

'How do you do, Mrs Ambers?' Joe inclined his head towards the elderly woman who, from her appearance, looked as if she were on her way to a Victorian tea-party. The coat she wore was long, the skirt being gored, taking its lines from a narrow waistband, while the bodice was buttoned up to the neck, the same being covered by a fur stole that seemed to be made up entirely of tails. Her hat was of faded green velour and her perky face seemed lost under its enormous brim.

Her reply to Joe's acknowledgement could have been heard as far away as the ticket barrier, 'Oh, how do you do, Mr Remington. You're the brother-in-law, aren't you? Yes, yes. And' – she now turned and looked at Elaine – 'this'll be the sister. Well, well, no resemblance, no resemblance whatever. Ha! ha! it goes like that. Now I wonder if Hammond is outside. Would you be kind enough, Miss Hughes-Burton, to see if he's there? He'll have a carriage, no motor. Sarah doesn't believe in motors; she's old-fashioned, as old-fashioned as the hills.'

'Yes; yes, of course, I'll see to it.'

As Betty was about to dart away Joe caught her arm, saying, 'Leave it to me;' then turning to Mrs Ambers he asked, 'Where are you for?'

'The Hall. The Hall, of course; Menton's place.'

'Oh. Oh yes.' He showed no surprise; unlike Elaine, who stared at the odd creature, thinking ruefully: Isn't it just like Betty to meet up with Lady Menton's cousin; she had

73

now remembered the name Ambers and its connection with the Mentons. This weird-looking individual was *Lady* Mary Ambers and known to be as flush with money as were the Mentons, and all too old to enjoy it.

The three women were walking towards the ticket barrier now and Elaine, in her most gracious manner, asked of the old lady, 'I hope you had a pleasant journey?'

'Journeys are never pleasant but this one was relieved by your sister here.' Lady Ambers turned her head abruptly and nodded towards Betty, who answered bluntly, 'Well, it worked both ways.'

'Thank you. Thank you. It's unusual to find an intelligent talker who doesn't turn out to have been a suffragette. You did say you weren't a suffragette, didn't you?'

'Yes, I did.'

'Good. Good.'

Joe was standing beyond the barrier, and at a respectful distance behind him stood David. However, standing in front of David was a smartly liveried middle-aged man and over the dividing iron railings Lady Ambers called loudly, 'Oh, there you are, Hammond. Good. Good.'

Inclining his head respectfully the man said, 'Yes, milady.'

And now there was a hold-up because her ladyship couldn't find her ticket. Having been forced to stand aside to let the other passengers through the barrier she fumbled with her handbag, and then with her purse, until Betty came to her side and said quietly, 'I think you put it down your glove.'

'Oh, yes. Yes, of course. Good Lord, you would think I was senile.' The reply was meant to be in a whisper and it amused the line of passengers.

They were outside now. David, carrying Betty's luggage, was shepherding them towards the car, while Hammond led the way along the kerb towards the shining but elderly carriage.

He held the door open wide for her ladyship to enter, but with her foot on the step Lady Ambers hesitated, stepped back on the pavement, looked along to where Betty was about to enter the car and cried, 'Miss Burton! Miss Burton! You must come and have tea with me. Do you hear! You must come and have tea with me.'

'Oh, thank you very much. Yes, I will. Thank you. Goodbye.'

Settled in the car, Joe let out a low rumbling chuckle. 'There's a character for you. I wonder what connection she is to the Mentons?'

'Oh, she's a cousin.'

Joe turned his head towards Betty as he said, 'Really!' Then he twisted further round in his seat as Elaine put in, 'She happens to be Lady Mary Ambers.'

'Lady Mary Ambers!' Joe nodded his head to each word. 'Well, well, this is the eccentric one. I've heard of her. She lives up to her name. Travels the world, doesn't she?'

He turned again towards Betty and asked, 'How does she do it? She didn't even know where she'd put her ticket.'

'Oh, she would have found it or someone would have found it for her. She's one of these people who'll always get by . . . But I didn't know she was Lady Mary. Nice of her, don't you think, not to press it. She said her name was Ambers, but that was all.'

'She looked slightly mad,' Elaine muttered.

Betty slanted her eyes towards Elaine as she said, 'Don't you believe it; nobody's mad who can survive three rich husbands.'

'She's been married three times?' Joe turned around again.

'Yes, and by all accounts they all adored her,' said Betty.

'You mean by *her* accounts,' was Elaine's response.

Again Betty gave Elaine a slanting glance, and she shook her head now, saying, 'No, she never mentioned them. But I've met her once before, although I don't think she remembered me and I didn't know even then who she really was. It was at a bun-fight Lena Bradshaw was holding for some charity or other, and Lena referred to her as Old Mary.'

'Well, you've been invited to tea and that's a double honour, if you did but know it.' Joe was now looking straight ahead through the windscreen, and after a slight pause he ended, 'You'll be the first one from Fell Rise to enter the portals of Menton Hall.'

'Oh, I won't take it up; it was just her way of being polite.'

'Don't be a fool! Of course you'll take it up,' said Elaine.

Now Betty's head came right round and she stared at her sister for a moment before she said on a small laugh, 'I'll send *you* in my place.'

There was an awkward pause, until Joe cried, 'I forgot to introduce you to David, Betty. Betty, David.' He bobbed his head from one to the other, and when Betty leant forward towards the open partition and said, 'Hello, David,' and he answered pleasantly, 'How do you do, miss?', Elaine closed her eyes tightly while pressing her back deep into the upholstery of the car, and behind her clenched teeth her tongue clicked the roof of her mouth as she exclaimed to herself, really! really! and the intonation had the sound of a curse. He was impossible, impossible. Introducing Betty to the chauffeur. What next! What next indeed! Betty might be cosmopolitan in her outlook but what must she think of the master introducing his sister-in-law to the chauffeur, and a coloured one at that.

2

Betty had been at the house for a week and, as Mike remarked to Joe, she fitted in like an old glove. And Betty, too, felt that she fitted in. She loved the house and garden; she loved the food – well, who wouldn't after having sampled Cousin Kathryn's fare for the past six months – and she liked the people about the place. In a way she liked Mike most of all; his bluntness caused her to erupt with laughter. And, of course, she liked Joe.

Elaine, she considered, was very lucky. But then Elaine had always been lucky; everything always turned out as Elaine planned it should; just as she had planned that she herself should and would stay with her. And at the present moment she had to admit she could wish for nothing more, for she was tired of moving from one place to another; she was tired of waiting on old ladies, and reading aloud; and she was tired, very tired, of condescension.

Relatives, she found, were the worst offenders in this respect, except, of course, Elaine. She could never remember her being so sweet, or so grateful; in fact, she couldn't remember the slightest feeling of empathy ever existing between them, but now all that seemed to have altered.

That there was a reason for her sister's changed attitude towards her had very quickly become apparent: Elaine was feeling lonely and lost amongst these people. As she said, they didn't speak her language, and she could never speak theirs and, what appeared to be very trying to her, Joe's friends weren't of the class to which she had been accustomed.

She had wondered more than once during the past few days if her sister had grown to love her husband. She couldn't possibly have loved him when she married him: she wasn't the kind of person to fall in love at first sight; and anyway, she was still suffering from the Lionel Harris affair. But she had done better for herself in marrying Joe than ever she would have done with Lionel Harris; or Major Lionel Harris, as he insisted on being called.

She was an early riser and it was just turned half-past seven on the Saturday morning when she made her way downstairs. The sun was shining, throwing broad shafts of light through the stained-glass windows on the landing. She had decided to take a walk round the garden before breakfast and was crossing the hall towards the front door when Ella came from the morning-room carrying a brass, helmet-shaped coal scuttle. Seeing her, she stopped for a moment, exclaiming, 'Eeh! miss; you're up early.'

'It's a habit, Jane, and I can't get out of it.'

'Well, the fire's blazing away in the breakfast-room, miss, and I'll get your breakfast early if you want it.'

'No. No, thank you. I'll have it at the usual time; I'm going to take a walk around the garden.'

'Do that, miss; it's a lovely morning, sharp though.'

'Yes, it is lovely. It's been a beautiful autumn; but we can't expect this kind of weather to last much longer.'

'No, you're right there, miss. Oh, and when the winds start an' the snow, my! it would freeze a brass monkey.'

'I bet it would. Well, I've got that to come.' She smiled at Ella now, then opened the door and went out, the while Ella, moving to one of the hall windows, watched her stride across the drive towards the terrace, before she herself turned and hurried to the kitchen.

'She's gone out, the miss, for a walk in the garden. By! but she's pleasant, isn't she?'

'Aye, she is that.' Mary nodded her head slowly. 'She's plain but she's very pleasant.'

'Well, I'd rather have her than some I could mention.'

'Now, enough of that. There, drink your tea and then get about your work . . . But what did you say? She's gone walking in the garden?'

They both turned now and stared at each other as the same thought struck them.

Betty had stopped by the lakeside. But rather than looking down into the water, she raised her head to the sky and drew in deep draughts of air, and as it filled her lungs she likened it to wine, for it made her feel heady, and good. It was odd, she thought, as she now walked round the lake, that she had disliked Cousin Kathryn's garden, and yet she already loved this one. But, she told herself ruefully, the reason wasn't really hard to find: Kathryn had had her digging or weeding, working like a horse every day. Here, everything was neat and tidy and you could walk round and enjoy it.

She made her way through an arch in the privet hedge and took a path to the left. It was new to her and led away from the kitchen garden and the greenhouses and into a narrow belt of woodland.

When she came to the end of the strip of woodland she found she had also reached the extent of the grounds, for here she came up against a fence. It was low, only three and a half feet high, and made of staves wired together. The path

79

itself ended at the fence but to the right of her was a patch of rough scrubland, with hawthorn and bramble, that had overgrown the fence in places.

She was about to turn and retrace her steps when a piece of sacking protruding from the bushes near the fence caught her eye. The fact that it didn't look like old sacking made her curious. Stepping from the path she approached the bushes and parted the branches to reveal a partly filled sack, its top folded over to cover its contents. Slowly she bent down and flipped back the top and her surprised gaze saw a loaf partly wrapped in paper, a brown-paper bag and below these carrots and onions and potatoes. She straightened her back and looked about her, then looked down into the sack again and, stooping, she opened the paper bag. It held a number of sausage rolls, some queen cakes and, wrapped in a piece of greaseproof paper, a solitary chop.

She fastened up the paper bag again, folded the top of the sack into the shape she had found it, then stepped back on to the path.

'Well, well.'

She walked now into the woodland and stood against a tree. The land in front of her and beyond the fence sloped away, and in the distance she made out the dark huddle of houses that was the village, topped by the pit-head, and the greater huddle beyond them that was the town. And she asked herself what she was going to do about her find. Someone in the house was evidently helping families down there. Well, from the little she had seen, God knew they needed help. But was it fair? It was Joe's money, or his father's, that was being, she had almost said, squandered. No, it was certainly not being squandered, and stolen wasn't the right word. Oh no! in this case stolen wasn't the right word.

Her thinking was checked by the sound of footsteps crushing the dry leaves, and now she moved behind the tree and pressed her back against the trunk and remained still. When the two figures passed by her she saw they were the half-caste chauffeur David and his wife. They were carrying two sacks each. She watched as they placed the sacks, not behind the bushes with the others, but in the open along by the fence. Then she saw the girl pointing towards some figures now approaching up the slope.

She was in a quandary: if she moved, David and his wife would hear her, for around her feet was a carpet of dried leaves; if she remained where she was, the men, for now she could see they were men who were approaching, could not help but see her.

The men had already seen her by the time she coughed, and it must have seemed like the crack of a gun, for it caused David and Hazel to swing around and stare in her direction.

In the seconds that passed as neither they nor Betty moved, the men had reached the railings and now they too, taking in the situation immediately, stared at her.

She forced herself to take a step from the trees and, nodding towards David, to say, 'It's all right, carry on.'

It sounded to her own ears as if she were back in the Army: It's all right, corporal. Carry on.

The deep breath David let out would not have been one of shame at being found out, but of a quick decision: turning quickly, he lifted up the sacks and handed them to the waiting men.

When each man was holding two sacks they all remained still as if formed of one body, then the oldest-looking among them, a thin-jowled, black-capped middle-aged man, nodded towards her and muttered, 'Thank God, miss.'

She stood as the men hurried away down the slope; watching them until they disappeared in a clump of bushes, only to emerge within a moment or so, pushing what appeared to be a square wheel-barrow, and she was quick to realise that the sacks would now be camouflaged.

She hadn't noticed David and Hazel walking towards her and she turned her head sharply in their direction when David said, 'He knows, miss. The . . . the boss, miss, he knows about it.'

'Oh well, that's all right then.' She smiled.

'But . . . but not the missis . . . not madam.'

Again she said 'Oh!' Well, this was no surprise; she wouldn't expect Elaine to play godmother to the pit people, for apparently they were anathema to her. She had soon learned that Elaine disliked them not only as a class, but more so because of Joe's attitude towards them; and, above all, she had learned that Elaine couldn't tolerate this dark fellow here, nor his wife.

'Well, don't worry; she won't hear anything from me. As long as her husband knows then, in a way, you are just . . . well, just carrying out his orders.'

She watched the couple smile at each other with a deep warmness, and the look in their eyes brought into life a peculiar feeling, the only feeling she was really afraid of, the feeling that had the power to grease the lock on the door of the closed room of her mind, the empty, starkly bare room wherein nothing existed but aloneness.

'They are having it very rough, miss. It's the bairns most of all, and the week-ends always seem the worse. They . . . they always looked forward to a bit of a dinner on a Sunday, so we do this every Saturday. Mary . . . I mean Mrs Duffy, saves us the bits and pieces from the house, and the boss says I can have the surplus from the garden. But even so I've had to cut down on their rations, for we never thought the strike would last this length of time.'

'How much longer do you think it will go on?'

'Oh, that's anybody's guess, miss. If they give in now they're finished, for good an' all, they're finished; it's a kind of war. One thing's certain: they won't give in for themselves nor yet for their wives, but it'll be the bairns that'll break the back of the strike; it'll be for them they'll give in.'

'But they're being helped, aren't they? I mean, there are people providing food?' She didn't say soup kitchens, as it sounded so much like condescending charity.

'Aye, yes.' David sighed now. 'People are kind. They do their best, but 'tisn't good enough to keep body and soul together. And you know, miss, it isn't only the food, it's the loss of pride. Somehow if a man has to beg or grovel for food, or be numbered two hundred and ten in a queue for it, it strips him of his manhood. Things like that shouldn't be allowed. We're all human beings whatever our work, or . . . or our colour.'

He naturally stood head and shoulders above his wife, but his making this statement seemed to increase his stature further, and she, putting her hand out and taking his gently, spoke for the first time, saying, 'David, David; miss doesn't want to go into all that.'

'Oh, but I do, I do. I agree with what your husband said.' Betty was smiling at Hazel and Hazel smiled back at her, and what she said now surprised and embarrassed Betty, for it was almost the same words as Mike had said to her yesterday, 'I'm glad you've come, miss, and I hope you stay a long time.'

'Thank you. Thank you. I'm . . . I'm glad to be here.' She smiled at them, then turned and walked up the path; and they walked with her; and when they neared the greenhouses where the path divided, she continued with them and a few minutes later, on a note of surprise, she said, 'Good gracious! there's the gates. I didn't know there was a path this way. And there's your house across the drive.'

83

'Would you like to come in and have a cup of tea, miss?'

Betty looked from one to the other; then her large mouth stretching wide, she said, 'Yes, I would. Thank you.' And her round brown eyes twinkling, she leaned forward towards them and added in a conspiratorial whisper, 'I don't suppose you have any sausage rolls left?'

For a moment David and Hazel looked at each other, then back at her, and now their joined laughter rang out loud on the frosty air.

And the echo of their laughter reached the house and it brought Ella upright from where she was emptying a pail of ashes on to the dry midden and she smiled as she thought, 'That's funny to hear first thing in the morning; I wonder what the joke is.'

And the sound of laughter wafted its way in through the open window to Mike's bed, where he was sitting propped up after a sleepless night and waiting impatiently for his breakfast; and it caused him to turn his head towards the window as he thought: Laughing at this time of the mornin'. What's there to laugh about at this time of the mornin'?

And the echo of it reached Joe as he crossed the hall to the dining-room, causing him to stop for a moment, then walk to the front door and open it. Somebody laughing like that at eight in the morning! It was a long time since he had heard laughter like that around here; not since he and David used to dive into the lake during the holidays. He closed the door quietly. Ah well, those days were gone, never to return.

And Elaine, pouring out her first cup of tea from the silver teapot, paused as the sound of the laughter came to her through the open window, and it reminded her strongly of a laugh that used to grate on her. Betty's laugh. Betty had a coarse laugh; what was termed a belly laugh. But surely she wasn't out at this time of the morning. She turned her head and looked towards the window. No, no. Anyway, what could she be laughing at in the garden? It must be some of those hobbledehoys from the village sneaking about to see what they could thieve . . .

Joe had almost finished his breakfast when Betty hurried into the dining-room, and she apologised both to him and to Ella, who had just entered the room carrying a fresh pot of tea: 'Oh, I'm sorry,' she said, 'but . . . but I went for a walk in the garden and the time slipped by.'

'You went for a walk in the garden?' Joe repeated the words slowly.

'Yes . . . Yes.' She sat down and lifted up the cover of the bacon dish.

'It was early to go walking in the garden, wasn't it?'

'Best time, I think.' She pronged two slices of bacon, a sausage and a piece of fried bread onto her plate.

Joe wiped his mouth on his napkin before he said casually, 'Which part did you get to? I don't think you've been all over it, have you?'

'I have now . . . This is lovely bacon, Jane,' she said, turning to look at Ella, who was standing as if stuck against the sideboard. 'We never get bacon like this in the south. It's what you call green bacon, isn't it? . . . You have large grounds.' She had brought her eyes back to her plate, and now raised them without moving her head and looked across the table towards Joe.

'Yes; yes, there's quite a lot.'

'I got right to the boundary this morning . . . And these sausages are good, too.' Again she turned and looked towards Ella, and Ella stared back at her, but didn't move or answer.

'Did you meet anyone while you were out on your early walk?' The question also sounded casual.

85

'Oh yes, yes.' She reached over now and lifted a silver jug towards her, saying, 'I think I'll have coffee instead of tea this morning;' then went on as she poured out the coffee, 'I ran into David and Hazel and—' Now she paused, placed the coffee jug back on the table, then screwed up her eyes as she ended, 'Funny, but I didn't catch the names of the others; the other men.'

Joe and Ella exchanged quick glances; then Joe, crushing his napkin between his hands, placed it on the table and, leaning forward, he said slowly, 'Betty.'

'Yes, Joe?' She waited. 'You want to say something?'

He ran his tongue around his lips, glanced again at Ella, nodded at her, which was a signal for her to leave the room, although at this point she didn't seem to understand, then swallowed deeply and remained mute, for he couldn't say to Betty in front of Ella, 'For God's sake! don't let on to Elaine about this.' But in the next moment he knew that there would be no need for that, for, after taking a drink from her cup, Betty said, 'I don't usually like coffee first thing in the morning but I've just had two cups of tea with David and Hazel, and the last of' – she paused and made the slightest movement of her head towards Ella as she ended – 'the sausage rolls.'

Again there was laughter, spluttered, smothered laughter on Joe's part, uninhibited on Betty's, although the sound Ella gave vent to was almost hysterical, and she hadn't subdued it fully as she crossed the hall.

Mike, sitting further up in the bed, said aloud, 'What's going on in this house this morning? It's like a pantomime.'

And Elaine, hearing the renewed laughter, muttered to herself with deep indignation, 'That's the girl; either Joe or Betty has been joking with her. I wonder what next. This situation is becoming impossible.' But then it wasn't likely to be Joe who had caused Jane so to forget herself as to laugh aloud, and at that pitch, because Joe knew her feelings with regard to the servants and he wouldn't upset her, not in her present condition. No, it would be Betty; she had a way of hob-nobbing with the servants, with anyone, in fact, below her own station. It would so often appear that she was more at home with the lower classes. Well, she'd put her into the picture straightaway: she wasn't going to allow that kind of thing to go on in this house . . .

But wait. She needed Betty. Oh yes, she needed Betty, and not only now, but would do for months to come; and when the child was born she would need her more . . . She'd better tread carefully; Betty was quite capable of taking up her bags and leaving.

She suddenly experienced a feeling of deep envy towards her gauche sister. Oh, to be able to take up your bags and go . . . with enough money to provide for your needs, to say farewell to this part of the country, and this house and everyone in it. Oh yes, this house and everyone in it.

3

'You're not going to accept?'

'Of course I am.'

'After her sending you a letter like that?' Elaine pointed to the sheet of paper in Betty's hand, and Betty laughed, replying, 'If she had written any other way I wouldn't have thought it was from her; it's characteristic.' She read aloud, ' "Come to tea on Wednesday four o'clock . . . just you. This place is like the North Pole; wrap up well. You remember me? We met in the railway carriage. Sarah'll likely not speak to you but don't let that bother you. Yours, Mary Ambers." '

'It's just like her.'

'What did she mean, just you? Did she think that I would go along with you?'

'No, of course not.'

'Then why did she say it?'

'I don't know, Elaine.' Betty now folded up the letter and put it in her pocket. 'She's an eccentric old lady,' she added.

'You're being invited on sufferance: you must refuse it; she says Lady Menton will likely not speak to you.'

'I'm not going to refuse it, Elaine; she's likely very lonely.'

'Nonsense. She's more likely bored and wants to use you as a form of excuse.'

'Most probably. Most probably.' Betty now turned towards the door, adding, as she opened it, 'Most people do.'

As the door closed behind her, Elaine called testily, 'Betty! Betty!'

Betty took no notice, but crossed the landing and went into her room. Jane had lit the fire, for the day was bitterly cold; in ten days' time it would be Christmas. She had never looked forward to Christmas, because she always felt sad at Christmas. She didn't know why, but even as a child she had felt sad at this time of year. Christmas presents and a Christmas stocking had done nothing to alleviate this feeling. She couldn't understand why; it was something deeply inborn in her. But now she was depressed, too, by other matters, things that she couldn't discuss with Elaine, such as the deep sympathy she felt for the miners down there in the village, and for all those others who'd had to return to work under worse conditions than they had suffered before going on strike. For seven long months they had stood out and now, as Joe had said last night, they were like an army that had surrendered to a merciless foe, and like conquered men they were bitter and full of hatred.

She had seen that hatred take on a tangible form a few weeks ago when she was passing through Fellburn. The miners had been fighting with the police, themselves protecting pitmen from another town who had come to work in the mine. The streets had been full of raging curses intermingled with cries of: 'Blacklegs! Scurvy swine! Backdoor bastards. Thieves! Taking the bread out of the bairns' mouths;' on and so on. And she had seen the blood running down thin rage-engulfed faces.

A month ago all the windows down one section of Joe's factory had been smashed in, and two of his men had been attacked in the dark and beaten up. Injustice created beasts: Mike had stated it well when he said that it turned fireside tom-cats into tigers.

But now it was all over there was a deeper sadness in the village and the town than there had been when the strike was at its height. She likened the situation to war-occupied territory. Admitted, there were many rough customers among the miners, but who wouldn't be rough when forced to work under such conditions as they had, and for so little money?

There were times of late when she wished she hadn't come here. Except for the time she spent in war service she had, for most of her life, lived among a class of people who, in the main, lived graciously. Even though, for some time now, she had found herself as an employee, nevertheless she had, in a way, been on the same plane as her mistresses. But since coming into this house she had been plunged into a different atmosphere, a strange atmosphere; yet despite it all she found herself in sympathy with it, and with those from whom it emanated, not only with Joe and Mike, but also with David and Hazel down in the cottage, who were quietly fighting their war against colour prejudice; and with Ella, who had been forced to change her name just to please Elaine; and with Mary and Duffy, both work-weary. And it distressed her to think that she felt more at ease in their company than she did in that of her sister.

Elaine had always been petulant, and marriage hadn't improved her; in fact, on more than one occasion of late it had been as much as she could do to carry on playing 'good old Betty' and not to turn on her and tell her exactly what she thought. But she had reminded herself that Elaine was well into her sixth month of pregnancy and was feeling unwell most of the time, or at least so she said. She slumped down in her chair and held her feet out towards the fire and chastised herself. She mustn't accuse Elaine of putting on her sickness, for at times she really did look ill.

She wished Christmas was over; she wished she had something definite to do besides soothing Elaine, and arranging flowers, and knitting, knitting, knitting. The only brightness in her days occurred when she climbed the stairs and had a natter with Mike, or when she talked to Joe; not that she often had the chance to talk to Joe, apart from at breakfast, or perhaps at late supper if Elaine had gone to bed. She liked talking to Joe. She liked Joe altogether. She thought he was a fine man, much too good for Elaine.

Betty rose abruptly from the chair and went hastily from the room and up the stairs to the top floor.

When she opened the sitting-room door she could see no sign of Mike, so she knocked on the bedroom door only to hear a voice from the observatory calling, 'I'm up here. Who is it?'

'It's me, Mike.'

'Aw, come on up, lass.'

She climbed the steep stairs into the conservatory, and there he was sitting on a straight-backed chair, a rug round his knees and an oil stove to the side of him, and she said immediately, 'What on earth brought you up here?'

'The view, lass, as always the view, for on a clear day like this it's something not to be missed. Look at that.' He pointed through the wide panes. 'You can see all the way to the river, even the ships going up and down. Look there.' He handed her a pair of binoculars and when she put them to her eyes, yes indeed, she could see the different shapes of the ships on the river.

She stood by his side and turned her head one way and then the other as she said, 'It is a most extraordinary view.'

'Aye, lass, there's not a yard of land for miles around you can't pick out from here. Me old dad knew what he was doing when he built this place.'

'He did indeed! But look' – she bent over him – 'it's dangerous for you to attempt those stairs alone.'

'I'm all right; I've arrived.' He spread out his arms.

'One of these days you'll arrive at the bottom.'

'Very likely, lass, very likely, and that'll put a quick end to it, and a good job an' all.'

'Don't be silly.'

'I'm not being silly.' He looked up at her now, his clear blue eyes fastened intently on her. 'I'm going to ask you a question. In the same position, which would you choose, a quick end or a long-drawn-out existence looking at your bones twisting up?'

She stared back at him, her face solemn-looking as she replied, 'I don't know; I wouldn't be able to answer that truthfully unless I found myself in your position. I only know that your going would leave a gap in a great many lives.'

'You think so?' He laughed a short amused laugh; then he shook his head at her and said, 'You're kind, lass, you're kind. But you know something? I've never been able to use all the fingers on one hand to count the friends I've had, the real friends. And I'm not the only one, because you show me the man who says he's got more than five friends in the world, real friends I'm talking about, mind, and I'll show you the biggest liar going. A man can have acquaintances by the score; in fact, we all tend to say, Oh, he's a friend of mine. But no, lass, friends, real friends, are scarcer than the radium that Madame Curie went after. By the way, I've been reading about her the day. Great woman, great woman; nearly went mad when her man died. And by the way, that's scarce too, the

92

element that makes a woman nearly go mad when her man dies.'

'Now you're being cynical.'

'Oh no, lass, no, I'm not. If she's young she takes it in her stride; if she's under fifty she dolls herself up and looks for another man; an' if she's over fifty she takes a housekeeping job and hopes.'

His head went back and his laugh was infectious, and she joined hers to it, and when it died away she dried her eyes and said, 'You're an awful man, Mike, but you're good for one, like some medicines.'

'Epsom salts or cascara?'

She flapped her hand at him; then taking a seat to the side of him, she said, 'I'm going out to tea on Wednesday.'

'Aye, where to?'

'The Hall, Lord Menton's place.'

He turned to her so quickly that he ricked his neck, and the pain was evident in his face. He gasped before he said, 'No kiddin', lass?'

'No kiddin', Mike.'

'Well, I'll be damned! Lady Menton asked you?'

'Oh no, no, not Lady Menton, the one I was telling you about, the eccentric one, Lady Mary Ambers.'

'Oh her; the one you met on the train?'

'Yes; here's the invitation.' She pulled the letter from her pocket and handed it to him, and as he read it his face stretched in glee as he exclaimed, 'Well, I'll be damned! I've seen some invitations in me time but that beats all. She must be a character.'

'Yes, she is. I'm rather looking forward to meeting her again.'

'Does . . . does Elaine know?'

'Yes. Yes, I told her.'

'How did she take it?'

93

He had poked his face towards her and she hesitated a moment before she smiled and said, 'Oh, she advised me to refuse it.'

'Aye, she would. But she wouldn't have given you that advice if she'd been included. You go, me lass. But mind, I'm going to tell you something.' He wagged his finger at her. 'If the conversation comes round to this house and me, likely you won't come back here, because me name's mud, as was me father's afore me. No, no, his name was clarts, which means the same, but it's a thicker kind, you know.' He jerked his head at her now, saying, 'By! I won't be able to wait until you get back to hear all about it. But mind you keep your end up; don't let them floor you.' He now put his head on one side and paused before he ended, 'But I don't think they could. Nor do I think they would want to; I don't think they'd want to floor you, 'cos you're not prickly.'

'Oh, you don't know me.'

'Don't I? I think I do. I knew all about you within a few days of your coming. I know people, Betty, I know people and' – he grinned mischievously at her now as he whispered, 'I know something about you that you try to keep hidden.'

'You do?' She was whispering back at him.

'Aye, I do. You've got a temper, but you've got it well under control. There's two Bettys, one under the skin and one on top of it.'

She didn't return his grin but she stared at him for a moment in silence before looking away and saying, 'You see too much, Mike; you're uncomfortable; you see too much.'

'Aw, lass' – he nearly upset himself from the chair as he reached out and grabbed her hand – 'I mean no offence, lass. I wouldn't offend you for the world. It was just that I wanted you to know that I recognise the depth in you. You're so damn pleasant to everybody that folks take you for granted. You're the oil on the wheels that makes things

94

run smoothly. You're the hearty good sort. That's on the outside. But underneath, there's you, the real one . . . I know you, you see, I know you.'

They were holding each other's gaze, and he was also holding her wrist with one hand and she was still holding his arm with her other where she had tried to steady him. She swallowed deeply in her throat, sniffed, blinked her eyes a number of times, then said briskly, 'Come on; it's about time you got yourself down those stairs.'

After a moment's hesitation he pulled himself to his feet, and, standing by her side, he laughed softly as he said, 'I'm stooped a bit, but I'm still taller than you.'

Again their gaze held, but she made no reply; she understood the meaning behind the words: he might be crippled yet he still considered himself a man. And indeed he was. Like herself, there was another being underneath his skin.

'Now look, stop arguing, Betty, you're going in style.'

'But it isn't a mile down the road, Joe, and I don't know how long I'll be there.'

'Well, if you're there until tomorrow morning David'll wait for you.'

'It's ridiculous. It isn't as if the roads were wet, and I like walking. You know I do. And what if I can't get away before five? What'll you do to get back without the car?'

'You let me worry about that. Do as you're told for once.'

'Oh, that's funny.'

'Yes, it is, isn't it?' Joe looked across the breakfast table towards her and said quietly, 'You're at everybody's beck and call; you never seem to have a minute to yourself.'

'How do you know? You're not here all day.'

'I have spies.'

'Oh, I've no doubt about that.'

95

'But they're nice spies.'

'And I've no doubt about that either.'

As they smiled at each other, he said quietly, 'I'm very glad you're here, Betty; Elaine's been as different again since you came. As she said, and rightly, there was no-one here who spoke her language. You *will* stay on until the baby comes?'

'If she wants me to.'

'Oh, she wants you to. We all want you to, particularly himself. You've scored a bull's-eye up there, I might tell you.'

'Oh, don't go on.' She flapped her large square hand at him. 'By the sound of it I'm qualifying for stripes.'

'Well, you could say something like that.'

'Nonsense! Anyway, about the car . . .'

'No more about the car. It'll be at the door at five minutes to three and David'll deliver you on the dot.'

'You're not thinking about buying a uniform for him, are you?'

'Well, that's an idea. I hadn't thought of it, but it is an idea.' He got to his feet now, glanced at his watch, compared it with the marble clock standing in the middle of the marble mantelpiece, altered the hands a fraction, then said, 'Well, I must be off. Goodbye, Betty.'

'Goodbye, Joe; and thanks for the car.'

He turned from the door and grinned at her; then, jerking his chin upwards, he said. 'We'll let 'em see.'

She rose from the table and walked to the dining-room window that looked out onto the end of the drive, and she stood there for about five minutes until she saw him descending the steps. She watched him pause at the bottom and look up into the sky, then pull the peak of his trilby hat firmly down over his brow and turn up the collar of his coat before stepping into the car and taking the wheel.

She stood at the window until the car disappeared from her view down the drive, then she turned about and slowly drew her teeth tightly over her bottom lip.

At three o'clock exactly David drew the Rolls to a stop at the bottom of the broad stone steps which led up to a stone balcony and thence to a front door, unusually shaped in that it had a rounded top, and as he opened the car door Betty discerned a twinkle in his eye.

After helping her to alight, he walked before her up the steps, pulled the iron handle attached to the wall, and waited until the door was opened before bowing slightly and returning down the steps to the car.

The footman was not in livery but he wore a black suit and a white collar and tie, which did nothing to disguise his position, for, his head slightly to the side and his voice holding a definite note of hauteur, he said, 'Miss Hughes-Burton?'

'Yes.'

'You're expected. Would you please come this way?'

'Thank you.' They were only two words but their inflexion brought the footman's head to a more level position.

Betty now followed him through a small hall, the floor of which was tiled and resembled that of a butchers' shop; then they entered the main hall. Here the walls from floor to ceiling were lined with a dark wood and, as if this wasn't depressing enough, animals' heads, mostly horned, seemed to protrude from the panelling in every part of the room that wasn't taken up by the windows, doors and the staircase.

The floor was covered in Persian rugs so worn in parts that they wrinkled under her feet.

She was now walking down a short wide corridor, and at the end of it the footman stopped, tapped twice on the door, opened it and announced in precise tones, 'Miss Hughes-Burton.'

'Oh, there you are. There you are. Come in. Do you know that your reply didn't come until eleven o'clock this morning? Come along, sit down; you look frozen. This is the worst part of the country in the world. Do you know that? Open your coat or you won't find the good of it when you go out . . . Bring in the tea, Rogers, and don't stint on the cakes.'

During all this Betty had walked up the long drawing-room and taken the proffered seat, the while unobtrusively taking in the room. In a way it was on a par with the hall; the only difference being that it was lighter, for this room, too, was a showcase for trophies and pieces of elaborate china and furniture, all representing travel. The china cabinets held rows of silver cups, whilst small tables showed off groups of ivories and Chinese figures and ornaments; the only homely touch in the room was the enormous Chesterfield suite, which had once been beautiful, having been upholstered in green velvet with a gold tasselled fringe, and which, in its faded old age, still gave off an air of comfort.

'How are you?' Betty inclined her head towards her hostess who, pulling a large woollen shawl closer about her shoulders, exclaimed briefly, 'Bored . . . bored to death. I would have been gone weeks ago but James is on his last legs and Sarah wants me to stay till the end. Why, I don't know; we fight like cat and dog. She's dull, nothing up top.' She now tapped her forehead, and all Betty could do was to remain silent and prevent herself from laughing outright and asking herself how a human being came to be like this, so utterly unself-conscious and oblivious to the age in which she lived, as was strikingly evident in her dress, which was even more old-fashioned than her travelling outfit had been, for it had a number of overlapping skirts. She couldn't see the bodice because of the shawl, but the cuffs

98

of the dress were at least six inches deep and were fastened with a long row of pearl buttons.

'How are you getting on along there?' The tousled grey head was jerked in the direction of the drawing-room door.

'Oh, very well.'

'Your sister good to you?'

'Yes, oh yes, very good.'

'They're a funny family she's married into, so Sarah says.'

'In what way do you mean?' Betty's tone was cool now.

'Oh well, you hear things, just rumours. And he, the father, coarse man, isn't he? Coarse man.'

'I find him a very intelligent man.'

'Intelligent, do you? Well! well! it isn't often you find coarse men intelligent. I prefer coarse men; they're always more interesting than polite, gentlemanly ones. Most of those turn out to have no guts. Two of my husbands were coarse, the first two.' She bounced her head now towards Betty, then exclaimed loudly, 'Ah, here it comes,' as the door opened and the footman wheeled in a trolley.

When the man had brought the trolley to the side of the couch the old lady peered down on it; then, picking up a minute sandwich, she opened it. 'Cucumber. Ah! Cucumber always give me indigestion; haven't you got anything else in the kitchen but cucumber?' She was staring up at the footman with her piercing gaze, and he replied in an almost soothing tone, 'There are egg and tomato below, milady.'

'Oh. Oh, that's all right then. Just leave it; Miss Burton will pour out. You're used to pouring out tea, aren't you?'

'Yes.' Betty smiled faintly. 'Yes, I'm used to pouring out tea.'

'Well, get on with it; I'm as dry as a fish. They had baked ham for lunch; it was salty.'

Betty poured out the tea from the heavy silver teapot into the paper-thin china cups, and when she handed Lady Ambers her cup the old woman said, 'Thanks, me dear, thanks. Oh, it is nice to have tea poured out for you and to have company. I miss company; someone to talk to. Have a sandwich. The egg are at the bottom. You heard what he said.'

'I'll have a cucumber one.'

'Please yourself; it's your digestion.'

Betty had barely sat down and was about to take her first sip of tea when she was startled by her hostess exclaiming, 'It must be a bloody life having to say, "Yes, ma'am" and "No, ma'am" to people. I don't mean footmen and butlers and the household staff. No, no; not them; they're servants, they were bred to it, as we were bred to accept their service. But I mean people like you, an intelligent, refined woman having to run after old bitches. And there are some old bitches about, I know that. I remember your telling me on the train that you were with Mrs Boulton-Westbrook. Well, if she was anything like her sister, I pity you. She had a companion for years; treated her like a doormat. Then when the poor thing took ill she let her go into a home, not the kind for distressed ladies but some place run by a council. You know the kind . . . well, perhaps you don't, but they're awful. I opened one once, and as I said to the mayor at the time, I wished to God I was closing it; terrible place, green-painted walls and wooden chairs. I wouldn't treat anyone like that. I've never had a companion up to now, never met anyone I'd want to live with, not any woman anyway, but now I think it's time I had a companion. I've been thinking about it a lot since I met you on the train. I like you, girl, I like you.'

She leaned forward and poked the blunt-edged silver tea-knife into Betty's arm. 'You've got a kind face and a sympathetic manner, but at the same time, I can tell, you wouldn't stand any nonsense from me. Now would you?'

As she grinned widely Betty, too, leaned forward and placed her tea cup on the trolley before bowing her head. She could hardly contain her laughter from bursting forth. Then she did let it ripple, but not to its full extent, as the old lady said, 'Do you want to laugh? Well, laugh; it's good to hear people laugh. I used to be able to make people laugh at one time. They'd always ask me to parties. I was the life and soul of any do but . . .' She suddenly stopped talking, placed her half-eaten sandwich down on the plate, let her head fall against the back of the couch; then she parted her lips wide, lifted up her bottom set of teeth with her tongue and extracted what might have been a crumb of bread or a piece of egg from her gums, wiped her finger on the tea napkin and said slowly, 'But there's nothing much to laugh at any more, especially here in this house. Sarah and James are old before their time. He's not eighty yet, and he's in his dotage, and Sarah only seventy-five and acting as if she were coming up to her century. And that's why' – she now brought her head forward and fixed her gaze on Betty as she ended – 'I would like you to be my companion.'

Betty remained silent, for she was engulfed in a wave of pity for this woman who had been everywhere, seen everything – at least so she had implied on the train – and who now was old and very tired and lonely.

'I'd be good to you; I wouldn't let you go into a home if you stayed by me. Have you any money of your own; I mean, an income?'

'No.'

'Nothing?'

'No; only what I earn.'

'Well, then, I would provide for you. Yes, I would, I would. I'd make an agreement. What do you say?'

What could she say? A moment ago she had wanted to laugh uproariously, now she was almost on the verge of tears. She swallowed deeply before she said quietly, 'I am most grateful for your offer, Lady Ambers, and . . . and under other circumstances I would have accepted it, and gladly, but, you see, my sister is going to have a baby early next year and I have promised to stay with her until then, and for a little time afterwards.'

'A little time after? Then what?'

'Well, I . . . I don't really know, but . . . but if your offer is still open I would be glad to discuss it again.'

'You would?'

'Yes; yes, I would. And thank you very much.'

'You're a nice girl.'

Betty lowered her head slightly, blinked, smiled, then said, 'I'm on my best behaviour today.'

The laugh the old lady let out sounded, Betty thought, almost as loud as her own when she got going.

'Have a cake?'

'Thank you.'

'You know . . . you know something?'

Betty waited.

'When I was in that train with you I thought that my travelling days were over, and me only sixty-seven.' She paused as if waiting to see what effect the statement of her age would have on Betty; but Betty didn't blink an eyelid, and she went on, 'I thought I'd have to spend the rest of my days looking at James slavering and listening to Sarah moaning. But after three weeks of it I know I couldn't stand it. And this house. Did you ever see anything so dull as this house? Then James took to his bed and, as I told you, I'm stuck here until he goes, and then it's back to an hotel. I live in hotels, you know, I haven't any settled home, but—' She now eased herself to the front of the couch and, putting out

102

her bony fingers, she clasped Betty's knee gently as she said, 'If you come with me, girl, I'll buy a house; we'll make a home, you and I. I've plenty of money, more than I know what to do with. That's what I'll do, we'll make a home.'

It was a situation with which at present Betty couldn't cope; at least not with words. She watched the old lady lean back again against the couch; she watched her look upwards as if she were again lost in thought as she said, 'Life is strange, isn't it? But George said to me: You'll find someone, Mary, who will love you and look after you; you'll never die alone. But who would have thought I would meet her in a train on a journey from London to Newcastle? Do you believe in fate?'

'Yes, in a way.' There was a slight tremble in Betty's voice which she couldn't control. 'I . . . I have the idea that life is mapped out for us from the start, yet at the same time I . . . I question why the roads on some maps are so rough and so hard.'

The old lady looked at her now in silence. It was the first silence that had fallen between them, and it continued while once more she put her head back and gazed towards the ceiling. But after a few moments Betty had to break it. Looking at her watch, she said quietly, 'Will you excuse me, Lady Ambers? But I must be going; the chauffeur is waiting for me and he has to pick up my brother-in-law from the factory at five o'clock.'

'Oh. Oh.' Lady Ambers now pulled herself slowly to her feet and, holding out her hand, she said, 'You have given me your word; it's a bargain.'

'It's a bargain. But . . . but I must impress upon you I must stay with my sister as long as she needs me.'

'Till after the baby is born?'

'Yes, till after the baby is born.'

'Well, then, let's forget about this Lady Ambers non-sense. Call me Mary. And look' – she was still holding

Betty's hand – 'do you think I might visit you now and again?'

'Oh yes, yes.' Betty smiled brightly at her. 'Of course; you'd be very welcome.'

'Well, I'll do that. When things get really on top of me I'll come along and see you . . . Will I have to write and let you know?'

'No, no, you needn't; just call when you feel like it.'

'And your sister won't mind?'

'She'd be delighted to see you.'

'From what I saw of her I didn't take to her much. But anyway, I won't be coming to see her, I'll be coming to see you . . . Ring the bell.' She pointed to a thick betasselled cord hanging by the fireplace, and after Betty had pulled it she said, 'Goodbye, Lady Mary. It's been a pleasure.'

'I'm so glad you think so, girl. It makes me feel I've still some life left in me. We had a laugh, didn't we?'

'We did, and thank you. Goodbye.'

The door opened, and when the footman entered, Lady Ambers called in a loud voice, as if he were already on the drive, 'See Miss Burton into her car, Rogers, and see she's well tucked up.'

'Yes, milady.'

As Betty walked across the hall behind the footman she was amused by the fact that even his back showed that his opinion of her had changed since he had opened the door to her.

David did not allow the footman to do the honours but himself saw that she had a rug over her knees before he took his own seat, and when they had passed through the gates he put his head back and said loudly, so that his voice would penetrate the closed windows of the partition, 'I hope you had an enjoyable visit, miss?'

Betty, bending forward, opened the window and said, 'Most enjoyable, David. And she's going to return the visit.'

'My! My!'

'Yes, that's what I say too, David: My! My!' She sat back and repeated to herself, 'My! My!' and then she thought, Poor soul. Poor old soul.

How would she like being companion to her?

She would like it very much. Yes, she would. And she had promised to make a settlement on her. Had anyone else ever promised to make a settlement on her in her life? No-one; apart from a small salary she had received from Mrs Boulton-Westbrook, she had worked for her keep among cousins and aunts since the war ended, and that was eight years ago.

Yes, she would enjoy being companion to Lady Ambers . . . Mary. No, Lady Mary. That would be better.

'Don't be ridiculous! Make a settlement on you? She's saying that until she gets you. They're skinflints, the Mentons, the Amberses, all that crowd; they're known to be tight-fisted. And you took it in?'

'Yes, I took it in. And I believe her. Anyway, why are you getting so het up? I'm not going tomorrow; I told you I'll stay as long as you need me.'

'But you'll hold her over my head.'

'What do you mean?' Betty's tone was indignant.

'Just what I say. If I lose my temper with you or say a word out of place, all right, you'll say, I'm off to the old crone's.'

'She's not an old crone.'

'What is she then? She's an eccentric old bag of rags.'

'She's a lady . . . she's a lady of the old school: she's straightforward and she's honest.'

'What do you know of her? Don't be stupid and gullible, Betty. You met her on the train, you've had a cup of tea with her, and now she possesses all the virtues.'

As Betty stared at her sister, Elaine cried, 'Go on, tell me that you haven't got to put up with me or my temper, you can walk out now.'

'And that's what I'm going to do.'

As Betty turned towards the door Elaine called in a voice that was just above a whisper, 'Betty, please, I'm sorry. Don't take any notice. I'm . . . I'm just afraid you're going to leave me.'

'And I am for the present.'

'Don't be mad at me.'

'I'm not mad at you. Go on—' Her tone softened. 'Go on downstairs; Joe will be in in a minute. And stop worrying; nothing has changed. And oh, I'd better tell you, she's going to call.'

As Elaine's mouth dropped into a gape, Betty left the room, closing the door behind her, and as she made her way to her room she thought she should be feeling quite pleased with herself that she was so much in demand, that she was wanted. But did it matter if you were wanted and needed by the whole world if there wasn't someone particular who needed you for yourself?

Oh, she wished that she had never come here. Life had been dull and hard before, but her feelings weren't ravished then, as they were now.

4

It was nine o'clock in the evening of 26 April, 1927, and Elaine was deep in labour, as she had been all day. The first pains had attacked her at five o'clock the previous evening and when the doctor saw her a short while later, he smilingly told her she had a long way to go yet and that it might be the morrow morning before she gave birth.

He was back in the house at nine o'clock the following morning and after examining her he again smilingly intimated that it could be a little time yet; but that she wasn't to worry, everything was all right; it was often like this with the first baby. He'd be back about noon.

Joe had engaged a nurse, and unfortunately Elaine had taken a dislike to her on sight, for she not only turned the bedroom into a replica of a hospital ward but she gave orders which she expected to be obeyed. 'Come on now,' she would say at frequent intervals, 'bear down, do a little work, he or she can't do it all themselves. You wouldn't expect it, would you? Come on now, bear down.' When she added practical help in the bearing down, Elaine screamed, and not for the first time during the last few hours; but this time she added between shuddering breaths, 'Get out! Get out! Joe! I want Betty. *Joe! Joe!*'

Joe burst into the room; then stood for a moment looking towards the bed, where the nurse was standing breathing almost as heavily as Elaine now, although still keeping her composure. She nodded her head at Joe and gave a peremptory wave of her hand as she said, 'It's all right. It's all right. It's just that she is proving a little difficult.'

Joe now came quickly towards the bed, where Elaine was holding her arms out to him, and as he gripped her hands he glared at the nurse and said, 'What do you mean, a little difficult?'

'Just what I said, Mr Remington. She . . . she won't co-operate, she's tense, all her muscles are tense, she'll have to let go before it will come; she's only prolonging the agony.'

'Agony. Agony. Yes, that's what it is.' The tears were streaming down Elaine's cheeks and she tossed her head from side to side and moaned, 'Oh Joe! Joe!'

'It's all right, darling. It's all right. It'll be soon over.'

'Send her out, Joe. Send her out. I want Betty.'

'She'll be here in a minute; she's only gone downstairs for a bite to eat.'

'I want Betty. I want Betty.' Her head was still tossing backwards and forwards on the pillow.

'All right, all right, I'll go and fetch her now. Only in the meantime, darling, try . . . try to do what Nurse says; try to relax and then it'll come.'

'It'll never come; I'll die. I'll die, Joe. I can't bear it. Do you hear? I can't bear it.' She now gazed pitifully up into his face, and he wiped the tears from her cheeks; then he stroked her hair back from her sweat-dripping brow. But the next moment he was gripping her hand tightly as she pulled up her knees and emitted a high piercing scream.

When he was pushed aside he made no resistance but hurried blindly out of the room, and he stood with his back to the wall by the side of the door for a moment, pressing his fingers on his eyeballs and swallowing deeply in his throat. Never again. Never again. He would never let her go through this again, ever. If she died he'd never forgive himself. But she mustn't die. The child mustn't die. He wanted that child. Oh yes, he wanted that child. Boy or girl, he wanted that child, yet not at the price it was costing.

He ran down the stairs now and burst into the dining-room, but before he had time to open his mouth Betty had risen from the table and, wiping the food from her lips with her fingers, she said, 'It's come?'

'No, no, Betty, no, no.' He bowed his head, then swung it from side to side. 'She wants you. She can't stand that nurse. Nor can I, for that matter. How much longer, Betty?'

'I . . . I don't know, Joe. But if it goes on like this I think the doctor will take her to the hospital.'

'What!' His head came up. 'When did he say this?'

'He said as much when he left, just before you came in.'

'What will he do for her there that he can't do here?'

'I . . . I think he may be contemplating a Caesarean.'

'Cut her up?' He screwed up his eyes.

'It's quite safe. He . . . he explained it to me.'

'Oh my God! Betty.' He was standing in front of her, and she took his hands and gripped them as she said, 'It's all right, it's all right. Try not to worry. The doctor . . . well, he didn't seem too concerned. He said this often happens.'

'Often happens?' As he let his head drop back on his shoulders she gazed at him. He'd had his twenty-seventh birthday the previous week but at this moment he looked like a man of forty. His face was grey, the lines across his brow had deepened, his dark brown eyes looked black and

109

were sunk in his head. His thick-set body, which in itself emanated strength, seemed to have sagged under his clothes. But it wasn't only during the last two days she had noticed the change in him, for she had seen it creeping on him during the past three months, when things had not been running smoothly . . . in the boudoir.

True, Elaine's tantrums would have tried a saint, and Joe, she had to admit, was no saint; he was obstinate, and stubborn, especially on matters that involved principle, and his principles, unfortunately, were centred mainly around the colour question as appertaining to David and the present predicament of the miners, especially of the Egan family, because, she supposed, of their connection with Hazel. She was puzzled herself at times about Joe's concern for the welfare of David and Hazel, and had been forced more than once to see the situation through Elaine's eyes, and even to sympathise with her attitude.

She patted his hands now, saying, 'It'll be all right, you'll see; this time tomorrow you'll be deafened by a squawking *bairn*.'

He answered her smile with a small grimace and said softly, 'I hope you're right, Betty . . . Have you had enough to eat?'

'Yes, yes, I was finished.'

'You haven't been downstairs ten minutes; you must be worn out.'

'Oh, don't be concerned for me, I'm as strong as a horse. Now look.' She patted his hand again. 'Go and have a drink, a strong one. Then go up to your father; he's almost in the same state as you. He was for coming down this morning but I stopped him, because I wouldn't have been able to keep him out of the room. And I can imagine what Madam Stiffneck would have said to that. Go on now, do as I tell you, go up to the top floor and hold hands.'

110

She left him now and went hurriedly from the room and up the stairs.

Before she reached the landing she heard Elaine's cry, and when she opened the bedroom the cry pierced her ears, and it was all she could do not to screw up her face against it.

'There, there. It's all right. It's all right, dear.'

'Oh, Betty! Betty! I'm going to die.'

'No, you're not. Don't be silly.'

'You don't know.' Elaine gasped for breath, then went on, 'You don't know what it's like. Never . . . never again if . . . if I live. Never, never again. Do you hear me?'

'Yes, dear, yes.'

'I'll make him swear, I will, I will, I'll make him swear, never again. O . . . h! . . .'

The doctor came again at half-past seven and after a few moments by the bedside he exclaimed brightly, 'Oh, well, now you're showing progress.' He turned to the nurse. 'This is good; she's showing progress.'

'How . . . how much longer?'

He looked down into Elaine's face, patted her cheek and said, 'It all depends on you, my dear. It all depends on you. Just keep working at it. I'm very pleased with you. You've been a brave girl.'

'Oh, shut up!'

The doctor raised his eyebrows slightly, turned from the bed and looked at the nurse, and the nurse gave a slight shake of her head as if to say, 'Well, what did I tell you?'

Betty was standing near the dressing-room door and, although she did not beckon to the doctor, he went towards her as if she had made some signal, and when they were close she whispered, 'Is it coming?' and he whispered back, 'It's showing signs.'

'She won't have to go into hospital?'

111

'No, no; I don't think that will be necessary at this stage. If she'd only help herself a little more, everything would be all right.'

'She has suffered a great deal.'

He looked at her quizzically for a moment; then, his voice still low, he poked his face towards her and said, 'That is what birth is all about, my dear.'

'Betty! Oh! Betty. Betty!'

She drew her fixed stare from the doctor's face and hurried towards the bed and, bending over Elaine, she took hold of her groping hands and said softly, 'There, there, dear. There, there. It's the last lap.'

'Rea . . . really? You . . . you mean that?'

'Yes, yes. Now try to let yourself go; sink into the bed and . . . and when the pain comes hang on to me and we'll pull together.'

'Pull . . . pull together. Yes, yes, pull . . . pull together. You don't know what it's like, you don't, you don't.'

'I've got a little idea.'

'O . . . h!'

'Now here it comes. Come on now!'

She had hardly finished speaking when she felt herself being roughly edged out of the way by the nurse, and now she surprised not only the nurse and the doctor but also herself as she twisted her head round and yelled, 'Get out of the way, you! Leave us alone. Go about your business.'

There was a long pause before the nurse replied and almost as loudly. 'This *is* my business.'

'Well, you've made a poor show of it from what I've seen. That's it, dear, come on. Come on, press harder. Oh, that's a good one.'

When Elaine's body gave a great heave before sinking back into the bed, Betty almost fell across her, for Elaine was still gripping her hand and the long nails had embedded themselves in her wrists . . .

And so it went on until two minutes before midnight, when the doctor, now in his shirt sleeves, the nurse, looking very dishevelled, and Betty, almost as exhausted as Elaine, gave one combined sigh as Joe's son came reluctantly into the world and immediately voiced his indignation when he was held dangling by his feet. And on the cry the door opened and Joe stood there, his weary face alight, his mouth open, his eyes shining, until the doctor, turning from where he was placing the child in a warm towel that Betty was holding out to him, jerked his head towards him and cried, 'Presently, presently,' and Betty holding the child gently to her breast, looked over the bundle and said, 'A boy, a boy, a beautiful boy. Go . . . go and tell himself.' And she jerked her head upwards.

Joe did not move for a matter of seconds, but stood looking towards the bed, where the nurse and the doctor now were both bending over Elaine, and Betty, speaking again and quickly now, said, 'Go on, go on, she's all right.'

When the door was closed, she let her gaze drop to the crumpled face peeping out from the folds of the towel. It was topped with hair, dark hair. Its eyes were blinking, its jaws were working: it was alive, it was a life. It was beautiful, oh, so beautiful.

The pain that went through her heart now was from the opening of an old wound, a remembered pain, a pain that was made up of frustration, longing, need . . . and envy.

5

After the birth, Elaine was in a very weak condition. She remained in bed for nearly a month and, contrary to what is the generally held theory, the memory of it didn't fade, for hardly a day passed but she recalled it and swore that she would kill herself rather than endure the same again.

At first Joe had assured her that she had no need to worry, that he was satisfied that it would never happen again, but as the threat was repeated daily he became not a little irritated by it, and even more so by the fact that his son never ceased to yell during his waking hours, and this he blamed on the artificial feeding, for Elaine had firmly refused to breast-feed the child.

A week after the birth the nurse had left, to the relief of all concerned, and from then both the care of the child and the nursing of Elaine had fallen on Betty's shoulders.

Another maid had been engaged. Her name was Nellie McIntyre. Seventeen years old, her main work was to assist Betty in the bedroom and to help in the nursery.

A guest-room across the landing from Elaine's bedroom had been turned into an attractive nursery, but it had one drawback: it wasn't far enough away to dull the yelling of Master Martin Remington.

But, on this morning, for once, the child was quiet, and he was gurgling at his mother as she held him in her arms.

'Isn't he beautiful?' Elaine glanced at Betty, and Betty, smiling down on them both, said, 'Wonderful.'

'If only he would remain like this.'

'He wouldn't be a boy then.'

'I wish he wasn't; I would have preferred a girl.'

'Really?' Betty's face showed surprise. 'I thought you wanted a boy.'

'No, no, Joe did; although quite candidly I didn't care much what it was when I was carrying; I only wanted it to be over. But oh God! if I had known . . .'

'Now, now, what did we say yesterday? No more going back.'

'It's all right for you, you didn't have to go through it.'

'And we've been through all that before too . . . Now you're better and you'll be downstairs within a day or two, and I'd like to bet you'll be dragging Joe to a dance before the end of the month, so let's hear no more of what you went through.'

'You're hard.'

'Yes, yes, I'm hard, very hard.'

'Oh no! Now don't you start.' Elaine screwed her face up as her son wriggled in her arms, opened his mouth wide and let out a high cry.

'Oh, take him, Betty. Take him. It goes right through my head.'

Betty lifted the child into her arms and rocked him, saying, 'There now, there now, what is it?' And as she walked the room, rocking him gently, his crying subsided and she looked down on him and upbraided him gently, saying, 'Those are crocodile tears; all you want is to be nursed. Yes, go on, laugh, laugh; you know I'm telling the truth.'

'Go and put him down in the nursery, Betty.'

'Well, if I do, you know what'll happen.'

As Elaine sighed, Betty said, 'I'll take him for his morning visit upstairs.'

'Well, don't be too long. And don't let Mike get too near him with that filthy pipe in his mouth. The other day the child's clothes smelt strongly of smoke.'

'You're imagining things; it was your own cigarette you were smelling.'

As Betty made for the door with the child in her arms she looked over her shoulder to where Elaine was now lying back in a chair placed near the open window, and she said, 'If you made an effort to have a stroll in the garden this afternoon it would do you good. The sun is lovely and warm.'

'This afternoon! I can hardly use my legs. Oh, you are hard, Betty, I've only been out of bed two days.'

Betty closed the door behind her, crossed the landing and mounted the stairs to the floor above, and when she pushed open Mike's sitting-room door she found the room empty, so she called, 'Hello, Mike! There's a visitor to see you.'

Mike was turning from his work-bench when she came to the door of the adjoining room, and she said to him, 'I'm not bringing him in there among all the sawdust and shavings.'

'Who's asking you to?' He came slowly towards her. Then gazing down at the child in her arms, he rubbed its hands with his first finger, and when the child gripped it, a look of pleasure passed over his face and, glancing at Betty, he said, 'He always does that. Does he do it to everybody?'

'No, no,' she lied firmly; 'he never does it to me.'

116

'Well, well. By! he's growing every day, isn't he?' He now moved slowly towards the big leather chair near the window and when he was seated he held out his arms, saying, 'Let me have him.'

After placing the child in his arms, she seated herself opposite and listened to him talking to it.

'Hi! young fellow-me-lad. By! you're going to be a spanker, and you know what? As soon as you can toddle you're going into that room over there.' He nodded towards the workroom. 'I'll put a knife into your hand and I'll have you whittling before you can talk, and if I have anything to do with it you'll grow up like your namesake, your greatgranda, at least in some ways.' He now looked under his brows towards Betty and laughed as he added, 'He was a caution, was me da. By! aye, he was a lad all right. When he was my age if he wasn't hitting the bottle he was chasing the lasses, or he was running from me mother because she was chasing *him*, and many a time if she had caught him she would have murdered him at that.' He put his head back now and laughed; then he asked, 'Have you ever seen anybody as daft as our Joe over a bairn?'

'Oh yes.'

'You have?'

'Oh yes, yes, Mike; I'm looking at him now.'

He did not take his eyes off her during the silence that followed this remark, and when he spoke again there was no jocularity in his tone as he said, 'I'm goin' to tell you something. When you first brought him up here and I saw him in your arms I thought to meself, It should be hers, she's a lost mother.'

'Oh Mike!' She was on her feet now, standing with her back to him and looking out of the window. 'You shouldn't say things like that.'

'Why not, lass?'

117

'Because' – she turned her head quickly to the side and looked back at him – 'they're hurtful.'

'I didn't mean it to be hurtful. I'm only telling you, lass, I think you're lost; you should be married and have bairns of your own.'

'Chance is a great thing.'

'Then all I can say is, there's a lot of bloody fools walking around.'

'What if I don't want to get married?'

'Aw, if you were to tell that to the cat it would scratch your eyes out. Every woman wants to get married.'

'No, they don't.' She was facing him fully now. 'There's scores, hundreds of women who don't need marriage, just as there are men made the same way.'

'Then they're not bloody normal.'

'To your way of thinking they may not be, but nevertheless it's a fact.'

'Are you one of them, is that what you're saying?'

She swallowed deeply before she replied, 'No, I'm not one of them.'

'Then you want to be married?'

Whatever her answer would have been to this she wasn't called upon to make it, for a tap came on the door and when she said, 'Come in,' the door opened quickly and Ella as quickly came across the room and said in a loud whisper, 'It's . . . it's Lady Ambers. She called; she asked for you. I . . . I said you were upstairs, and when I went you weren't there. And the missis, she told me to take her up, and she's with the missis now. I . . . I thought I should tell you.'

'Thanks, Jane. Thank you. I'll be down directly.'

'Lady Ambers! My! my! we're going up in the world. That's the old girl that wants you to go along of her, isn't it?'

'Yes, that's her.'

'She's likely come for her answer. What are you going to do?'

'What do you think?' She lifted the child from his arms and as she walked hurriedly towards the door he called after her, 'Don't you dare. Do you hear me?'

She made no answer, but hurried down the stairs and made her way to the bedroom, pausing for a moment before opening the door and entering the room.

Lady Ambers was sitting opposite Elaine and she immediately cried at Betty, 'Oh! There you are. There you are. And the child in your arms. It suits you. Why haven't you come to see me? I wrote to you; didn't you get my letter?'

'Yes, and I answered it.'

'Well, I never received a reply. Likely it wasn't posted at this end, or if it was, somebody nicked it at yon end; you can't trust anybody. Let me have a look at him.'

When Lady Ambers craned her wrinkled neck up out of her mink stole Betty did not bend towards her but said, 'I think his mother is the one to show him off,' and with that she placed the child on Elaine's knee. However, her tactfulness did nothing to soften the expression on her sister's face. She saw that Elaine was on her high horse and she didn't have to make a guess at what had put her there, for Lady Mary, she imagined, was an expert at hoisting people into this position.

'He looks healthy. Who does he take after?' She lifted her eyes from the child to Elaine and said bluntly, 'Not you; I'd say his father. Yes, I remember him; I met him at the station. Roughly handsome individual if I remember correctly. Yes, roughly handsome. Men are more attractive when they're roughly handsome. People who are too handsome or too beautiful lose something. For my own taste, give me a plain individual; they're always more interesting, like your sister there.' She now nodded towards Betty, who compressed her lips and made a slight motion with her head at the split compliment; and the next moment she understood the reason for the expression on Elaine's face, for the old lady went on, 'If you've got to live with anyone for any length of time, good looks can become an irritation. They intrude; they make you aware of age. But personality, no, that entertains you. And you know something?' She now stubbed her finger over the baby's head and towards Elaine's breast as she ended, 'That's the greatest asset in life, to be an entertainer; in one way or another to be an entertainer.' Now she twisted her head round and thrust her chin up towards Betty and demanded, 'When will you be ready to leave?'

'Oh now, Lady Mary . . .'

'Never mind, Oh now, Lady Mary, you told me you'd come to me once the child was born.'

'That isn't quite correct. I said I would stay here as long as I was needed.'

'Well, she's all right, and up.' She did not deign to look at Elaine now but thumbed towards her. 'And she's quite old enough to look after herself and the child, I should say. And I notice servants running about; I've seen a man and two maids already, as well as that black man who is the chauffeur. You have as many here as Sarah has.'

'She's not leaving.'

Now the old lady jerked her head in Elaine's direction and she stared at her for a moment before she said. 'You've said that once already but, as I've already asked you, do you rule her life? She's an independent woman, she can go where she likes; and if I know anything she'll go where the need is most, and I think that my need is greater than yours.' She now nodded her head at Elaine; then, quickly turning her attention to Betty again, she said, 'Well, what about it?'

Betty walked slowly forward until she was standing against the old lady's chair and she said softly, 'I'm very sorry but . . . but I can't leave her just at present.'

They stared at each other. Betty's expression was sad and the old lady's, at that moment, was slightly pathetic, yet her voice was as strident as ever as she demanded, 'Are you here for life then?'

'Oh, no, no; I can go . . .'

'She's here for as long as she wishes to stay. She's my sister and this is her home,' Elaine said stiffly.

The old lady now drew herself to her feet with Betty's assistance, and she adjusted her stole, smoothed her brown silk gloves over the backs of her hands, gave her body a little shake, very much like a hen would do after a dust bath, then turned on her heel and walked out of the room.

Betty did not look towards Elaine before she followed Lady Ambers, and once out on the landing she hurriedly caught hold of the old lady's arm, saying gently, 'That is the wrong way; the stairs are this way.'

Lady Ambers did not speak until they reached the hall and there, making an effort to subdue her voice, she said, 'I find your sister an objectionable person. I knew at our first meeting that I shouldn't like her. She is a selfish creature; it shows in her face, petty and peevish. I know the type, I've met scores of them. You're a fool. Do you know that?' She was poking her face towards Betty now. 'And a double fool for allowing yourself to be used. But there'll come a time, you mark what I say, young woman, there'll come a time when you want to be away from here and the claustrophobic atmosphere of that room. She pretends the boot's on the other foot, but I could read through her. Do you know what she said to me? She said you had more need of her than she had of you. Her tune was different before you came in: it was then as if she were conferring a favour on you, and I picked it up and told her that, from my short acquaintance with you, you weren't the kind of person to accept favours lightly. If you had been sensible you and I would have been away into the sunshine long before now . . . I'm leaving tomorrow. It seems that James doesn't want to die and Sarah is getting on my nerves. They're so old-fashioned, so behind the times. Well, miss, I'll keep in touch because—' Her voice dropped almost to a murmur and, looking straight into Betty's eyes, she said, 'I don't know why this should be, but I've got a strong feeling that you and I will come together through a reciprocal need. I've only had this feeling once before in my life and it turned out to be correct.' She bounced her head now, then took two paces towards the door, stopped again and looked at Betty, saying very quietly and formally, 'Goodbye, Miss Burton,' and Betty answered, 'Goodbye, Lady Mary.' Then keeping a short distance behind her, she followed her through the door that Duffy was holding open, and down the steps to where her man, Hammond, waited beside the carriage door.

Not until the carriage had disappeared around the curve in the drive did she turn about and go back into the house, and as she crossed the hall and made for the stairs Ella appeared as though from nowhere, saying quietly, 'I've popped you a tray in the breakfast-room, miss, sandwiches and that.'

Betty paused, nodded at the girl, then said, 'Thank you, Jane. Thank you.'

In the breakfast-room she sat down by the side of the table and, reaching out absent-mindedly, picked up a sandwich from the plate and nibbled at it. But after the first bite she hastily replaced it on the plate; she didn't like to eat sandwiches in the middle of the morning. It was kind of Jane to bother, but she had indicated to her before that she wasn't very fond of sandwiches.

At this moment, she was experiencing a deep feeling of regret and a strong wish to be in that carriage bowling along the road, sitting by the side of that strange but entertaining old woman, that vital old woman, that wise old woman, and – now she gave an audible small mirthless laugh – that utterly tactless old woman.

It was strange the way she had made the prophecy that they would need each other some time, and it was a little frightening, too, because she felt there was truth in it . . . And Elaine had indicated that, in a way, the boot was on the other foot, hadn't she? And that she wasn't so much needed as needing? Well, perhaps she was right in that assumption, because she did have the desire, above all things, to be one of a family. She *needed* to be one of a family; she *needed* to belong to some place, to someone. But at the same time, Elaine needn't have put it like that. But then Elaine had never been able to give freely: she had always taken, grabbed with both hands, and when she did give, it was reluctantly . . . Was she like that with Joe? she wondered.

She had risen from the seat and was about to go from the room when she realised she hadn't touched the coffee. It would upset Jane if she didn't make a show of eating and drinking, so she finished the sandwich, ate a biscuit and washed them down with the cup of coffee, then went upstairs. Before she reached the landing she heard the child crying, and as she went towards the bedroom door Nellie emerged with the baby in her arms, and she said to her, 'Put him in the cot; I'll be there in a moment or so.'

Inside the bedroom, they looked at each other in silence, and Betty made no move to break it until Elaine burst out, 'Well! Say something. Tell me what you're missing, what you've given up for my sake.'

When Betty still made no reply but went to a chest of drawers and took from the top of it a small pile of freshly laundered nightdresses and bed jackets and arranged them in the middle drawer, Elaine cried at her, 'How you can even tolerate her I don't know. She's a horrible creature, a frump. Her clothes stink with age; she's a poisonous old witch; and she's half mad.'

'She's not half mad.' Betty swung round. 'If you were half as wise as she is, you'd do. Nor do her clothes smell with age. They may be old-fashioned but they're beautiful clothes; she's a nice person, a thoughtful person.'

'Thoughtful? Don't be silly; she's as selfish as they come.'

'Then there's a pair of you. At least with her I'd know where I stood: I would receive a salary; I wouldn't have to wait for a few pounds to be doled out to me when the mood took her.'

She wasn't aware that the door had opened. Even when Elaine's gaze was switched from her to the side, so deep was her anger, so loud her voice, coupled with the child's crying coming from the nursery, it smothered the soft opening of the door, and when she swung round and saw Joe standing there, she wished for the earth to open up and swallow her. She put her hand over her mouth and, dashing past him, went from the room.

Slowly, Joe closed the door behind her. But he didn't make his way towards Elaine; he just stood looking at her over the distance, and she cried at him, high and peevishly, 'Now don't you start! I've had enough for one morning. That dreadful woman's been here trying to take her away. She upset me and . . . and when I told Betty she was a poisonous old witch, she got on her hind legs in her defence.'

Now Joe began to walk slowly across the room and when he stood in front of her, he said quietly, 'I don't know anything about that, but I just heard the last bit. Do you mean to say you haven't been giving Betty anything all these months unless she asked for it?'

124

'No, no; you've got it wrong.'

'Then you explain it.'

'Whenever she needs anything I give it to her.'

'But she's got to ask for it?'

'Well' – she tossed her head impatiently – 'I can't always remember.'

'I've doubled your allowance since Betty came. Perhaps you remember my saying that I didn't like to offer her a wage but I'd leave it to you. How could you! How could you be so mean!'

'Don't you dare speak to me like that. Don't you dare suggest I'm mean; it never crossed my mind. I . . . I say to her, there's money in the drawer if you need it.'

'And how much do you keep in the drawer? Two pounds? Five pounds? A hundred pounds a month now goes into your private account. Well, from now on it'll go back to fifty and I'll see that Betty doesn't have to beg for what is hers from now on.'

'Joe! Joe!'

He paused by the door and turned towards her. The tears were raining down her face; she was lying back in the chair now, her two hands cupping her cheeks, and she whimpered, 'Don't . . . Don't be like that, please. I can't bear it. I tell you, it was just thoughtlessness on my part. Only a few weeks ago I bought her a dress and coat and . . .'

He was back at her side. 'All right, all right. Stop it! Stop it!'

'Don't say I am mean.'

'All right. All right.'

'And . . . and don't let her go. Don't let her leave, will you?'

'I certainly won't let her leave if I can help it. But it's up to you; you're the one that can either keep her or make her go.'

'I'll be thoughtful. I will, I will, Joe. I feel so weak, so tired. I'm . . . I'm not selfish. Say I'm not selfish.'

'You're not selfish. There now; dry your eyes.'

'You don't think I'm an awful person?'

'No; I could never think you're an awful person. You know what kind of a person I think you are.'

'I love you, Joe.' Her arms came round his neck and brought him to his knees by her side, and when his head lay pressed between her scented breasts she stroked his hair and murmured, 'I'd die if you stopped loving me,' and he murmured back, 'Then you'll live for ever, for ever and ever.'

6

From her sitting-room window Elaine could see over the far
hedge the top of the car as it approached the gates; then because of the trees on the drive it was blocked from her view,
but she knew that if it continued towards the house without
stopping she would see it again by the time she had counted
fifteen seconds. Today, however, as yesterday and the day
before, it did not reappear at the end of her counting.

Yesterday he had been fifteen minutes late for lunch and
his apology had been: 'Sorry; I've been held up.' It had been
as much as she could do not to ask him if he was held up
for the same reason as on the previous day.

This was too much. What was it about those two that
attracted him . . .? But there weren't two; for the past three
days there had been only one, that girl, for her husband had
been in hospital since Monday with an ear infection.

Well, she wasn't going to stand for it. It was one thing
for him to go down there openly, but now he was doing it
on the sly . . . Held up, indeed!

As she hurried from the room and ran across the landing,
Betty's voice came to her from the foot of the attic stairs,
calling, 'Is anything wrong?' And she answered briefly,

'No,' then continued running down the stairs, out of the front door and down the drive.

She had rounded the bend and was in sight of the cottage when she saw them. Joe had hold of the girl's arm and they were walking down the pathway, quite close together.

She stopped on the grass verge and stood in the shadow of a tree. She watched as her husband took hold of the girl's hands, bringing them together on a level with his chest, then bending towards her. She could not see what he was doing, for he had his back to her; but even if they had been facing her and within a few yards' distance she would have been unable to see clearly, for the rage that was filling her was misting her eyes. For this to happen under her nose in their own garden! She had given him everything, nearly died in giving him a child; and now that child was but three months old and what was he doing?

She did not see their parting. The next thing she was conscious of was the car coming towards her, then stopping beside her.

'Hello, Elly! Were you coming to meet me?' There was a surprised note in Joe's voice, and when she did not move he said, 'Come on, get in. What's the matter?'

When she still made no movement, he sprang from the car and hurried over the verge towards her.

'What is it? What's the matter, dear?' When his hand came out to touch her she struck it a blow with the side of her hand and the force behind it gave the lie to its delicate appearance.

He did not move away from her, but pressed his head well back into his shoulders and narrowed his eyes as he asked quietly, 'What's this all about?'

'How dare you! How dare you stand there and say to me, What's this all about? Three days this week, and I've . . . I've just seen you with my own eyes.'

128

Joe gaped at her before looking in the direction of the cottage. Then, returning his gaze to her, his mouth opened wide and he let out a bellow of a laugh; at the same time his arms went about her and he hugged her to him as he almost sang, 'You're jealous. You're jealous. Wonderful! Wonderful! You're jealous!'

When she struggled fiercely in his embrace he let her go; but he was still smiling when she said harshly, 'Don't treat me as an idiot. I could understand you having an affair with someone of your own class but . . . but with that man's wife.'

The smile had gone from his face. He half turned his head away from her while his eyes still held hers, and he put up his hand in a warning gesture as he said, 'Careful. Careful, Elly, because you could be sorry for what you might say.'

'Are you telling me I'm blind? Is it usual for the master to be so attentive to his chauffeur's wife as to take her hands and fondle her?'

He let out a long sigh as he said now quietly, 'Yes, under the circumstances it was usual. I had just come from visiting David in hospital, where he told me the good news that Hazel was going to have a baby. What you saw me doing was trying to reassure her, to allay her fears as to what the child might go through. Would he be treated the same as his father because of his mixed blood? She was sad and troubled also because her people are not pleased at the prospect of her having the child.'

They stared at each other in silence now. Her breathing was easier and she gave a characteristic lift of her eyebrows as she exclaimed, 'Well, that's understandable; who would want another chocolate-coloured . . .' The gasp she gave on the last word became almost a cry as she shrank back from Joe's uplifted hand. He stayed it in mid-air, and she took two slow steps back from him; then her hands groping at the trunk of a tree, she moved some way around it before giving out a cry and running away up the drive.

She slowed her run to a walk as she mounted the steps to the house, making a great effort to regain her composure in case she should encounter the servants; but she met no-one until she burst into her sitting-room and saw Betty.

'What on earth's the matter?' Betty took her by the shoulders and, peering into her face, said, 'What is it, what's happened? You're trembling like a leaf.'

'He . . . he was going to strike me, Betty.'

'Who?'

'J . . . Joe.'

'Don't be silly; he's not in.'

'He . . . he will be in a minute.'

'What did you do?'

'I . . . I went down to meet him. He . . . he was with that girl at the cottage. I saw him holding her hands, bending over her. When I accused him, he said he was comforting her because she was going to have a baby. And . . . and when I made the remark that . . .' She swallowed and swung her head from side to side.

'Yes? Go on. What remark did you make?'

'I . . . I said it would be another chocolate-coloured . . .'

'Oh, Elaine!' Betty interrupted.

'Well, it was nothing to say.'

'I think it was; you know that he thinks a lot of David.'

'And why? Why does he think of lot of David? That's what I want to know.' The tears were running down Elaine's cheeks now.

'They were brought up together. Joe has a lot of compassion in him for . . . for the underdog.'

'Underdog! He's no underdog; Joe treats him as an equal.'

130

'And will continue to do so.' Hearing Joe's voice, Betty turned sharply towards the door; but Elaine did not even glance towards it as she rushed into her bedroom and banged the door behind her.

Betty paused for a moment, facing Joe in the doorway, and said softly, 'Go easy on her.'

'I think I go too easy.' His voice was thick, his words muttered.

'She said you were going to strike her. You weren't, were you?'

'Yes, I was.'

She looked away from him, her face puckered, and as she now moved past him she murmured, 'I don't understand you.'

She was walking towards the head of the stairs when the dinner gong sounded; at the same time there came a loud ringing of Mike's handbell from above. She looked first one way and then the other; and having decided to answer the latter, she was crossing the landing in the direction of the attic stairs when the nursery door opened and Nellie appeared, saying, 'Oh, that bell, miss; it's woke him up.'

Betty nodded towards her. 'I'll see to it,' she said. 'Give him his bottle.'

'It isn't time.'

'Nevertheless, give it to him. I'll be down shortly; keep him quiet.' She was now running up the attic stairs; at the top she thrust open the sitting-room door and exclaimed straightaway, 'Oh, stop that row, Mike! You've woken the child. You'll have to get an electric bell installed; that one makes such a racket.'

'Well, you've taken your time in coming. What was all that about down there?'

'What do you mean?'

131

'Her, running down the drive, then dashing back as if the devil was after her; and our Joe getting out of the car as if he were the devil himself, his face as black as thunder. Come on, come on, what's up?'

'He'll likely tell you himself.'

'He won't, or only half the story. Now look, put me in the picture or I'm going down there to find out for meself.'

Betty drew in a long deep breath, then said, 'Apparently Hazel had told Joe that she was going to have a baby and when Joe told Elaine, she . . . she came out with a silly remark.'

'Hazel is going to have a baby?' Mike's voice was low now.

'Yes. Is there anything surprising in that?'

Before Mike answered he turned himself round in the chair, pulled himself upwards, then with the aid of his stick walked to the window, there saying, 'No, there's nothing surprising in that, nothing to cause a hullabaloo between those two either.' He turned his head to the side and so wasn't looking directly at her as he asked, 'What was the silly remark?'

She paused a long moment before she said, 'It was something to do with Hazel producing a coloured child.'

'The bloody silly bitch! The empty-headed ninny!' He banged the stick on the floor now, then leaned forward and supported himself on the window-sill with his hand. 'Why, in the name of God! did he have to go and marry a narrow-minded, vain, silly little bitch like her?'

'Mike! Please! Please! Mike.'

'All right, you can say Mike as much as you like, I know she's your sister, but let me tell you something: I'd rather see him married to a whore, because at least she'd have a bit of humanity in her.'

132

Betty's voice was stiff and low as she came back at him, saying, 'She's still young; and what you seem to forget is that she's still living in a foreign atmosphere, as it were. She can't please you all.'

'She doesn't need to please us all; she's only got one to please.'

'Well, she tries hard to please him.'

'Does she?' He now thrust himself round to confront her: 'Let me tell you something, Betty: the only one your sister pleases is herself; everything she does is aimed at number one. He can't see it yet because he's blinded by his feelings, his needs, and at the same time he's fascinated by her because she's of a different class. And I know what I'm talking about. Men of our type can be fascinated by women of her type. His mother was as much like her as two peas in a pod; and whereas I came to me senses very quickly, his is going to be a slow awakening, because he doesn't want to open his eyes to the light. Perhaps it's just as well, because it can bowl a fellow over and leave him scarred for life if he comes to too quickly. Do you know what I advocate, lass? And I'm not jokin', mind you, no, I'm not jokin'. Trial marriages, that's what I advocate. And 'tisn't the day or yesterday I said that; I was twenty-two when I first voiced it, and a middle-aged bloke almost jumped on me, told me to take me coat off. It wasn't till after I found out his only daughter was living with a bloke. "Good luck to her," I said. But just think on it, Betty. It would do away with a lot of heartbreak, don't you think? because who knows what they are taking on when they shackle themselves for life, eh? Who knows, I ask you, who knows?'

She said quietly, 'In this case, *they* should have done; neither is a child.'

'She is.' His voice was high now. 'She sees herself as a bloody little flapper, and she'll go on seeing herself like that

133

until she's an old woman. I know the type. I tell you I know the type.'

Betty's eyes narrowed and her voice held a note of scorn as she said, 'Then, thinking about her as you do, why are you so two-faced in her company? You're always so pleasant to her.'

'It's like you to hit the nail on the head, isn't it? Aye, all right, I *am* two-faced, but I look at it this way: he's got enough to put up with; I'm not going to add to it. He thinks I like her. Let him go on thinking that, but I've got to speak me mind to somebody, an' who better than you, 'cos you don't like her either.'

'Mike! . . . she's my sister and . . .'

'Aw, come off it, lass. Don't take that tack with me; don't tell me you take that bloody, unintelligent way of looking at things. This business that we've all got to try to be little Christs and love each other makes me sick; in the widest sense it makes me sick; but when it's pumped into you that because you're born of the same mother an' brought up in the same house you've got to love every damn member of the family, God! On the face of it, imbeciles would think with more reason. You show me a family where all the members love each other all the time, and I'll show you a family of hypocrites . . . Go on, get yourself away.' He turned from her now and flapped his hand backwards towards her. 'Go on downstairs and play the self-effacing attendant to your bitch of a sister, and while you're at it remember that you shouldn't condemn others for being as big a hypocrite as yourself.'

Betty turned about and left the room; but outside the door she stood for a moment, her head bent, her eyes closed, her fingers moving backwards and forwards across her brow. The self-effacing attendant. Yes, he, too, had hit the nail on the head; that's what she was, the self-effacing attendant.

134

She liked Mike. Yes, she liked him very much, but too often in his presence she felt she was in an operating theatre being roughly dissected. She was getting weary of it all. It was as if she were living on a battlefield in the midst of four different camps: the camp in the kitchen; the camp on the first floor; and this one-man camp up here; then the camp down in the cottage. And it was strange, but that camp, which was apart from the house and which appeared to be the happiest, was the cause of most of the dissent in the house.

At this moment she had the overwhelming desire to be with Lady Mary, for then she would have to please but one. A self-effacing attendant she might be, but with Lady Mary she'd be at the beck and call of someone who'd pay adequately for the duties of an attendant, not someone who'd make her feel she should consider it her good fortune to serve, as did her sister.

She had just reached the landing when she saw Elaine and Joe descending the main staircase. They were walking close together: he was looking down at her and she up at him. As Mike had said, it would be a slow awakening . . . Perhaps he would never awake.

Well, she hoped she was big enough to wish that he might sleep for ever, but human nature being what it was that might be difficult too.

All life was difficult, and it wasn't today or yesterday she had discovered that.

PART THREE

I

It was Christmas Eve, 1928. The house was ablaze with lights. There was a roaring fire in every room and to keep these supplied young Pat Collins, David's helper in the garden, had been hard at it all day, carrying wood and coal from the ground-floor rooms to those in the attic.

The hall was hung with holly and mistletoe and in between the two long windows of the drawing-room stood a seven-foot Christmas tree decorated with candles and glass baubles, and around the tub in which it stood was an array of gaily wrapped parcels.

There was an air of excitement running through the whole house, and Ella, hurrying into the kitchen, said to Mary, 'You know something? The feelin's more like New Year's Eve than Christmas.'

Mary was putting the finishing touches with an icing tube to a number of small cakes, and she said offhandedly, 'I've told you, like last year, haven't I, because she's from the south: they don't pay very much attention to New Year; it's Christmas with them, whereas we only think Christmas is for the bairns, and New Year's the time for jollification.'

'It's a pity he's not really old enough to appreciate the

tree. By! she's done it bonny. I'll say that for her. And it looks as if we're in for some good presents an' all.'

'I've told you not to be nosy, Ella, haven't I? I told you to keep away from that tree, didn't I?'

Ella turned to where Duffy was sitting in a straight-backed wooden chair to the side of the fire, his feet on the fender, a pipe in his mouth, and she laughed at him as she flicked her hand in his direction, saying, 'Aw! Uncle Jimmy, what do you think I've got eyes for? And speaking of eyes—' She lowered her voice and moved to the table and, leaning across it towards her aunt, she exclaimed in a loud whisper, 'There'll be some eyes on her bust the night.'

'Bust?' Mary stopped squeezing the icing tube and said, 'Bust? What are you talking about?'

'Oh, what am I talking about? It's a pity you can't see it; she'll have a cloak on when she comes downstairs. Eeh!' She put her hand over her mouth now as she straightened up and, looking to the side, nodded at her uncle as she finished, 'You'd fall flat on your face if you saw her, Uncle Jimmy.'

Duffy had taken the pipe from his mouth and slowly he brought one foot after the other off the fender before he asked, 'What do you mean, fall flat on me face?'

'Her chest, her bust' – Ella now pointed with a stiff finger to each of her breasts – 'they're practically hanging out.'

'Ella! Mind your tongue.'

'It's a fact, Aunty Mary: she's got her frock on and there's hardly any top to it at all; it's a square neck and there they are like plum duffs sticking out. I . . . I stared at them through the mirror and she said, "Is there anything wrong, Jane?"' – she mimicked the question – 'an' I said, "No, ma'am. No, ma'am." And when I left the room I heard Mr Joe come out of the dressing-room and she said something to him, but I couldn't catch it, and then she laughed . . . She's mucky.'

140

'I've told you to watch your tongue. You'll come out with something one of these days an' she'll overhear you.'

'Let her . . . Eeh!' She reached out, picked up a small broken cake from the table and after biting into it she shook her head slowly and looked to the far end of the kitchen as she said, 'I don't know what Mr Joe's thinking about to let her go out like that where other men will see her.'

Mary now lifted the tray of small cakes and, turning about, walked towards the sideboard with them, and as she passed her husband they exchanged glances that said a great deal.

Ella was about to speak again when the kitchen door opened and Nellie McIntyre entered, and she, coming straight to Ella's side, asked in a shocked tone, 'Did you see her?'

'Aye, I did. What do you think of her?'

'What do I think?' Nellie shook her head until her white starched cap slipped to the side; then looking from one to the other, she brought out, 'I'll tell you what I think, an' I'm not going to apologise to you, Mr Duffy, for saying it. I think that if she had shown her bairn her breasts like she's showing them off the night, it wouldn't have cried so much.'

There was a moment's silence before Ella, slapping Nellie on the shoulder, burst out laughing and said, 'Eeh! you! But you're right, you're right. She is, Aunty Mary, she is, she's right.'

Mary brought her plump body up straight, placed her folded hands at the line where her waist should be, then said, 'There's nobody arguing with either of you, but it would be advisable to keep your opinions to yourselves and remember that you're in a good job and also that her word goes.'

The two girls looked at each other, sighed, and together they left the kitchen, but in the hall Nellie took hold of Ella's arm and pulled her along the corridor and into the morning-room. There, closing the door behind her, she whispered, 'I heard Miss Betty on at her.'

141

'About her breasts?'

'Aye. Well, I think it was, 'cos she said, "It's only a small dinner party, Elaine, and the Leveys are very conservative," and then the missis said, "It's about time they were livened up then, isn't it?" Then Miss Betty said, "This isn't London, Elaine," and the missis answered, "No, you're right; they're so . . . provincial, they make me sick. If you don't make your own life here you'll die." Then Miss Betty said, "Has Joe seen it?" and the missis answered, "Of course he has." Then Miss Betty said, "But not on you. Don't aggravate him, Elaine." And then the missis laughed and said, "My breasts aggravate him! Oh, what do you know, Betty?" Then I had to scoot across the landing because Miss Betty came out of the room in a hurry.'

'They're not taking Miss Betty with them then?'

'No. No, well, she never goes out with them, does she?'

'No, she doesn't. But this being Christmas Eve and a party . . .'

'She's got a new frock on.'

'Huh! Miss Betty?'

'Aye, it's woollen, it's a soft pink colour. She looks nice in it . . . well, as nice as she'll ever look. You can't believe they're sisters, can you?'

'No, one looking like a doll an' t'other like a horse. But I know which I'd rather have if I had to have me pick.'

'Me too. Oh aye, me too.'

They nodded at each other, then like two conspirators, they crept from the room.

It was nine o'clock. The house was quiet. They had been gone for over an hour now, having left amidst laughter and Joe saying, 'I wish you were coming with us.'

She hadn't believed him; nor had she reminded him that she hadn't been asked, but she'd thought it was kind of

142

him to say that. He was kind, was Joe. Behind his explosive and somewhat irrational behaviour there was a deep thoughtfulness. It was this very thoughtfulness that seemed to make him irrational. Mary, Jane and Nellie had gone to the village to visit their people. It would have been quite some walk, but David had come back from Egan's house, where he had left Hazel, to take them in, so there was only Duffy, Mike, the baby and herself left in the house, and it felt strangely empty.

She had brought her own supper from the kitchen, but instead of eating it in the dining-room she had taken it into the drawing-room and eaten it as she sat to the side of the blazing fire, while all the time her eyes were held by the Christmas tree.

Next year, Martin would be running round the tree; he'd be playing on the floor with trains and motor cars and building brick houses; in her mind's eye she could see him quite plainly. She loved the child; even feeling at times he was more hers than Elaine's. If caring and attention could be taken to imply parenthood, then the child was hers. And yet she had no doubt that Elaine loved him, at least when he was happy and smiling.

After finishing her supper she lay back in the chair and gazed about her. How many Christmases had she spent alone? How many Christmases had she spent in other people's homes? Through how many Christmases had she experienced the intensified feeling of aloneness? A while back Mike had said that we couldn't all be Christs and love everybody. He was so right, you could really love only one person. There were different kinds of love, but the love that she wanted, and the love that she needed, could be supplied by only one person.

She recalled the Christmas Eve before last very clearly. She had been in her cousin Kathryn's cottage and had experienced a deep longing to meet someone who really needed her. She hadn't thought: I wish I could fall in love, because that would have been disastrous. But here was another Christmas Eve and her situation *was* disastrous.

She pulled herself to her feet and, walking slowly to the side of the fireplace, she looked at her reflection in the circular gold-framed mirror hanging there. Her hair looked nice: it was a dark tawny-brown colour, coarse, and like all coarse hair had a natural wave in it. Her eyes were brown and round, but they weren't large; her nose was straight, but it *was* large; her mouth was her best feature, it was big too but the lips were full and shaped quite nicely. But these large features needed a large frame and her face looked too big; yet it wasn't too big for her body, because that was big too. It was bad enough being five feet nine tall, but to have breadth with it, and that breadth covered with flesh, was too much. Yet she wasn't fat. No; that was one thing she determined she wouldn't be, fat; she was careful what she ate and she very rarely drank anything alcoholic.

And then there was her name, Beatrice. It sounded big; it seemed to fit her frame; but it had been reduced to Betty. and Betty sounded girlish, and she had never been girlish.

She closed her eyes for a moment before swinging round from the mirror and picking up the tray and hurrying from the room. When she pushed the green-baized door of the kitchen open with her buttocks she saw that Duffy was asleep in the chair by the fire, and so she gently placed the tray on a side table near the door; then, quietly leaving the room, she climbed the stairs and entered the nursery.

The child was fast asleep in his cot. He had kicked his bedclothes down and his plump legs lay on top of them. One fist was doubled and pressed into his cheek. Bending over him she gently replaced the bedclothes, then softly she

144

put her lips to his brow which, as always when her flesh touched his, stirred the ache in her heart.

After making up the fire and replacing the guard she went to her own room. It was very comfortable, with everything there she could wish for, and she had the desire now to sit quietly by the fire until she heard the girls return, then go to bed. But there was Mike. He was up there alone and he would be expecting her; it was Christmas Eve and no-one should be alone on Christmas Eve.

She drew a comb from the middle parting through each side of her hair. She had always parted it in the middle, imagining it tended to lessen the length of her face. Then taking a clean handkerchief from a drawer and sprinkling a few drops of perfume on it, she placed it up the cuff of her dress, then went out and mounted the attic stairs . . .

'I thought you were never coming.'

'I had one or two things to see to.'

'But they've been gone this hour and a half.'

'Yes, yes, I know.' She raised her eyebrows and nodded at him. 'But I need to wash sometimes and to change and sit down and look at myself and think.'

He laughed gently now, saying, 'Well, come and sit down here.' Then pulling himself forward in his chair, he pursed his lips, nodded his head slowly as he ran his eyes over her, then commented, 'I like that, it suits you, shows off your figure. You've a good figure, you know.'

'So has a camel . . . at least other camels think so.'

'Ha! ha! ha!' His laughter was high and loud. 'You do me good, you know that, Betty? You always do me good, 'cos you've got the gift of laughing at yourself, and that's a priceless asset.'

'Well, I always like to share a joke.'

'Aw, lass. Aw, lass. Come here. Look.' He pointed out through the uncurtained window. 'Look at that sky up there.

145

See them stars? Isn't that a sight? You know, at one time a sight like that would have frightened me, but not any more, because I know that one day I'll be somewhere along that lot.'

'Huh! I thought you didn't believe in God.'

'Who's talking about God? God's got nowt to do with that.' He was stabbing his finger now towards the window. 'Well, not the bloke that you and others think of as God.'

'How do you know whom I think of as God?'

'I don't.' He nodded at her. 'But we'll have to get on to that subject some time . . . Why didn't you go along with them the night?'

'Because I wasn't invited.' She lowered her head down towards him now.

'Everybody's invited to the Leveys. He's a good fellow; they're a nice family. You've met them.'

'Yes, yes, I know that, and they've told me to drop in any time, but . . . but that's a politeness, a sort of . . .'

'Not this side of the country 'tisn't. If people say drop in, they mean drop in . . . Are we going to have a game?'

'Yes, yes, of course.'

She brought a small table from the wall and placed it in front of him, then opened the envelope top and from a drawer underneath took a pack of cards. This done, she sat down opposite him and as she began to shuffle the cards she said, 'Are you coming down tomorrow?'

'Aye, I suppose I'll have to make it, Christmas dinner and all that. A lot of bloody palaver; no meaning left in it.'

'You should come down more often; you stay up here too much.'

'What is there to come down for? And what can I see from the drawing-room, or the dining-room? And if I was on the first floor the best view only takes in part of the garden and the drive. No, this is my abode from now till the end.'

'Don't be silly.'

'Who's being silly? I'm not pitying meself, don't think that; this is a world of its own up here; I have two workshops, a bathroom, a bedroom and this.' He waved his hand around the sitting-room. 'Who would want for more?'

'You're too much alone up here.' She had finished dealing the cards, and he picked his up and looked at his hand before saying, 'If you can't stand your own company you're hard put to stand anybody else's.'

'You're cutting yourself off. How long is it since you went to the factory?'

He put his head back and thought. 'Two and a half, three years.'

'Aren't you interested in it any more?'

'Yes and no.'

'What do your mean by that?'

'Well, speaking plain, I wanted to give Joe his head, see what he could do on his own; I didn't want to shackle him in any way. I wanted him to use his own ideas, and if I'd been on the spot I know I couldn't have helped but say, Well, it's been done this way for years and that's how it's going to be done for many more, or words to that effect. I would have had to show who was still the boss. Well, when I'm out of the way I don't lose face when some of his ideas turn out better than mine.'

As they looked at each other and smiled she shook her head slowly and, using his tone of voice, she said, 'You're a queer fella.'

'Aye, that's been said afore, lass, I'm a queer fella. Look, before we start, bring over that tray.' He pointed to the sideboard. 'It's Christmas, so let's start the way we mean to go on . . .'

It was now half-past eleven and she had been downstairs three times during the past two hours or so, twice to see to the child and the third time when she heard the girls returning. On this occasion she had gone into the kitchen and, her mouth wide, her eyes bright, she had said, 'Merry Christmas,' and they had all turned, the four of them, and looked towards her and chorused, 'Oh, the same to you, a Merry Christmas, miss.' Then they had all laughed together and she had left the kitchen feeling singularly happy.

Now she was sitting before the fire close to Mike's chair, her slippered feet stretched out and her hands cupping the back of her head. She gave a quiet laughing gurgle in her throat before saying, 'You know, I feel a little drunk.'

'Well, keep at it, lass; we've got a long way to go yet, the bottles are still half full.' He pointed to the table at his side on which stood three bottles, one of port, one of whisky, and one of gin.

'They say you should never mix your drinks but it's a nice feeling to feel drunk. I've never felt like this before, Mike. I could like everybody . . . everybody.'

'I thought you always liked everybody, Betty.'

'Oh no, Mike.' She turned her head on her hands. 'Oh no. You said yourself I'm a hypocrite, and I am, I'm two-faced.'

'Not you, Betty; you're the straightest piece of woman I've come across in me life.'

'Aw no, no, you're wrong, Mike. I am, I really am, I'm two-faced, 'cos sometimes I want to stand on my hind legs and tell Elaine exactly what I think of her, but do I do it? No; I just say: Yes, Elaine; and, No, Elaine; and, You're right, Elaine.'

'That's not being two-faced, lass, that's diplomacy. That's what you call diplomacy.'

'Yes, yes, I suppose you're right.' She sighed and nodded at him. 'Yes, it's diplomacy. That's how I'll look at it in the future . . . diplomacy. But I'm still two-faced. Oh yes, I'm still

148

two-faced.' She lowered her hands from behind her head and joined them on her lap and, gazing at them, she went on, 'I'm two-faced because I play at being good old Betty, and I'm not a bit like that inside. I envy Elaine. Do you know that, Mike? I envy her because she's got Joe . . . and Martin . . . and this grand house. She always got everything she wanted, Elaine, and . . . and I should be glad. I tell myself I should be glad, but I'm not. I'm not, Mike.'

Mike now leaned forward and put his hand on her knee and he looked into her eyes as he said quietly, 'You're lost, lass; you should be married.'

'Yes. Oh I know that. Oh I know that, Mike, but who'll have me?' She gurgled again in her throat.

'Anybody who wasn't a bloody fool, lass. You know something?' He squeezed her knee now as hard as his gnarled fingers would allow. 'If me body weren't twisted an' I was ten years younger I'd ask you meself.'

At this she let out a deep rollicking laugh; then leaning towards him, she said, 'And you know what? And you know what, Mike? If I were ten years older and had any sense left I'd take you up on that and say, Thank you kindly, sir. And you know something else, Mike?' Her eyes were twinkling and her lips pressed tight for a moment and she hiccupped and gave a spluttering laugh before she whispered, 'I'm going to tell you something. It's funny, it really is; but you know what I've always secretly wanted to be? You'd never guess. You'd never guess in a thousand years . . . Some man's mistress! Isn't that funny? I've never dreamed of getting married; no, oh no; just being some man's mistress. Now I ask you if that isn't the limit. I've pictured myself sailing round a magnificent bedroom, my own bedroom, mind; everything had been bought for me, all expensive stuff . . . no expense spared.' She stopped now and drooped her head towards her chest to check her rising laughter, then went on, 'I'm always dressed in a flowing negligée, yards and yards of crêpe-de-chine. No, no! not crêpe-de-chine, wild silk, the most expensive wild silk. And then he comes in, the hero, the fellow that's paying for the lot. And you know something? Do you know something, Mike? I have never been able to put a face to him, not once. I've never been able to put a face to him, and perhaps I know the reason.'

She now straightened her back, her laughter sliding away, and picked up her half-empty glass of port from the table and looked down into it before she added, 'The farce always ends up by me looking in the mirror and seeing myself as likely he would see me, and so it's on those nights that I ask myself why. And then I answer myself: " 'Tisn't fair," I say, " 'Tisn't fair." And I get sorry for myself because, as I see it, no matter what a woman looks like on the outside the mechanism underneath is the same. Don't you think so, Mike? The same emotions boil behind the plain and the ugly as behind the beautiful. Isn't that true? In fact I've come to the conclusion that the passions hidden behind the plain fronts are the stronger, oh, by far the stronger. Years ago when I used to look at Elaine I used to tell myself for my own comfort that God had worked it out evenly to His way of thinking: To those with beauty He gave no brains, and He compensated the plain ones with a lot of grey matter and personality. But' – she smiled weakly now as she nodded at Mike – 'I used to think it was blooming unfair of Him not to let us have a choice, because I know what I would have plumped for . . .'

'Betty.'

'Yes, Mike?'

'Now listen to me, Betty. Listen carefully.'

'Yes, Mike.'

'You listenin'?'

'Yes. Yes, Mike, yes, I'm listening.'

'I want you to marry me. Now, now, listen, I'm serious. I'm not old as age goes, I'm fifty-two, and I'm not all that useless as a man. You know what I mean. Marry me, Betty.'

'*Oh . . . Oh*, Mike.' She swallowed deeply, closed her eyes tight, lay back in the chair and remained utterly silent; nor did she do anything to stop the tears raining down her cheeks. Not until she had gulped deep in her throat did she speak, and then her voice was a mere whisper as she said, 'We're both tight. Don't forget that, we're both tight, Mike, but . . . but nevertheless I thank you. I do, I do indeed, and from the bottom of my heart, because it's the first proposal I've had in my life. Men . . . men sort of like me, I know, and women use me, but no-one has ever loved me. We are a type, women like me, we are a sort of worker bee to the queens of this world . . . like Elaine, and to some men we . . . we are pals, sort of, and so I'll never, never . . .'

'Stop your nattering; I'm . . . I'm not all that far gone, in fact I'm not far gone at all. I can hold me drink an' I'm sober enough at this minute to know what I'm after. I mean it. Will you marry me?'

She rose to her feet now and stood looking down at him as she wiped her tears from around her chin, and when she could speak she said softly, 'Oh, Mike. Mike!'

'Will you?'

'Ask me again in the morning, Mike. Good-night.'

'All right then. Good-night, lass; and never fear I'll ask you again in the mornin', Christmas mornin'.'

She walked unsteadily towards the door and opened it quietly, then turned and said softly, 'It's been the best night of my life.' Then she went out and down the stairs and into her room. She didn't undress but dropped slowly on to the bed and, burying her face in the pillow, she cried as she had never cried before in her life.

2

'Happy Christmas, Elaine.'

'Oh. Happy Christmas . . . Oh, my head! My head!' Elaine pulled herself up in bed, then said, 'What time is it?'

'Ten o'clock.'

'Good Lord! . . . Oh, I couldn't face breakfast.' She waved away the tray that Betty was about to put on the bed table. 'A cup of tea, that's all . . . where's Joe?'

'Outside, I think; he's been up and about for some time now.'

'He's inhuman.'

'What time did you get in?'

'Two . . . three, I don't remember, I can't remember.'

'Did you have a good time?'

'Yes, yes.' Elaine opened her eyes wide. 'Surprisingly, yes. There were two nice men there. One was a doctor who turned out to be Lena Levey's brother.' She narrowed her eyes and squinted up at Betty, saying, 'What's the matter with you? You look as if you too had a night out on the tiles. Didn't you sleep?'

'Yes; yes, I slept, but I was up rather late' – she jerked her head backwards – 'playing cards with Mike.'

'Oh, fast and furious living, playing cards with Mike. How's the master of the house?'

'Oh, happy, smiling. You'd think he knew it was Christmas.'

'Oh, here's the second master, or is it the third?' Elaine flicked her fingers towards Joe, who was now entering the room, and Betty, turning from the side table where she had just poured out a cup of tea, asked him, 'Do you want one?'

'No, no.' He shook his head; then, going to the bed, he sat on the side of it. He did not look at Elaine as he groped for her hand, but he kept his eyes on Betty as he spoke, 'I've just seen Father.'

'Oh yes?' Betty turned her head to the side and looked at him.

'He told me some news.'

'Did he?' Betty now came to the bed and handed a cup of tea to Elaine, and she, taking it, tried to draw Joe's attention to her as she demanded, 'What news? What do you mean, news?'

Still Joe did not take any notice of his wife but, staring at Betty, he said, 'If you need a blessing you have mine.'

When the heat swept through her whole body, it brought the sweat oozing out of her pores, and she wetted her lips as she was about to say, 'I don't need your blessing, Joe, it's misplaced,' when Elaine, putting the cup sharply down on the side table, demanded, 'What *is* this? What's happening?'

Now Joe did turn towards her and, smiling, he said quietly, 'Father's asked Betty to marry him.'

No-one could have adequately described the look on Elaine's face at this announcement, for it was a mixture of amazement, horror, disgust . . . and anger, yet when she spoke her tone in no way corresponded with her expression,

153

for her voice was flat, her words mundane: 'You're joking,' she said.

Before Joe had time to reply, Betty, her face and manner as stiff as her voice now, cried, 'Why should he be joking?' She had meant to laugh the whole thing off; that is, even if Mike remembered what he had said to her last night, for on awakening this morning it had taken her some time to recall the incident; but the look on her sister's face, in fact, her complete attitude, which spoke of furious anger, aroused in herself a defensive bitterness, and she added now, from deep within her throat, 'Is it so strange that a man, any man, should ask me to marry him?'

They were staring at each other as if Joe weren't present, and Elaine, her voice matching her expression, cried, 'Yes, it is. In this case it is. He's an old man and crippled and he's . . .'

'And what, Elly?' Joe had risen from the bed and was staring down at her. 'Go on, why don't you say it? He's not your kind of man, no matter what age he is; he's uncouth, rough, coarse.'

'Oh my God!' Elaine put her hands to her head, and lay back and closed her eyes, but she had hardly touched the pillows before she was sitting up again, staring at him and demanding, 'Do you mean to say you're for this?'

'Yes, every step of the way. Betty, here' – he jerked his head over his shoulder – 'she needs someone, and he needs someone, they both get on well together.' He now bent towards her and, his face grim, he said, 'I can't understand you; there are things about you that simply amaze me. I thought you'd be delighted. Don't go!' He swung round as Betty made for the door, but she took no notice of him and as the door clashed behind her, leaving the room filled with the expression of her feelings, he turned again to Elaine and, shaking his head slowly, he said, 'You're a cruel little bitch.'

154

'And you are a stupid, bull-headed fool.'

He had been standing stiffly, but now the upper part of his body moved slowly to the side, rather like the slow-motion action of a boxer about to deliver a side blow. However, his hand got no further than the second button of his coat, and gripping this he twisted it as he stared at her and listened to her hissing at him: 'Don't you know what this means; haven't you any foresight? You have a son, you seem to forget that. If they married it is not impossible that they might have children, and where would you stand then? Have you thought about that?'

'You mercenary little bugger!' The way he said 'bugger' didn't sound the same as when it came through his father's lips, and it was the first time he had used the word to her. Her head pressed deep into the pillows, and her voice still coated with bitterness, she hissed at him, 'I won't have it. I won't stand for it; there can't be two mistresses in this house. She's angled for this. I should have known.'

He straightened up now, took in a deep breath, stretched his neck out of his collar, then said slowly, 'You're right there: there could never be two mistresses; we'd have to move.' And on this he turned slowly about and left the room, leaving her sitting bolt upright in the bed, her large white teeth nipping savagely on the long painted nail of her middle finger.

'You're a fool.'

'Yes, I know I am, Mike.'

'You like me, don't you?'

'There's nobody I like better.'

'Well, I wouldn't be difficult to live with and I wouldn't ask much of you.'

'I know that. I know all that, but such a decision . . . well, it would cause complications and far-reaching consequences.'

'Aw! To hell with that for an excuse! As you likely know, I told our Joe and he was for it. He could have said, "My God! are you in your dotage, man?" but he didn't. Even knowing that money-wise he and his would stand to lose, he said nowt of the sort. What he said was, "I hope it comes off, Dad, but if it does, mind, I refuse to call her step-mother." You look het-up, lass; you've been having words.'

'Yes, you could say I've been having words.'

'Well, I needn't ask who your opponent was; and I bet it was about this very subject, because, if it *had* come off, she'd have her nose put out, wouldn't she?'

'Yes, she would. But what we both seem to forget is that what hurts her, in the end hurts Joe.'

'Aw, damn that for reasoning. Well—' He hobbled to the window, leaned on the sill with one hand and scratched his head with the other as he said, 'Nice Christmas box to be turned down flat on the second proposal of me life.'

When he slowly turned his head to look at her, they both smiled, and he said, 'Come here,' and when she was standing by his side he turned his back to the window-sill and leaned his buttocks against it for support, then taking her hand, he said, 'I want you to promise me one thing as a sort of compensation for the dirty trick you've played on me.'

'What's that?'

'You won't go and leave us; you won't go off to that Lady Mary, whatever her name is. You said you had a letter from her last month telling you she was looking for a house, and not too far away from here, I understand. Well, I have me own ideas what she's up to. The old are always selfish and she's a determined old faggot, if ever there was one; so I want you to promise me one thing: no matter what the atmosphere is down below' – he made a face towards the floor – 'you'll not leave here.'

'Oh, Mike, that's a tall order. Anyway, when I wrote to her I half promised that I'd go and stay with her for a week or two on my holiday.'

'Oh well, there's nowt against that. Take all your holidays with her as long as you regard this as your home.' He now jerked her hands and brought her nearer to him, and, staring into her eyes, he said, 'I can't do without you, lass. I look back and life seemed empty afore you came into it. I can't explain me feelings: I'm past passionate love; I would say I'm past love of all kinds; but then I've never laid such stock on love as I have on liking, and by! I like you, lass.'

When she bowed her head and stood mute he whispered thickly, 'Aw, don't cry. Don't cry. And yet in a way it's good to see a woman cry because of something I've said to her. Do you know something? The last woman I saw cry over me was me mother. Come on. Come on, dry your eyes, else if our Joe sees you he'll think we're already married and I've been indulging in the privileges of wedlock and hammerin' you.'

'Oh Mike, Mike!' She sniffed, blew her nose, then added, 'By the way, I never wished you a Happy Christmas.'

'Happy Christmas, lass.'

'Happy Christmas, Mike.' Slowly she bent towards him and placed her lips on his, and for a moment she was held against him so fiercely that they almost overbalanced.

Seconds later she was on the landing and making for the stairs. He had said he was still a man, and from that brief embrace she could tell he was still very much a man.

She was a fool. Oh, she was a fool. She had thrown away the only chance she would know in life of being a wife, the mistress of a house . . . and of being held tightly in a man's arms.

3

∽

'Isn't it a beautiful view?'

'Wonderful. Really wonderful.'

'Don't you think I was clever to find this house?'

'You're clever in all ways, Lady Mary.'

'Yes, yes I am. There's no false modesty about me; yes I'm clever in all ways, always have been. I was clever in the buying of it. Because it was furnished I pretended I didn't want it, not my style, I said; and I knew they hadn't time to clear it and get it to an auction because they were due to leave for South Africa in ten days. Their idea had been to let it furnished, but they'd had no applicants. I must have appeared to them at first like a godsend; then' – she now bent towards Betty and slapped her knee as she ended – 'I was the last resort. And then there was Nancy, and their cook, Mrs Bailey, from the village thrown in, so I bought Valley View cottage: beautiful outlook overlooking the Teviot; that's what they put in the advertisement. And here I intend to stay for the rest of my life . . . that's if I have a good companion.'

Betty looked at the old lady, who was sitting in a wicker chair on the lawn that was bordered on two sides by a blaze

158

of colour. Beyond these were banks of bushes and trees, and straight ahead, beyond a long sloping grass meadow, flowed the river, not big as rivers went, but gleaming and twisting like a gliding eel.

Behind them stood the house. Part of one gable was covered with Virginia creeper, its leaves pink with the promise of scarlet here and there, and from the other gable were hanging great festoons of wistaria leaves indicating that the blossom must have weighed them down in the spring.

There were eight windows to the front of the house, two at each side of the front door and four above door level, all deep set in the rough stone wall. Although it was called a cottage it had eight main rooms, besides the kitchen quarters, and a long attic, whose windows looked out onto the back of the house.

Betty had arrived late the previous evening, her reception by the old lady not only touching her heart, but warming her and soothing her frayed nerves, and she had to admit that her nerves had become frayed over the past months. From that anything but joyful Christmas Day up till just a few weeks ago there had been a noticeable rift in the relationship between herself and Elaine, and she knew that if she hadn't been so useful to her sister, or if the child had been easy to rear, or again, if there wasn't the obstacle of the real master of the house, Elaine would have politely given her her marching orders long before now.

Then a few weeks ago Elaine's attitude had changed; in fact, there had been two or three times when it seemed as if she was about to apologise for her behaviour. Once she had grabbed hold of her hand and had begun to say something, but before Betty could ask her what was wrong she had turned and rushed away into the garden. She hadn't followed her, for she recognised this as an echo of her sister's childish strategy; as a child, when she was at fault, she would

159

attempt to apologise, then run off and lock herself in the schoolroom, and by the time she was coaxed to come out, you would find yourself apologising to her.

She had thought that Elaine would greet her news that she was going to spend two or three weeks with Lady Mary with relief, yet, although she hadn't openly stated that she didn't want her to go, her manner had spoken for her.

During the summer months, Elaine had fallen into the habit of travelling up to London on her own. Sometimes she stayed with her Uncle Hughes-Burton, at other times with a school friend. Betty was surprised that Joe hadn't objected to these visits, which often kept Elaine away for two or three nights at a time; but on these nights he himself didn't return from the factory until eight or nine in the evening. And then there were his visits to the Brookses, which had become more frequent since Hazel's baby was born in April, strangely, on the same day that Martin was born two years before, a coincidence which had incensed Elaine. Betty recalled Elaine's anger at the time when Joe, stopping the car at the gates on the sight of Hazel sitting outside nursing the baby, had got out, taken the child in his arms and brought it back to the car, saying, 'Isn't she beautiful?'

And undoubtedly Hazel's baby *was* beautiful. And there was very little sign of the father's colour about her.

Yes, she had to admit to herself that there were times when she saw Elaine's point of view with regard to Joe's affection for David and his wife. Granted he and David had been brought up together, granted he had compassion for the man, but even so his treatment of him and his wife was unusual: it was as if he loved them . . . loved him. When this thought had first occurred to her, she had felt some embarrassment, yet it gave her an insight into Elaine's feelings on the subject and she couldn't help but be in sympathy with her on this issue at least . . .

'What are you thinking about, staring ahead like that?'

'Oh, nothing . . . everything; it's so peaceful here, so restful.'

'Too restful at times. That silly Miss Watkins imagined I had come here to die. She was preparing for the funeral, I think.'

'It was likely her concern for you.'

'Concern, huh! She should never have called herself a companion; she was more like a politician: one would imagine it was she herself who had pushed the flapper vote through. She actually waved the newspaper above her head that morning last summer, yelling, "We can do it at twenty-one!" Lady Mary now leaned forward again and, gripping Betty's hand, she muttered, 'Do you know what I said to her?' And in a hoarse whisper, her expression one of glee, she went on, 'You know what I said to her? "Be quiet! woman. You're forty and by now you should know that you can do it at any age, past fourteen, that is."'

As she lay back in her chair, her face turned to the sky, laughing unrestrainedly, Betty held her hand over her own mouth while her body shook.

Straightening herself up now, the old lady continued her tirade against her former companion: 'Her mother was a suffragette: rights for women, equality, and the like; fools the lot of them, fools. I would never allow any man to be equal with me. Mentally any woman can outshine and outwit any male if she has sense enough to put her mind to it. Equality! Do you know something, girl? My father was a bully and my mother was a terror. The servants hated him and loved her. If a servant disobeyed him or as much as spoke before he had given him leave, he would whip him, literally whip him off his feet. He could flick a whip like any of those cowboy men. I thought of him the other day and what his attitude would have been to Mrs Bailey when she stood by the dining table, her bust sticking out so much with pride that I couldn't see her face, and told me that her son had got to Oxford, "He's going to Ruskin College, ma'am," she said, her tone suggesting that I had tried to stop him. Mind, I had to stop myself from saying, "Well, it's a working man's college; you find no gentlemen there." But there's a lot of my mother in me and so I said, "You must be very proud, Mrs Bailey," and she said, "Times are changing, ma'am. Yes, by! they are that. An' not afore time. Nobody'll look down on him." It was then I thought of my father and that whip and I became sad for a moment at the realisation that indeed times have changed; no-one would have dared to speak to their mistress like that in my father's time.'

'I'm sure she meant no offence.' Betty's tone was cool.

'Why do you always defend these people? You know, in some ways you're like my mother, only she was a beauty and she had charm . . . Oh! Oh! I'm not insulting you, you've got charm. Even though you can't lay claim to good looks you've certainly got charm. But my mother was a character. They were both characters. Do you know what? They used to fight like cat and dog. Talk about the poor on a Saturday night, my parents could have out-yelled and out-bashed them hollow.'

She now lay back in her chair and once more she turned her face up to the sky as she went on, 'I remember one time. It was after a house party. Irene, that was my sister, and Ned, my brother – he was killed in India – we were looking through the top balcony. We always got up when they were having a go, and this time it was my father's turn. He was going at my mother for flirting with some fellow. I can see her now. She came sailing out of the bedroom, her head in the air, her face bright with impish laughter, saying, "You know what you can do, Henry, you can kiss my backside," and my father bellowed, "I wouldn't kiss what I could kick," and we watched him lift his boot and plant it

162

on her hefty buttocks and away she went sprawling flat on her face. Then you know what he did? He picked her up and carried her back into the bedroom. They loved each other. Yes, they did, very much. It was a happy house. Wherever we lived, as long as they were together, it was a happy house. I hate mealy-mouthed individuals. don't you?' She brought her head up and glanced towards Betty, but Betty merely smiled at her and waited for the rest, and it soon came.

'Sarah, you know, Lady Menton, she's mealy-mouthed. Oh, isn't she just! At least since she married James. Prayers for breakfast, dinner and tea. But she was a different girl when we were all in India; Sarah was no prim memsahib then, oh no. She didn't wear four flannel petticoats then, sometimes not even one. We used to go to the hills, you know, in the hot weather.' She now twisted around in the chair and looked fully at Betty and her face crinkled into myriad wrinkles as she began to sing softly in a croaking quiver the parody on *If Those Lips Could Only Speak*.

'If those hills could only speak
And the husbands could only see,
What a wonderful, wonderful picture
Of im-mo-ra-li-ty.'

They were laughing again unrestrainedly, and now Betty said, 'You're a wicked woman, you know, Lady Mary.'

'I know I am and I take that as a compliment, girl. By the way, I was thinking: how would you like to learn to drive a car?'

'I can drive a car. I drove a truck for some time during the war.'

'You did? Well! well! That's marvellous news. I'm going to buy a car and you will help me choose it, and you'll

163

drive me all about this beautiful countryside. I've always been given to understand that there were no places worth seeing in the North. Well, now I've seen them for myself, I can tell you in truth you can keep the South; this is more like me.' And she waved her hand in front of her as if to encompass the whole countryside. 'It's rugged beauty, with very few soft spots. In a car we can go to Hawick that way' – she thrust out one arm – 'or to Kelso that way' – she thrust out the other arm – 'or back to Kelso and over the border again across those wild moors and fells. They drove me that way and the grandeur was breathtaking. I never knew such places existed before, and I've travelled in my time. What car do you fancy?'

'Now, Lady Mary' – Betty's voice was low, her words spaced – 'I told you, didn't I? A fortnight, three weeks at the most.'

'Well, we could go lots of places in a fortnight to three weeks.'

'But what would you do with the car afterwards?'

'I'd' – the old head wobbled from side to side – 'I'd engage a chauffeur.'

'Where would you house him?'

There was silence for a moment, then the face wrinkled again into glee, and now she was holding Betty's knee as she said, 'I'd make him sleep with Nancy on the peril of having his legs whipped from underneath him.'

As she laughed quietly and helplessly Betty said, 'Under those conditions he'd be bound to give in.'

'Isn't it nearly tea-time?' And to the abrupt question Betty replied, 'No; there's more than half an hour to go yet; there's time for a nap.'

'Who wants a nap? I want to talk.' Nevertheless Lady Mary laid her head back against the chair and became still, and within a few minutes she was dozing.

Betty looked at her. The dress she was wearing had been fashionable forty years ago. It was one of a score to be found lying in trunks in the spare room. She understood that the old lady's habit was to take seven out at a time, wear a different one every day of the week and continue in this way for a month; then replace them with another seven. On her own admission she was a wealthy woman, so why did she dress like this? Likely because she wanted to look different and so attract notice to herself; dressed in today's fashion she would appear, until she opened her mouth, to be just another old lady.

Why did she like her? At times she had a bitter tongue, and her imperious manner could be very off-putting unless you understood what was behind it. She liked her, she supposed, because she did understand what was behind it: loneliness, a wasted life, a keen mind that saw the futility of living but nevertheless experienced a fear of dying, a need to be cared for and loved.

Well, she could care for her and she could love her. She would find her easy to love. So why not, why not stay? What was more, Lady Mary wouldn't go back on her word, she would do as she said and provide for her. Now that she was past thirty, the years would go by quickly, so very quickly; before she knew it she'd be forty, then fifty; and then what?

On Christmas Eve she had thrown away a sure form of security, and now she was being given a second chance to alleviate one worry in her mind at least. Was she going to be a fool for the second time? And how different it would be living here; the very setting oozed tranquillity. And there'd be no irritations. Oh, the old lady's tongue wouldn't be an irritation, more a form of amusement. But the main release would come from not seeing Joe, nor hearing him, nor sitting opposite him at breakfast.

165

Sometimes she thought everyone in the household must know how she felt about him; yet she knew that this was wild imagination; no-one knew how she felt. She hadn't herself realised the extent of her feelings until the moment she had placed Martin in his arms.

She asked herself what it was about him that had caught at her heart from their first meeting. It wasn't his looks, even though she loved to sit and stare at his face and watch the way his lips shot widely into a smile or laughter. Was it the look in his eyes? For they were kind eyes, except when he lost his temper and the light in them deadened like cooling steel. It wasn't that he stood out dramatically from other men in looks or stature; yet he did stand out. His personality affected people; to some he was a nice fellow, to others he was bad-tempered, a hard man. But all seemed to agree on one point; he was no fool. And yet he was blind where Elaine was concerned. But was he? Since overhearing their quarrelling she had begun to think that he knew more about her sister than she had imagined. Perhaps the truth was he wanted to remain blind. Mike had once said something to this effect, something about his not wanting to wake up.

And then there was Mike. If she left the house she would miss Mike, because there had daily been growing in her a feeling for Mike that was almost akin to love, yet wasn't love; at least, not love as she knew she wanted love; still, it was something that she would miss if she were to lose contact with it.

She sighed and lay back and looked over the calm scene before her. She'd let it all settle in her mind for the next two weeks before making a final decision about moving in with Lady Mary.

4

As it turned out, she was forced to make her decision after just six days.

Betty and Lady Mary were sitting in the drawing-room awaiting the hired car that was to take them into Kelso. Lady Mary had definitely made up her mind she was going to buy a car, one that would fit them, she had explained. For the past two days Betty had tried to persuade her from taking this decision to its practical conclusion, but she remained adamant: 'All right,' Lady Mary had said, 'if you are not going to drive it, it doesn't matter; I shall hire a chauffeur, a gentleman one. Look at the newspapers! Ex-officers are still throwing themselves about right, left and centre to become employed: Gentleman, late of the so-and-so regiment, will accept any position. Didn't I read that out to you last night? This country's heading for total collapse, and it's that Labour Party's fault and the strikes they cause. In my day everybody was fitly employed, each man to his station; now Mrs Bailey's son goes to Oxford. Huh!'

When the sound of a car coming on to the drive at the side of the house came to them, they both rose to their feet, and Betty, opening the door to allow Lady Mary to pass into the small hall, remarked, 'I think it's going to rain. Do you think you should make the journey?'

'Don't try to put me off, girl. And stop thinking I'm buying this car to induce you to stay.' She turned and confronted Betty, and she, looking straight into the old lady's blue eyes and smiling faintly, said, 'It never entered my head.'

'Liar!'

'Well, you should know.'

'Huh! Huh!' The chuckle came from deep within Lady Mary's throat; and then they were at the front door, and there stood a man, but not the chauffeur of the hired car.

'Why, Joe!'

'Hello, Betty. Good morning, Lady Ambers.'

'What do you want?'

'I've . . . I've come to see my sister-in-law.' His tone was polite but stiff.

'She's on holiday.' Lady Ambers now took Betty's arm in an effort to thrust her back into the hall, but Betty, covering the hand gently, said, 'Come and let us sit down for a moment. Come in, Joe.'

Protesting loudly and her words almost unintelligible, the old lady went back into the drawing-room and when she was seated Betty turned to Joe, who had come no further than the doorway, and asked quietly, 'What is it? What's wrong?'

'I've . . . I must talk to you, Betty.'

'You can say what you've got to say here; there's no secrets between her and me. She's going to stay here; she's made up her mind,' said Lady Ambers defiantly.

'Please, please, Lady Mary.'

'Aw! girl.' Now the old woman thrust out her hand and grabbed at Betty's, saying pathetically, 'You don't want to go back there, I know you don't; you've been content here. We get on well, don't we? We do, don't we now?'

'Yes, yes, we do, very well.'

'Then why be persuaded to go back there and be everybody's servant?' She now turned and looked up at Joe, saying, 'Oh, you can look as angry as you like, my man, but it's the truth. I keep my eyes and ears open; I heard a lot while I was with Sarah, along the road.'

Joe drew in a long slow breath; then, looking at Betty, he said, 'I must speak with you alone.'

'Yes, yes. Please excuse me a moment, Lady Mary. Now, now.' She patted the hand that was still gripping hers. 'You must realise that my brother-in-law wouldn't have come all this way unless the matter was urgent . . . Please.'

The grip was slowly relaxed; the old head was turned completely away; and Betty, hurrying past Joe and from the room, motioned him to follow her.

Both having swiftly climbed the shallow oak stairs, he followed her to her bedroom, and, she, opening the door, stood aside for him to pass her; then closing the door behind them, she asked quickly, 'What is it? What's happened? . . . is it Mike?'

'No, no.' He shook his head. 'It's . . . it's Elaine. She's . . . she's in a state.'

'State? What kind of a state?'

He closed his eyes for a moment, nipped at his lip, then said, 'She discovered she's pregnant again and she's tried to do everything she can to get rid of it. I didn't know until yesterday; I mean, what the real trouble was. I knew she'd been taking medicine, stomach medicine. She . . . she had indicated she had trouble with her bowels. I . . . I came across a letter just by accident. She was lying on the bed sweating. I went to her handkerchief drawer and there it was tucked between them. Well, naturally, it intrigued me. I read it. It was from this school-friend of hers arranging to have somebody do an abortion. I went berserk, and when she said she intended to go through with it I told her . . . well' –

169

he thrust out his head and turned towards the window – 'I threatened to divorce her and . . . and give the reasons why; and oh, so many other things besides. And then last night' – he turned towards her again – 'I found her on the bed and bleeding. I got the doctor immediately; she' – again his head moved in desperation – 'she must have tried to bring it away herself. Have you ever heard of any such thing?'

'Oh, dear God!'

'The doctor wanted to put her into hospital, but she refused to go. She kept telling me to come for you. She promised me she wouldn't do anything more if I would bring you back.'

'Oh, Joe.' Her face was screwed up as if in pain.

'You'll come?'

'Of course, Joe, of course.'

She watched his shoulders slump as he came towards her and when he was standing close to her he took hold of her hand, saying, 'We've missed you. Nothing's the same: Father's lost; there's been trouble with Ella again; she cheeked Elaine and she wanted me to dismiss her, but . . . but I couldn't. I explained to her there's three out of work in Ella's house. It's odd, you know, Betty, but she doesn't seem to understand the situation; I mean, of ordinary people. Somehow I don't think she ever will. How is it you can see their side and she can't?'

'I . . . I suppose it's the business of being kept in the nest for too long.'

'Well' – he nodded at her now, smiling wryly – 'it's just as well for all of us that you were pushed out early on.'

She had to withdraw her hand from his, saying now, 'I must pack. Would . . . would you mind going downstairs and talking to Lady Mary; try to explain. If . . . if you tell her everything, she will understand; she's really a very understanding person when you get beyond her sting.'

170

'All right, I'll tell her as much as I can.' He turned towards the door, then stopped and looked at her. 'Had . . . had you made up your mind to stay?'

She had already turned to pick up a case, and she looked down at it as she said, 'Yes. Yes, I had, Joe.'

'Oh dear.' He turned slowly and went out.

Less than ten minutes later she entered the drawing-room again to see Lady Mary sitting bolt upright in her chair. When she looked at her the old lady did not say, 'Well, you're going then;' nor did she voice any reprimand, but, lifting her hand, she beckoned Betty towards her and said, 'I can understand that you've got to leave now, but remember, I'll go on waiting for you to come back, and I mean, to come back for good. But in the meantime I shall buy that car and hire that chauffeur and I shall send it down to that house to bring you here for a few days at a time. You will come?'

'Yes, yes, I shall come, Lady Mary. And thank you, thank you so much for being so understanding.' She now leaned forward and kissed the wrinkled cheek; but there was no response from the old lady; nor did her position alter in the slightest; all she did was to champ her lips together, gulp some spittle down her throat and say, 'Well, if you're going, get yourself away; I've never believed in sobbing farewells.'

'Goodbye, Lady Mary.' Betty turned slowly and walked up the room. And Joe, too, said quietly, 'Goodbye, ma'am. And thank you for your understanding.'

Left to herself Lady Mary's stiff back bent forward; her hands, which had been flat on her lap, curled inwards. Then, her eyes blinking the moisture back into the sockets, she exclaimed aloud, 'Blast all empty-headed, selfish, pregnant women!'

5

Elaine's second child was born on the last day of March 1930, and when Betty held her in her arms she shuddered as she moaned inwardly, 'Oh no! No!' and whatever exclamation she might have been about to utter was silenced by the doctor as with a look, he indicated to the nurse that she take the child out of the room.

When Joe saw his daughter, he said, 'Oh my God!'

When after twelve days no-one would bring the child to Elaine she got herself up and went to the nursery, and when she saw what she had given birth to she screamed and fell into a dead faint.

After a month, by which time the child had made no effort to move its limbs, the doctor confirmed there were definite signs of brain damage.

It was left to Betty to see to the child. From the first moment she had taken the flannel over the harelip, and had wiped the matter from the corners of the small eyes that were set at an angle in the domed head, and had gently washed the right leg that resembled a piece of twisted rope, she knew that as long as this child lived she'd be bound to the house.

Strangely, the only one not repelled by the sight of the child was Martin. He would stand by the side of the cot, chattering away to it, and he would always begin with, 'Hello, little girl.'

The child had not been christened, nor had she been given a name. When Martin had said to Betty, 'Nice baby,' she had replied, 'Yes, she's a nice little girl; she's your sister.' From then on he had called her 'little girl'.

In the works it was known that Remington's classy wife had given birth to a monstrosity. Few of the men had known of such an idiot, for surely an idiot it must be. There might be some in Bog's End who were not very bright, but they weren't idiots. No, by God! They left that kind of thing to the high-breeders.

During the following months the atmosphere in the house changed, becoming charged with gloom from Mike's quarters down to the kitchen; while on the first floor war raged.

Joe understood Elaine's feelings, because he knew how he had felt that first moment when he had looked on the child. So, for six months, he bore her outbursts of grief, her prostration when, for days on end, she would remain in bed, and he also accepted her sudden change of attitude towards their first-born, for whereas previously she had left him almost solely to the care of Betty and Nellie, she now monopolised the child. But when she decided that her son must sleep in their room he put his foot down. Even her suggested compromise that Martin should have a room to himself was met with a firm, 'No!' because, as he pointed out, Martin was the only one in the house who saw their daughter as normal: to him she was a baby, and as yet he did not see the difference between her and other babies.

Up till then he had not accused her of being the cause of the child's deformity, because when he had put the question to the doctor as to why such an event had occurred, the answer had been evasive: such children appear in all families, the doctor had said; the cause wasn't really known.

Not until the child was a year old, which was in March 1931, did he openly accuse her of being the cause of the baby's deformity . . .

Apart from worries at home Joe was experiencing additional problems at the factory. The orders for packing-cases and such-like had dropped to almost half of what they had been in 1927. Unemployment in the country was rife, with almost two million people out of work. The previous week he himself had had to lay off half a dozen men, and there was the likelihood that another half dozen would have to go within the month if he didn't bring off that York order.

A few years before it seemed to be only the miners that were hard hit, but now it was every industry.

This worry alone would have been quite enough to cope with without the complexities he had to face with his wife and the tragedy that lay immobile in a cot in the nursery. So his mind was in anything but a peaceful state when he arrived home at six-thirty on this particular evening to be informed almost immediately by Ella that the mistress had gone into Newcastle.

'Really!' He smiled at Ella. 'Did she order a taxi?'

'Yes, Mr Joe.'

'Miss Betty didn't go with her?'

'No, Mr Joe . . . Miss Betty's up in the nursery.'

'Thanks, Ella.' He still called her Ella.

He hurried up the stairs and into the nursery, and Betty turned from the cot, saying, 'Oh, hello, Joe.'

Instead of answering her greeting he said, 'Ella tells me that Elaine's gone into Newcastle.'

'Yes, she suddenly took it into her head this afternoon.'

'Didn't she want you to go with her?'

174

'No.' She scraped the spoon around the bowl and gently placed the contents in the child's mouth; then going to the basin in the corner of the room, she wetted a flannel and on her way back to the cot she said, 'It's a good sign.'

'Yes, yes, it is. Did she say why she was going?'

Betty didn't answer until she had dried the child's face and had lifted up the side of the iron-railed cot and dropped it into place. The precaution of the railed cot was not so much to prevent the baby from falling out as to stop Martin from climbing in beside it. And now she turned and looked at Joe and said slowly, 'No, she didn't.'

'Perhaps she just wanted to go out, to see the shops.'

'Yes, yes, perhaps that was it.'

They stood staring at each other, he waiting for her to say something, she thinking, She'll likely tell him about the telephone call herself. If she doesn't, then it's just as well I haven't mentioned it.

'How's himself?'

'He has what he terms the hump. I tried to persuade him to come downstairs; he's alone too much up there and . . . and I can't get up as often as I would like.'

'I know that, Betty.'

She started visibly when he caught hold of her hands, saying, 'What would we do without you? They say that there are compensations in life, and by! you've been a compensation to everybody in this house.'

'Oh' – she jerked her hands away, her face unsmiling – 'don't start pinning wings on me. I do what I do because I like it. I wouldn't do it otherwise; I have my selfish side; I'm allowed to be human.' She was making for the door when he said in a perplexed fashion, 'I'm sorry, Betty, I . . . I was only trying to tell you . . . well, how grateful I am.'

She stood with her back to him for a moment; then,

turning to him and her expression soft now, she said, 'I know; I'm sorry I was so sharp. I'm . . . I'm a bit on edge today.'

'You're tired.' He was moving towards her again. 'You must have a break. Go up to Lady Mary's for the week-end, and tell her I sent you. That might put me in her good books. To go and fetch you away once was bad enough, but to repeat it was unforgivable in her eyes. She hates the sight of me.'

'Oh no, she doesn't; she quite likes you.' She now assumed Lady Mary's voice and manner as she said, 'You're quite ordinary but a pleasant-enough fella. And that, I may tell you, is high praise from her; you should hear what she says about her male relations, Lord Menton in particular. Anyway' – she nodded at him – 'I think I shall take a break just for a couple of days. Are you going upstairs?'

'Yes; I was just on my way.'

'Bring the tray down with you, will you? It will save Jane's legs.'

'Yes, right-o.'

They went out of the room together, Betty making her way to the dining-room and the kitchen to see that everything was ready for the evening meal, and Joe to the upper floor. It was part of the pattern of the day.

Ella was sounding the gong for dinner when a taxi drew up at the front door and, at the same time, Joe came down the main staircase. When he opened the door Elaine was mounting the steps and she looked up at him and said, 'I hope I haven't kept you waiting for dinner.'

'No, no.' He smiled at her. 'The gong's just sounded; I'll tell Mary to hold it back until you're ready . . . Had a nice time?'

'Yes. Yes, very nice.' She walked past him and up the stairs, and he paused to look at her for a moment before following her. And when they entered the bedroom he closed the door behind him and asked quietly, 'You feel better?'

'A little.'

She took off her coat and hat, then went to the dressing-table and, sitting down, drew a comb through her hair before she added, 'I . . . I would feel better still if you'd agree with what I've decided to do.'

He came and stood behind her and looked at her face reflected in the mirror, and he asked quietly, 'What have you decided to do?'

She now moistened a pad of cotton wool with an astringent, wiped her lips with it, then said quietly, 'Put her in a home.'

'*Put her in a home?*' His face was screwed up as if he didn't know to whom she was referring, and he repeated, '*Put her in a home?*'

'Yes, that's what I said.' She now swung round on the stool and, her hands gripped tightly together on her knees, she gazed up at him and in a pleading voice she said, 'Let me do this, Joe. I've . . . I've been to see a . . . a Dr Rice, who has a home for such thi . . . children, outside Newcastle. He says he will come and see you and . . . and her.'

He hadn't moved, nor had his expression altered much; only his eyes darkened, and now he said slowly, 'Why didn't you call her "the thing", as you were about to do? So you're going to throw her out, put her in a home!' It seemed now that his body was pushed, so quickly did he move backwards to the middle of the room from where, his jaw thrust out and his voice a growl, he spat at her, 'No, you don't! Oh no! you don't. For once in your life you're going to shoulder a responsibility; and she's your responsibility as well as mine . . . she's your daughter.'

She too was on her feet now, and her own anger almost

177

matched his as she cried back at him, 'She's *not* my daughter! I don't think of her as my daughter. She's not human. She was a mistake from the beginning. I knew it, I knew it. You should have let me get rid of her then.'

'Well, all I can say is you tried your best and what she is now is the result of that best. I don't care what any damn doctor says about its happening to anyone, what you did to yourself you did to her. She's yours, and as long as I've got any say in it she'll remain yours, and in this house.'

'You're inhuman. You're almost like her.'

'Well then, you've got the two of us on your plate.'

'You're vile, you're common, raw . . .'

He made no answer to this, only stared at her, and now she cried at him, 'I hate you! I loathe you!'

The muscles of his face twitched as if he had been struck a blow. He passed one lip hard over the other, gathered spittle into his mouth, swallowed, then said, 'Well, now I know where I stand, don't I? And now I'm going to tell you where you stand. You tell your Dr Rice to keep away from here, because if he puts his nose in the door I'll tell Betty to go. And I don't think she'll be sorry, because she's worn out. Then you'll have to take on the real responsibility of your daughter. If you don't, there's an alternative; but we'll come to that later.' And on this he turned from her and walked slowly from the room, and into the bathroom.

Some minutes later he mounted the attic stairs to his father's room and almost collided with Betty as she was about to leave.

Mike, standing in the middle of the room leaning on his stick, looked towards his son as he asked, 'Who declared this war?'

Joe wiped his face with his handkerchief and blew his nose heavily; then he said, 'She's been to some fellow in

Newcastle, a Dr Rice; she wants to put the child into his home.'

'Oh?' Mike shifted his stick an inch or two on the carpet, looked down at it, and said again, 'Oh?' Then casting a sidelong glance at Joe, he added, 'Well, as I see it, and as things are, it seems sensible to me.'

'What!'

'Don't bawl, lad. Don't bawl. I understand how you feel, but I can see her point.'

Joe's eyes were wide, the amazement showing on his face; and now he turned and looked at Betty as if for support, but she, after a moment of answering his glance, looked away from him and her voice was merely a mutter as she said, 'Yes, I can see her side of it, too. She's likely thinking of Martin and the impression on him as he grows older.'

'She's not thinking of anyone but herself.' Joe's voice was loud again. 'How many times to your knowledge has she shown any interest in the child since it was born, eh? Tell me that.'

'I don't know.' Her voice now was no longer a murmur and she was staring straight at him. 'What I do know is that you are both bound to see the situation from different angles.'

'Tell me one thing, Betty, just tell me this: if she was yours, would you put her in a home and leave her there to lie until she dies, which could be tomorrow or next year or ten years' time; would you?'

As she looked back into his taut face she blinked, then jerked her head to the side before turning and going towards the door, saying, 'She's not mine, so I can't give you any answer to that.'

The two men looked at each other in silence until Mike said, 'I say again, lad, I think she's right.'

Joe did not come back at his father now but, turning to the

179

side, he sat down heavily in a chair, placed his elbows on his knees and dropped his face into his hands, and from between his fingers he said, 'I couldn't do it. I couldn't do it.'

Presently, he straightened up and turned to Mike, who was now seated near the window, saying, 'I was talking to Jack Farrow yesterday. They have a four-year-old mongol child and he said there's been more happiness in their house since the child was born than ever before. It's brought them closer together, and the other children think the world of it.'

'Yes, yes, I've heard that said afore, but your daughter is not a mongol, Joe; the doctor gave me the straightforward answer the other week when I asked him how she'd be classified. He said there was no heading under which they could put her; in fact, medically speaking she was nothing.'

'Oh, my godfathers!' Joe's cry and his action, as he rose, of turning his head to the side as if away from something frightful caused Mike almost to castigate him, saying, 'Aye, you can be horrified but you've got to face it, and in facing it you've got to understand how Elaine's looking at the situation.' In a calmer tone, he went on, 'There's one thing you mustn't do, though; you mustn't let the child cause a permanent rift atween you; that is if you still care for her . . . Do you?'

Joe stared at his father, although he wasn't seeing him, he was seeing Elaine as she had been a few minutes before, saying to him, 'You're vile, you're common, raw.' Did he still care for her?

There was really no need to ask the question, for the very sight of her at times burned him up; he felt he wanted to lose himself in her, strip off the veneer and bury himself in the woman he imagined to be underneath, the woman he was for ever trying to unveil; the woman, the mature woman, he felt would emerge one day . . . Did he love her? He opposed her, he frustrated her, he fought with her, but all the while . . .

180

yes, yes, he loved her. And tomorrow, even tonight, he would go to her and tell her how sorry he was for upsetting her, yet at the same time knowing that he would never comply with her wishes, whether they be about the little girl or the two down in the cottage for whom the hate that had been kindled in her on their first meeting had never abated.

He turned now and walked out of the room without answering Mike's question.

6

There were many times during the following year when the unreasonable demands made on her, not only by Elaine but also by Joe and Mike, made Betty wonder just how she controlled her temper; if she hadn't had Lady Mary's house to fall back upon she didn't think she would have been able to carry on.

Physically she was strong; but the twenty-four hours' responsibility of the nursery fell on her shoulders, and it was beginning to tell. Nellie was a great help, but she openly admitted she didn't like to handle the child. As she said, she could do anything with Master Martin but not with *it*.

Then Mike, whose arthritis worsened during the winter, laid almost as much claim to her attention as did the child, but he approached it in a different way. 'Come up here and rest,' he would say. 'Come up here and get the weight off your feet.' But most of the time her visits would be taken up with manipulating his back and shoulders, and making sure he did the exercises the doctor had set him to keep the joints of both his fingers and toes free. He didn't mind grabbing at a ball with his hands, but he objected strongly, as he tried again and again to pick up a pencil with his toes

. . . And then there was the evening card game. So often she just wanted to get to her room and lie stretched out on her bed, but the thought of him up there alone, and fuming, would drive her up the attic stairs.

As for Elaine, her sister worried her, for she was with-drawn, and sulky with it. She never spoke of the child lying still in the nursery, the child that never cried; she never visited the nursery and saw to it that her son spent most of the time elsewhere. It would seem that she had developed a possessive passion for the boy, but the whole household was aware that her aim was to keep her son away from his sister as much as possible.

Whatever the situation might be between Elaine and Joe, Betty could only guess at, for there were no rows now, no raised voices in their sitting-room, yet she knew from the look of Joe that the situation wasn't good.

And Joe made his own demands on her. Whereas at one time he would say, 'Go and have a break; go and see your old girl,' he had, over the past few months, made no such suggestion. It was as if he would have her live in the nursery all the time. He would come into the room, stand by the cot and gaze down on the child; sometimes he would lift her limp hand or turn her head on the pillow, aiming to get her eyes focused on him. At times his finger would trace the harelip, then move over the flat cheekbones to the domed head. At such times, when he stayed by the cot longer than usual, she could feel his pain, his compassion, and when he turned his face to her and she saw the sadness deep in his eyes, her heart would ache for him, although in a different way from usual.

'Aunty Bett.'
'Yes, darling?'
'When will the little girl come out to play?'

183

'Oh.' Betty looked down at Martin, who was mounting the stairs by her side, his hand in hers, and she said, 'Not yet awhile; when she's a little better.'

'When?'

'Perhaps next year.'

'At Christmas when Santa comes?'

'Yes, yes; perhaps at Christmas when Santa comes.'

'I'd like her to play with me now, Aunty Bett.'

'Well, she's sick at present.'

'She doesn't talk to me.'

'No; no, not yet. You see she doesn't know any words.'

'Well, I could show her with my books.'

Betty opened the nursery door, then paused for a second as Martin tugged his hand from hers, crying, 'Daddy! Daddy!'

Joe opened his arms and the boy leapt into them, and Betty said, 'I didn't know you were in; the car's not outside.'

'I had a puncture just below the gate; David's seeing to it.'

'Daddy. Daddy.' The boy was pulling Joe's face round to his. 'Aunty Bett says the little girl will talk next . . . next year, and she'll play with me, but, Daddy, I want her to play now.'

The boy twisted himself about in Joe's arms and leaned over the iron rail and bent down into the cot, and Joe held him there for a moment and allowed him to stroke the child's face; then lifting him up again, he placed him on the floor. But the boy, as though he would not be outdone, shook the cot bars until they rattled as he cried, 'Put her on the rug, Daddy! Put her on the rug!'

'No! Martin. Leave go. Stop doing that!' As Joe unloosened one small hand from a rail the child grabbed at it with the other until Betty, going to him, said, 'All right, all right, if you're a good boy I'll put her on the rug; but just for a moment, mind.'

184

'You think that's wise?' Joe asked the question in a muttered aside, and she answered in the same way, 'I can't see that it can do any harm to either of them; he won't always accept her as she is now; in fact, it's a wonder it's lasted this long.'

Joe stood aside and watched her lift the side of the cot out of its slot, lower it, then gather the small limp form into her arms, saying as she did so, 'Put the pillow on the floor, will you, Joe?'

A moment later he stood looking down at his daughter lying on the cushion. She looked like some immature gargoyle, while his son, kneeling by her side, his face showing rapt pleasure, appeared to him for a moment like a seraph newly born out of the celestial hierarchy. It was like beauty and the beast being played out by infants, only in reverse.

There were times when he couldn't bear the situation and this was one of them. As he turned abruptly away, Betty, who was on her knees by the side of the pillow, checked his leaving by saying, 'Joe?'

'Yes?' He stood with his back to her.

'I'd like to get away this week-end.'

It was a few moments before he replied, 'All right. I'll be here; I'll see to things.'

'There's no need for you to put yourself out, you know that; Nellie can manage and Jane will give a hand.'

'Yes, yes, I know; but I'll be here, nevertheless.'

He had opened the door when she spoke again. 'I must have a break, Joe.'

He turned now and looked at her, saying softly, 'Of course. Of course, Betty. I know that. I . . . I ask too much of you. But . . . but I can't help it. Somehow I don't want her to be left alone; it's as if she's . . . well, she's telling me she doesn't want to be left alone. It's stupid, I know, but there it is.'

185

Her throat was tight. She opened her mouth to speak, but couldn't. When he had closed the door behind him she put her hand on the child and its rapid heart-beat matched her own for a moment. What was to be the end of it? She still had no answer to this oft-repeated question that covered more than the problem of the child, and in the next instant she was startled by Martin, saying, 'Why does the little girl look funny, Aunty Bett? She's . . . she's not like other little girls, or their dolls; she's got a funny lip, and her eyes aren't straight.'

Only a moment or so ago she had said he wouldn't always accept her as she was now; well, he was now apparently seeing her for the first time as she really was and it was likely she would appear more odd to him as each day went by.

Quickly she picked up the child from the floor and placed it in the cot; then she lifted the side of the cot and dropped it into place; and when she turned from the cot Martin was standing in the middle of the room staring at her, his face solemn; and, as if he were aware of what she was thinking, he said softly, 'Even if she *is* funny I still want to play with her, Aunty Bett.'

7

Joe entered the drawing-room and walked towards the couch where Elaine was sitting reading before the fire. The April evening was chilly; there had been a frost last night and from the feel of the air another one was promised tonight.

He stood with his back to the fire observing her. She had glanced up when he had entered the room but now she had returned her attention to the magazine. She looked thin and, he thought, peaky; there was no doubt she was suffering as much as he was, even if it was in a different way, but why couldn't they share their suffering? At twenty-six she was more beautiful than when he had first met her, yet at the same time she didn't seem to have developed in any way, still appearing to be a flapper of twenty-two, or twenty, even eighteen.

He said softly, 'I'm sorry I've got to go out. I had forgotten about the meeting when I let Betty go.'

She looked up. 'Let her go! Betty's not a servant; you don't *let* her go.'

His teeth ground against each other; then slowly, he said, 'I didn't mean it that way; you know exactly what I meant.'

Her eyes were again on the magazine and he stared hard at her for a moment before he added, 'We're going to make George Bailey a director. I did tell you, didn't I?'

She showed no interest, so he went on as if he were being forced to defend the foreman: 'He's a good man. He's worked hard for us for years; he deserves it if anyone does.' He glanced at his watch, then said, 'Well, I must be off, but I won't be long; a couple of hours at the most.' Yet he did not immediately make for the door; instead, stepping quickly to the couch, he sat down by her side and, gripping her hand, he brought it to his mouth and rubbed his lips across the knuckles; and then, his voice soft and appealing, he murmured her name, 'Elly. Elly.'

She turned her head slightly to the side and away from him. 'You'll be late for the meeting,' she said indifferently.

'Elly. Look at me.' Gently he brought her face towards him and, his hands cupping her cheeks and his voice throaty, he said, 'Let's try. We need each other; I'm . . . I'm lost without you.'

'Whose fault is that?'

'Mine, I know, I know, but it'll never happen again, I swear; there's ways and means of preventing it, on my side, permanently; I'll take the necessary steps; anything, so that we can be one again, really one again. I . . . I can't bear this life, being separated from you.'

She moved her hand in his and, her eyes downcast, she said, 'Go . . . go to the meeting; we'll talk about it later.'

'Darling. Oh, darling.' He leaned forward and buried his face in her neck for a moment; then he kissed her on the lips. After passing his hand over her mat of straight, shining hair he rose to his feet, standing for a moment and smiling gently down at her; then reluctantly he turned from her and went out.

When she heard the car moving down the drive she rose from the couch, switched off the side-table light and walked to the window. The twilight was deepening and the full moon was already bright in the high sky. After a moment she returned to the couch and sat staring into the fire. She sat like this until the half-light in the room gave way to darkness; then she rose and went out into the hall and up the stairs.

She did not go into her own room, nor yet into the nursery, although she paused for a moment as she passed the door. She could hear Nellie moving about inside and Martin chattering. He should be asleep by now; it was more than an hour since Nellie brought him to the drawing-room to say good-night.

She went on and up the stairs and tapped on Mike's sitting-room door, and when she entered she found the room empty; but then Mike appeared in his bedroom doorway in his dressing-gown.

'I just came to see if you needed anything.'

'No, no, lass; I have everything I want.' He hobbled into the room, saying now, 'Sit yourself down. How're you feeling?'

She didn't do as he suggested but answered, 'Much the same.'

And to this he replied, 'Aw well, that doesn't show an improvement, does it?'

'What do you expect?'

'What do I expect?' He turned his head and looked at her. 'Well, since you ask I'll tell you. I think you should put up a fight: accept the situation and say, There it is, but it isn't going to down me; I've got me life to live, and I've got to help Joe to live *his* . . . You're not alone in this, you know, lass.'

'I'm well aware of that.'

'Well, if that's the case, you want to tell yourself it isn't the

189

end of the world. These things are happening to people every day and they've got to be borne; what can't be cured must be endured. Me mother used to say that, an' it's true.'

Her nose gave a slight twitch and she said, 'Are you sure there's nothing I can get you?'

'No; I've all me wants, lass, thank you very much. Joe's had to go back to the works?'

'Yes, to a meeting, I understand.'

'Aye, to a meeting. He's got worries there an' all. He's putting Geordie Bailey on the board. Of course, that's just a face-saver, when all's said and done, to give people the impression that things are looking up, when in fact they couldn't be much worse. If he doesn't get more orders in soon, it'll be a job to keep the payroll going. You see' – he nodded at her now – 'worries never come singly; and what he needs now at the present moment is help. And I'm no bloody use to him; so, as I see it, lass, it's up to you.' He looked straight into her face; and she returned the look fully for a moment, then said, 'If there's nothing I can do for you, I'll say good-night.'

'Good-night.'

Her leaving was as abrupt as his farewell, and when she reached her own room she stood leaning against the door for a moment, her fists clenched by her sides.

It was some ten minutes later before she felt her tense muscles relaxing. She had undressed and put on a black-top lace nightdress and over it a black negligée; then she went into the sitting-room and lay on the chaise-longue which was placed at right angles to the fireplace. The house seemed very quiet, empty in fact: Duffy and the cook were in the kitchen; Mike was in his loft upstairs; Martin was asleep in the nursery – she did not include the other child in her thoughts at that moment; it was Jane's night out, and Nellie would be down to supper and chatting away to the Duffys.

And up in the Border country Betty would be chattering away to that horrible old woman.

They all had someone to talk to except herself. She was alone, misunderstood by everyone, and mostly by her husband. He had urged that they should come together again. What did that mean? Oh, she knew what it would mean, and she didn't believe for a moment that he would ensure he would not make her pregnant again. He had cheated her twice and he thought too much of his manhood, his virility, to keep such a promise. He'd promise anything to get back into her bed again . . . And she had to face this: she wanted him back because she needed his affection; she needed to be fondled, to be caressed, petted, but what she didn't need was what he termed loving. It sickened her. She realised now that it had done from the very first . . . Would she have felt like this towards Lionel? No, no; she didn't think so, for there was all the difference in the world between Lionel and Joe. There was a roughness, an uncouthness about Joe, who took after his father.

She walked slowly into the bedroom. That girl Nellie hadn't been in to turn the bed down. She was supposed to take over Jane's duties when she was off; she should have seen to it before she went down to supper. She walked to the window with the intention of drawing the curtains. The moon was bright now; the garden looked mysterious, romantic. Romantic! She scoffed at the word. Once upon a time there had been romance in her life . . . but now there was nothing.

As her hand went up to draw the curtain a movement to the side of the house bathed in the moonlight caught her attention. Someone had run past the gable end and towards the elm tree. She reached for the cord hanging to the side of the bed and switched out the light; then she was standing close to the window.

191

Really! It was the girl, Nellie, and a man. They were canoodling. How dare she! Going down to supper indeed! This is what must happen every night. Just wait till she came upstairs.

She turned from the window and looked across the darkened room towards her sitting-room. The children were alone in the nursery. She had never thought of them as the children before; only the child, and that meant Martin . . .

It seemed that she had been standing still for an eternity, frozen to the spot, with her heart racing as if it would jump through her ribs, before she glanced upwards. Mike was in his attic kingdom. The Duffys were in the kitchen: Duffy was getting deaf and he never came up the stairs unless he had to, and Mrs Duffy was too fat and doddery even to attempt them. The house had never been so empty of people; this floor particularly had never been so empty.

It seemed, even to herself, that she flew from her room and into the nursery; and when she paused, breathless, by the side of the cot she had no recollection of having opened the door.

She did not immediately look into the cot, but peered through the dim light shed by the red-globed nightlight standing on a side table and towards where her son lay in his bed near the far wall. She could just make out that he was lying on his side, and it appeared that he had one hand, the fingers spread wide, across his face.

For a matter of seconds she stood perfectly still, her head turned, watching him; then she looked down on her daughter. Even as she did this her hands were gently lifting the side of the cot out of its sockets and, as if her body were floating, she glided round to the other side of the cot and, putting her hands through the rails, gripped the mattress . . . Then she put her hands to her head to shut out the sound of the soft thud as the child's body hit the floor . . .

192

As if in a dream she found herself back in her room again and standing near the bedroom window. Nellie was still under the elm tree, clasped in the man's arms. She stood and watched them for almost two minutes before she turned from the window. She felt no sense of guilt; in fact, at this moment she assured herself she had done a very good and brave thing, she had done what the doctor or Joe or someone should have done before the child had had time to breathe.

But what about Martin? Well, no-one would ever blame a child for wanting to play with his sister. She had heard Nellie telling Jane that Betty had had them on the rug together again today. No-one would hold the 'accident' against Martin.

Once more she turned to the window. There was now no sign of the girl and the man. She walked into the sitting-room again and stood looking towards the door. When she heard that girl come on to the landing she would open it and confront her.

She was amazed at her own coolness. Then her coolness vanished and she put her hands to her throat as she heard an ear-splitting scream, and she knew it hadn't come from the girl but from her son.

In response to Joe's frantic telephone call Betty arrived back in the house at ten o'clock the next morning. Lady Ambers, true to her word, had bought a car and engaged a chauffeur; and after Betty had directed him towards the kitchen, saying, 'Make yourself known; I'll come and see you in a moment or two,' she ran up the steps and into the hall.

Ella was coming down the stairs and, on the sight of Betty, she exclaimed, 'Oh! miss. Eeh! it's been awful.' Doubtless she would have enjoyed giving Betty first-hand details, but at that moment Joe emerged from the dining-room. He didn't speak but moved hastily towards Betty and, taking her by the arm, led her into the drawing-room.

'How did it happen?' she asked, as she took off her hat and threw it onto a chair and turned to let him help her off with her coat.

'Martin,' he said. 'He must have dropped the side of the cot down. How he managed it, the Lord only knows; he couldn't have stood on the cracket, for that was still in Nellie's room. We've always kept it out of his way, you know.'

'Where was Nellie?'

'Having her supper. She said Martin was fast asleep when she left him. Apparently she was on her way back when she heard his screams from the landing, and when she got into the room there he was on the floor, the child in his arms, and screaming as you've never heard a child scream. He was still screaming when I got home. He must have been trying to lift her from the cot, and when that wasn't possible he tugged at the mattress and, of course, she rolled on to the floor. There was a big bruise on the side of her face.'

'How long did she live?' Betty sat down now on the edge of the couch, staring at her hands, which were gripped together on her knees.

'She went at half-past three.'

'What did you tell the doctor?'

'What could I tell him? There was Nellie's version. She would have talked anyway. And Elaine had seen the whole thing. She had rushed in with Nellie and picked up the boy, but she couldn't pacify him. It was as if he were in a nightmare: he fought and struggled and screamed until the doctor gave him a sedative.'

'How is he now?'

'Strangely, he's all right this morning. As I said, it was just like a nightmare. When I told him the little girl had gone to heaven – that's the only thing I could think of to say – he didn't seem at all perturbed, but he asked for you. "I want Aunty Bett," he said.'

'And Elaine?'

'I'm worried in that quarter. She's quiet; I think she's blaming herself now for her attitude to the child. Last night she seemed to take it calmly, too calmly for normality.'

'It's likely the shock.'

'Yes, I suppose so. Dr Pearce said it's the best thing that could have happened. And perhaps I might have agreed with him, but it's the way it's happened, because even if the picture is obliterated from Martin's mind, which it appears to be now, some ignorant biddy is bound to bring it up in later life: Nellie will tell her mother, and her mother will tell the neighbours, and a child will hear it, and that could be it.'

'Oh, you're exaggerating, Joe. Anyway, it was an accident; it could have happened with any two children.'

There was silence between them for a moment; then Betty got to her feet, saying, 'I'll go up and see her.'

Without another word, he opened the door for her, and she went up the stairs to Elaine's room.

She was surprised to find Elaine dressed. They stared at each other across the width of the room, and it was Elaine who spoke first. 'I'm not going to say I'm sorry it's gone,' she said.

'I wouldn't expect you to.' Betty looked from her sister's white face to her twitching fingers and she felt a moment of deep compassion for her. She might say that she wasn't sorry her child had gone, but nevertheless she was deeply affected, so she went and put her arms around her, and immediately she was amazed at the result, for Elaine, her body trembling from head to foot, burst into a torrent of weeping and lay against her like a child searching for comfort from its mother.

195

'There, there. It's all over. Come on, now; don't cry like that.' And yet even as she said the words she was thinking that the outburst was the best thing that could happen to Elaine, it would release the tension in her. 'Come along, dear, and sit down,' she said, leading her to a chair.

But when she was seated Elaine still clung to Betty, who now pressed her sister's head into her waist and stroked her hair and was murmuring gently to her when Elaine burst out, 'Everybody hates me.'

'Don't be silly.'

'You do at times.'

'No, I don't. I have never hated you. Get vexed with you, yes, but I've never hated you.'

'Joe does.'

'Oh, Elaine, what's the matter with you? Joe loves you. Not many men would put up with what Joe's had to go through.'

'There you go.' Elaine pulled herself away from Betty's embrace and, pressing herself back into the chair, she whimpered, 'Nobody sees my side of it; nobody. Do you know something? I loathe everybody in this house, apart from Martin . . . and you.'

Betty now stared down at her sister and she thought with not a little pain that the 'and you' had been added more by way of diplomacy than truth. Her voice was low when she answered, 'That's a pity, then.'

Now Elaine turned on her, crying, 'Oh, the way you talk. You're so smug; you would never think any wrong thoughts or do anything bad, would you? Good old Betty. Everybody says, good old Betty. You inveigle yourself into people's good books. You're two-faced.'

'Be quiet! Elaine.'

'I'll not be quiet; this is my house. I'll speak when I want to speak. I'll shout if I like; I'll scream; I'll scream at old Mike,

196

and the second master, Master Joe, Master Joe, Master Joe, and that dirty filthy black man and his loose-living wife. Oh, I know what I know . . .'

'Elaine! I've told you to be quiet.'

'What is it? What's the matter?' Joe suddenly burst into the room, and Elaine screamed at him now, 'I'm telling your dear Betty that she's smug, two-faced, like you, like you all.'

When Joe stepped forward her screaming rose to an ear-splitting pitch: 'Don't you touch me! Don't you dare touch me!'

He stopped in his stride, glanced at Betty, then was about to speak when Elaine put her hands to her breasts, gasped and fell forward over the arm of the chair.

A few minutes later, when they had laid her on the bed, Betty whispered hastily, 'I'll phone the doctor.'

'What is it?'

'It looks like a heart attack.'

An hour later, when the doctor had examined Joe's wife thoroughly he reported that there was nothing physically wrong with her. His diagnosis was nervous hysteria.

Nervous hysteria. Joe had never heard of it. What was it?

And so the doctor explained it as merely a nervous symptom which made it appear that the patient had had a heart attack. It was often the forerunner of a nervous breakdown, and in this case it wasn't surprising, for she'd had two severe shocks in the past year. He had sedated her for the time being, he said, and he'd call again in the morning. In the meantime rest and freedom from worry and irritations were the best medicine for her.

Joe accompanied the doctor downstairs and as he opened the front door for him he asked tentatively, 'How long will this state last, do you think, doctor; I mean, the hysteria?'

The doctor rubbed his chin, then glanced back over his shoulder and up the stairs as he said, 'Oh, the hysteria will only occur at intervals, and it all depends if the state she's in now develops into a breakdown. Then . . . well, six months, a year' – he now looked straight into Joe's eyes – 'two, three, who can say? It all depends on the severity and how far the patient is able to help herself to work out of it. But anyway, it's early days yet. But I'll know more tomorrow after I have had a talk with her.'

He was on the top step when he turned to Joe again and said, 'She's inclined to be pampered, isn't she?' and without waiting for any reply to this he ended, 'Well, if she's in for a breakdown I'd cut down on that; a little astringency might be more beneficial for her. See you tomorrow.'

Joe watched him get into his car before he closed the front door, and then he kept his hand on the knob and stared at the grained wood as he said the words to himself: Nervous hysteria. Breakdown. He had heard of people having breakdowns but had never come into contact with them, and people connected with them didn't talk about them. It seemed to be a kind of disgrace: people didn't treat it as an ordinary illness but more as a stigma. Poor Elaine.

He turned slowly from the door and made his way towards the stairs. And he had to be astringent with her. Well, he would have thought that was the last thing a doctor would advise for anyone in her condition.

Was he at fault? Yes, yes, he supposed he was: if she had never been made to bear the children she would never have been like this. Of course he was at fault. Well, he'd have to make it up to her. But certainly not with any astringent treatment; what she needed now was to be loved, cared for; and that's the treatment she would get. Between them he and Betty would bring her back to health again, and it wouldn't take years; no, not if he had anything to do with it.

He bounded up the stairs now as if, with his love for her, he was about to create a miracle.

8

Joe achieved what he had set out to do in a surprisingly short time. Within six months of her attack Elaine appeared to be back to normal. As his father unfeelingly put it: if soft-soaping and coddling had done the trick then she couldn't have been all that bad in the first place.

Joe had been more than a little annoyed by his father's attitude to Elaine's condition from the very beginning: women didn't have breakdowns in his day. They hadn't time to have breakdowns in his day; in his day women had to work for their keep. Just look at the life his own mother had endured without resorting to a breakdown.

At one point Joe retaliated by saying, 'Then why didn't you choose a pack-horse for your wife? From what I remember, my mother didn't even know what a tea towel was used for. And looking back, I can't recall hearing you telling her to knuckle under, or to get off her lazy backside, or other such colloquial terms to remind her of her duties.'

To this Mike had bawled, 'Get the hell out of it afore I knock you down the stairs!' and from his expression he had looked both capable of and intent upon carrying out his threat.

Yet such had been Elaine's condition at the beginning of her illness that almost four months passed before Betty was able to have a break and spend a week-end with Lady Ambers. But now it had been arranged that she should take a long week-end once a month, and during the time she was away Joe would make it his business to stay almost continually by Elaine's side.

Even before the beginning of her breakdown he had for some time slept in the dressing-room. The fact that she could not bear to be left alone for any length of time during the day, but rejected firmly – even up to the present time – his presence in the bed puzzled him somewhat and irritated him more than he cared to admit.

Only last night he had played it gently with her. 'Let me lie with you,' he had said. Then the look on her face had made him reassure her immediately and he added, 'Nothing will happen, I promise you; I just want to lie near you and hold you like this,' and he had demonstrated by putting his arms around her where she lay deep among pink frilled pillows, which were her latest fad, for the bed linen now all had to be coloured. But his pleading had been in vain. Moreover, it had tended to upset her, so again he had retired to the dressing-room and lay, as he often did, with his hands behind his head, staring into the pale blur of light that came from the shaded lamp in the bedroom.

However, in this sleepless state he was finding it more and more difficult to quell his irritation by coating it with the sympathy and compassion he still doled out to her as the remedial medicine. He had been patient, God knew he had been patient, but he had needs. How long was it since they had been together, really been together; two years? He couldn't go on like this much longer, but of course he mustn't upset her. He must have release of some sort, though. Well, he could go into town; not Fellburn, though; that was too near. Newcastle, perhaps? Oh God Almighty! he didn't want to start that game. What if he picked up something? Look at Harry Codshaw. But there were other types of women. They said Alec Benbow had one in Gateshead; her husband went to sea. But Alec Benbow was a swine, because he had a decent wife and four children.

No; it would have to be Newcastle and a whore. But he still couldn't see himself going there; and yet to start the other line of business you had to know someone who would be compatible and, of course, available, and all the women he knew were married, and apparently happily so. The only unmarried woman he came in contact with was Betty.

Betty! Betty!

For the next few minutes his thoughts raced through untrodden channels of his mind, leaping back into scenes that had held no significance at the time, but which now brought a warmth into his being that turned into a heat that intensified until, as if they had suddenly been doused by a wave of ice-cold water, he sat bolt upright in the bed and gripped his head with his hands.

My God! What next? After all she had done for them, wearing herself out looking after the little girl. Not only had she nursed Elaine for months now, but had silently put up with abuse from her in the early days of her illness; and now he would repay her by saying, 'How about you and me getting together, Betty?'

He rose from the bed and put on his dressing-gown, and now went quietly out through the dressing-room door on to the landing, down the stairs and into the kitchen, where he brewed himself some coffee. By the time he returned upstairs he had come to a decision; he would go into Newcastle at the first opportunity.

It was just on three o'clock when Miss May Pringle, who

acted as Joe's secretary and who had been with the business since his grandfather had started the venture in Fellburn, came into his office with the afternoon cup of tea, and after placing the tray to his hand and saying in a no-nonsense manner, 'Drink it up before it turns to dishwater,' she paused, looked down at his bent head and said, 'Have you heard the latest?'

'What's that?' It was a second before he lifted his eyes towards her. 'Everything I hear is the latest.'

'Yes, it's funny that, isn't it, but I can understand your not having any knowledge of this first-hand, 'cos I only heard Big Wolsey and Cunningham yapping away behind a partition in the store not a minute ago. It appears there's a new firm starting up.'

'New firm? What kind of a new firm?'

'Same line as this.'

'Same line as this? Nonsense!'

'All right, it's nonsense.'

'I would have heard something about that if there were any truth in it.'

'Well, you've heard of Baxter's Boxes of Peterborough, Tilbury, et cetera, et cetera, et cetera.'

'Baxter's coming here?'

'Yes, so they say. They were saying there were some men looking over the spare ground that lies between the railway bridge and that row of houses. There's quite a bit of land there, you know. And they said it was Baxter's men who were thinking of buying it. Of course, it's going muck-cheap now, and if they start building they'll have the labour muck-cheap an' all.'

Joe put his pen down and stared up at Miss Pringle, then said slowly, 'It's likely just a rumour: those two men are reds; they want to unsettle the rest of them.'

'Yes, you may be right, but on the other hand there might

be something in it; there's never smoke without fire.'

'Their stuff's shoddy: our people wouldn't go to them; I mean, our customers.'

They stared at each other, and Joe, nodding his head, said, 'Don't say it, I know, for a penny a box cheaper they'd barter their souls.'

'Drink your tea.' She was pushing the cup towards him when the wail of the siren passed over the town. It was a sound like no other: the hooters in the dockyard, the hooters in the factories, large and small, had their own particular sound, but when the pit siren sounded its wail spelt disaster.

For a matter of seconds neither Joe nor Miss Pringle moved, nor was there any sound of saws or hammers or grinding lathes coming from the shops.

Miss Pringle was the first to break the silence. She put her knuckles to her mouth as she said, 'Oh! not another one.' Miss Pringle knew all about pit disasters. Her father had been killed in one, as also had the boy she had been planning to marry.

Joe took her arm, saying, 'Now, now; it might just be something slight.' From experience he knew that Old May, as his father called her, could weather any emergency except a pit disaster. 'Go and sit down,' he said, 'I'll take a run along there and see what the situation is. Now, now, stop shaking.' He shook her arm, then said briskly, 'It's your turn to drink your tea. Then don't forget there's that batch of letters to get off, and if we're going to have opposition from another factory we'll need to be on our toes, won't we?'

His brusqueness worked to some degree. She took her hand from her mouth, replying sharply, 'All right! All right! All right!' and marched out of the office.

A few minutes later he was in the car making for the pit-head, as seemingly was everybody else in the town, for the pit village housed only a third of the miners employed in the mine.

He couldn't get the car anywhere near the gates, nor, when he got out, could he get much information, because everyone was asking questions, and there was no-one to give any clear answers, except that there had been an explosion and it was thought part of the mine was flooded.

Seeing the impossibility of getting further information at the moment, he got into the car and drove home, though not right up to the house. Driving straight to The Cottage, he found David trying to console young Elizabeth, who was crying for her mother.

'Have you heard anything?' David asked immediately.

'No, nothing specific. I couldn't get near the gates to see. They say there's been an explosion and there's water in.'

'Hazel's in a state: old Dan's on this shift, and Willie and Fred an' all.'

'They'll be all together?'

'I don't rightly know, but I wouldn't be a bit surprised; they're all face workers.'

'Willie and Fred are the married ones, aren't they?'

'Yes.'

'Still, it mightn't be as bad as we're anticipating.'

'God! let's hope not . . . There, there; now stop crying. Come on, don't let Mr Joe see you're a big baby.'

'I want me mammy.'

'I'll tell you what.' Joe now dropped onto his hunkers before the little girl and, taking her hand, he said, 'How would you like to come and play with Martin? You know you like to play with Martin, don't you?'

'Yes.' The tears were blinked away and a slow smile spread over the round, pretty face.

'Well, then, your daddy will take the car and bring your mummy back straightaway from your grandma's and in the meantime you'll come up to the house with me and we'll all have a fine game in the nursery. What about it, eh?'

Elizabeth's smile widened. She glanced coyly up at her father now, and David said under his breath, 'You may need the car if . . .'

'I don't need it.' Joe kept his eyes on the child's face. 'Get yourself away, and if you can make use of it down there, do so.'

From the corner of his eye he could see David standing still, and he said now abruptly, 'Go on, man, before the waterworks start again.'

'Will I get my coat, Mr Joe?'

'Yes, get your coat, dear.'

'The one with the hood?'

'Yes, the one with the hood.'

As the child ran into the bedroom, David took his own coat from the back of the door and as he put it on, Joe said, 'Tell Hazel not to worry about her; she'll be all right, and she can stay the night up there if you're not back.'

'Thanks, Joe.'

As her father went out of the door Elizabeth came running from the bedroom in a red mackintosh coat with a hood attached, and Joe shaped his mouth into a large amazed, 'O . . . h!' before he said, 'My! My! don't you look bonny.'

'Granda bought it for my birthday.'

'Your granda certainly knows what suits you. Come on then.'

He heard the car turning in the road as he lifted her into his arms; then having gone out the back way, he cut through the garden to the house.

He still held the child in his arms as he went across the hall and up the stairs, and as she looked about her in curiosity, for it was the first time she had been inside the house, the hood fell back from her head.

He had just reached the landing when Elaine's sitting-room door opened and his wife emerged, followed by Betty.

They both stood and stared at him and the child for a moment, and as he approached them he began to talk. 'You would have heard the siren, so you know what's happened.' He spoke in a kind of aside and chose his words: 'There's three of the *E-G-A-N-S* down there, all on the face, I understand . . . You see who I've got here?' He bounced the child in his arms. 'She's come to play with Martin, haven't you?'

When he looked at her, the child, more out of shyness than anything else, pressed her cheek against his, and at that moment the nursery door opened and Martin, his face bright with surprise and pleasure, cried, 'Oh, it's Elizabeth! Look! Mummy, it's Elizabeth.'

'*No!* Go back into the nursery, Martin, this moment . . . *No!*' The 'no' was directed with deep emphasis towards Joe.

'What do you mean, no?' His voice was quiet now. 'Haven't I told you what's happened. Hazel and David have had to go to the pit-head.'

At the mention of the names Elaine's face seemed to blanch; her eyes grew wide and her lips left her teeth as if she were about to yell. Her eyes were riveted on the two faces while her mind cried at her that it was what she had suspected all along, and now she had proof of it. She had seen the child occasionally but had never really looked at her closely. Moreover, she had forbidden Nellie to take Martin anywhere near the cottage; and Joe had previously known better than to bring the child into the house. Now there he was, the child in his arms, and who could deny her parentage? Her eyes, her mouth, her nose, even the shape of her face was his. Her voice rose to a screech as she cried, 'Take her away!'

'Elaine! Elaine! come, come . . .' Betty was holding her firmly by the arms in an endeavour to turn her around; and Joe, putting the now frightened child on her feet, pushed her towards Martin and then shoved them both into the nursery and closed the door on them; then, moving to Betty's assistance, he almost carried Elaine into the sitting-room.

When, with a strength that gave a lie to her languidness, she thrust them both off, they stood staring at her helplessly for a moment as her hands went to her heart. Then, as they caught her before she fell, they looked at each other, and their eyes spoke the same words: 'Oh, not again.'

Two days later the bodies of Dan, Willie and Fred Egan were brought out of the pit and Elaine resumed her break-down, although this time she had to depend only on the ministrations of Betty, for she would not tolerate Joe near her; in fact, she herself locked both the outer door to the dressing-room and the door to her bedroom at night, and opened them again only in the morning.

She had only to resort to this twice in order to keep him away from her. The first time it happened he had taken his fist and hammered on the door, while he yelled, 'Open this door, do you hear? or I'll break it down.' He wasn't going to be made a fool of in his own house.

The next night, when he found the doors locked, he just quietly tried the handles, then turned about and made for the end bedroom on the landing.

It was strange, Mike remarked, that she was helpless enough to have Betty dancing attendance on her all day, yet she could get out of her bed at night to lock the doors and then again in the morning to open them. Wasn't it about time he woke up?

Yes. Joe decided, it was about time he woke up.

A week from the night he had reached the decision in the kitchen, he paid his first visit to Newcastle. He also got into the habit of downing a double whisky before going to bed. And so a new pattern was set.

PART FOUR

I

Between the years 1931 and 1938 the atmosphere in the house changed yet again. Whereas during the year the little girl had lived, the feeling of pity and compassion had been overall, and even after Elaine's first breakdown there had been added deep concern and unstinting love, from the day of the pit accident, compassion and love had been swept away, never to return.

It took a year for Elaine to recover from her relapse, but the pattern of life for Joe did not change; there remained the ever-present probability of further relapses, and so he had no need to make excuses about refusing invitations, or even about him and Elaine being seen together.

As time went on, it was imagined by many that Elaine's frequent trips to London were really sojourns in private clinics, but here they were wrong. She did stay in London, but she enjoyed her trips there, and she made no bones about telling Betty that but for these breaks her life would be intolerable. And on this, Betty agreed with her.

Betty's existence over the years had followed much the same pattern as previously, the only change being the length of her stays with Lady Ambers; they were sometimes extended to a month, for the old lady was now much more frail, though only, it should be said, in her body, for her mind was as alert as ever, and Betty often felt like succumbing to her persuasive attempts to get her to leave the house altogether . . . But then, there was the boy, and Mike . . . and Joe. Hardly a day went by but Mike expressed his need of her; and, in a less demonstrative way, so did Joe.

Elaine still needed her too, for she had to have someone to whom she could talk and recount the details of her visits to London; and, of course, she needed someone to take care of her son in her absence.

That Elaine loved her son, Betty had no doubt, and she seemed to prove this by demanding that he be in her company for every moment after he came home from school. The only time she didn't want him near her was when he had his screaming fits. And of late these had increased. On three occasions this last week he had raised the house in the middle of the night and had lain in a lather of sweat and fear. Even so, Betty hoped they would never indicate to the boy the real reason for his nightmares, for she felt that Martin was such a sensitive boy that a revelation of that kind could be very harmful to him.

The doctor had said he believed that Martin would grow out of his problem, but over seven years had passed since the first one and the fits of screaming were still as intense as they had been on that first night; and now that he was growing rapidly and was very tall for his age, the fits seemed to take their toll of his strength. This worried Betty.

When she mentioned her worries to Joe he admitted that he too had been concerned for some time about the boy's health, and he told her that Marcus Levey had suggested he go to his brother for advice. What he expected or even hoped this might be he hadn't indicated to Betty, but he stressed that he was out of patience with Dr Pearce's view that time would do the healing.

On this particular day in early December 1938, Betty was walking up the drive with Martin. David had met the boy from school and herself from the town, where she had been doing some shopping, and now as she and Martin walked briskly towards the house they continued the conversation they had begun in the car.

'But he's sure of it, Aunty Bett,' insisted Martin. 'You see, his father is a Jew, being Mr Levey's brother; and they have cousins who have come over from Germany, and one of the cousins had a newspaper and knew everything about what was going on, and he's sure there's going to be a big war.'

'Well now, that's silly talk, because I'm sure you know that Mr Chamberlain's been over to Germany, and Mr Hitler and he have come to an agreement which has done away with all this talk of war . . .'

'Manny says his father says his cousin says that the people in England don't know what they're talking about.'

Betty put her head back and laughed; then, looking down at him, she said, 'Have you done Frederick the Great at school?'

'Frederick the Great? Well, I don't think so, no.'

'Well, I remember learning something he was supposed to have said. It goes, "My people and I have come to an agreement which satisfies us both. They are to say what they please, and I am to do what I please." And I think that holds good today. People will always say what they please, what suits them, but crowned heads nearly always do what they please, even if they lose their heads in the doing.' Again she laughed; and now Martin laughed with her as she ended, 'So it's no good us worrying one way or the other, is it?'

'No, I suppose not.' He now put his head on one side and his expression was thoughtful as he said, 'I'm not sure if I would like to go to war: I don't like killing things; rats or even beetles. In biology the other day John Dolan said I was a cissy because I hated looking at the inside of a rat, but I'm not a cissy, am I, Aunty Bett?'

'Of course you're not, you're a very boyish boy, as your ripped trousers have proved at times.'

'Elizabeth said she wouldn't mind if there was a war.'

'Elizabeth said that?' Betty paused in her walk, and the boy looked up at her, nodding emphatically, saying, 'Yes, she did, because then she'd be able to go and be a nurse.'

'But she can be a nurse without there being a war.'

'But she wouldn't be nursing wounded soldiers, and that's what she wants to do, nurse wounded soldiers.'

'Oh? When did Elizabeth say this?'

They were walking on again and the boy answered immediately, 'Oh, last night when we were down by the greenhouses and . . .' He stopped abruptly and cast a quick glance up at Betty; and she returned his look.

'You won't tell Mummy?'

She shook her head, then said, 'But you do know you've been forbidden to go to the cottage.'

'But I wasn't at the cottage, Aunty Bett, I was down by the . . .'

'It's all the same.' Her voice was quiet now. 'You know what your mother means, don't you?'

The boy was looking ahead now and his voice was stiff and with an adult tone to it as he said, 'I like Elizabeth, Aunty Bett. I've always liked Elizabeth and I'm *not* going to stop speaking to her. Anyway—' He now jerked his head and looked up at Betty as he went on, 'Father's never said I shouldn't talk to her, or go to the cottage. Father likes Elizabeth, he likes her very much, and he likes Hazel . . .

214

and David. I . . . I don't see why people should be disliked just because they're black; David can't help being black. Anyway, Elizabeth isn't black, so what does Mother keep on about? I don't understand it. I would like her to tell me why she doesn't like her. I did ask her once, but she got into a temper and became ill.'

'Martin—' Betty drew him to a stop as they reached the curve in the drive and, bending towards him, she said softly, 'Don't pester your mother with questions like that. And don't go out of your way to see Elizabeth when your mother is at home. When she's away in London . . . well, I can't keep an eye on you all the time, can I?' She now grinned at him, and slowly he grinned back at her, then in a very unboyish fashion he suddenly reached up and put his arms around her and hugged her, and as she held him tightly for a moment he said, 'Oh, Aunty Bett, I wish *you* were my mother. I do, I do.'

They were standing apart now; her eyelids were blinking, and she swallowed deeply before saying, 'Now, that's very nice of you, Martin, but . . . but don't repeat it ever again because . . . well, your mother loves you very much and she would be greatly hurt if she even imagined you thought such a thing.'

'I'm . . . I'm sorry, Aunty Bett.'

'Oh, don't be sorry' – she put out her hand and gently touched his cheek – 'it's the nicest and best thing that's ever been said to me – believe that, Martin – and I'll always treasure it, but . . . but don't say it again, just in case . . . you understand?'

'Yes, Aunty Bett.'

They walked on again, and as they rounded the bend she said, 'Look, there's your grandfather waving to you,' and the boy looked up towards the observatory and waved his hand wildly back; then as they approached the house he said, 'I nearly had a fight about Grandpa yesterday.'

215

'A fight? Why was that?'

'John Dolan and Arthur Brown both said he was a mystery man and that likely he had committed a crime, else he wouldn't stay up there in the glasshouse all his life. They said he had been there since he was a young man.'

'What utter nonsense! Didn't you tell them that he suffers from severe arthritis and can hardly walk?'

'Yes, I did, but Arthur Brown said that was just a hood-wink. I would have belted him if he'd been on his own, but John Dolan was with him and he's bigger than me and it would have been two to one. You know what they said, Aunty Bett? They said he had food put on a lift and winched up to him from the outside. John Dolan said he had seen it actually happening. Oh, I could have bashed his head'. . .

As they entered the house Betty was laughing heartily as she said, 'You know what they must have seen? The scaffolding in place when they were re-pointing the walls and putting the odd slates on the turret. John Dolan was one of the boys who came at the time and collected the windfalls with you, wasn't he?'

'Yes, he was.'

'Well then, that's what he saw. He's got an imagination, has Mr John Dolan. You remind him of the scaffolding when you next see him.'

'Oh, there you are. You're late.' They both stopped as Elaine came down the stairs, and it was Betty who answered as she glanced at her watch, 'I don't think so; he's come straight from school and I from the town.'

'That might be so, but I saw the car come into the drive over five minutes ago.'

Betty only just prevented herself from exclaiming loudly, 'Oh, God in heaven, woman!' What she forced herself to say was, 'We decided to walk the last bit, Elaine, and we stopped to look at the blue tit's nest.'

As Betty looked at her sister, so smart, so petite, she wondered how one such small body could hold so much animosity. She also thought that people such as Elaine brought a sort of virtue to lying. She watched her now put her arms around her son and lead him towards the stairs, saying, 'I've been thinking: how would you like to come to London with me next week to do the Christmas shopping?'

'But we don't break up until the twentieth, Mummy.'

'Oh, I could write and ask the headmaster to excuse you; it would only be for a few days.'

'But I've got a test and have to do homework; and then there's the school play, remember? It's *The Tempest* and I'm one of the . . .'

The boy's voice trailed away as his mother's arm was pulled abruptly away from his shoulders. Left standing on the top stair, he watched her hurrying towards her room before he turned and looked back down into the hall where Betty was still standing. And when she shook her head at him and pointed, stabbing her finger forward, he recognised and reluctantly obeyed her implied meaning and followed his mother into her sitting-room.

2

'When is she coming back this time?' asked Mike.

'Well, as far as I know, next Friday,' replied Betty.

'Why, of course; she'll have to give herself time to titivate the place up with jingle bells and tinsel, won't she? It's a farce.' Mike turned to Betty, who was pouring out the tea at a side table, and he repeated, 'Do you hear what I say? It's a farce, because there's no Christmas spirit in this house any more. How in the name of God our Joe sticks her is beyond me. And his life. What life has he got? I once said to him, don't make the same mistake as I did, lad. That was when he was first married. Well, he didn't; the mistake he made was in marrying her in the first place.' He now took the cup from Betty's hand and, nodding at her, he went on slowly, 'And I did make a mistake, a very big mistake, lass. I'll tell you about it some day afore I die, if you haven't guessed it already.'

She stared back at him and said, 'No; I haven't made a guess at any particular mistake you've made.'

'What do you mean, particular?'

'Just what I say.' She returned to the table and lifted her own cup; and only when she was seated did she continue,

'You've always made mistakes, and one of them was to isolate yourself up here. Oh yes, I know, I know' – she closed her eyes now – 'it's the view. But I don't think it's only the view that keeps you stuck in these rooms.'

'So you have been thinking about my particular mistake?'

Her eyes now stretched slightly and she said, 'Is your staying up here connected with that . . . your particular mistake?'

'Aye, in a way you could say it is; but only in a way.'

'Oh, it sounds interesting.'

'Don't start laughing, lass, for it's no laughing matter.'

'I wasn't laughing.'

'You're amused.'

'Mike—' She now leant towards him and said slowly and definitely, 'If I didn't laugh at myself, and others at times, I'd go mad. Do you realise that?'

He stared back at her before he replied quietly, 'Aye. Aye, I do. If anyone's had a wasted life it's you; and I've helped to make it so these last few years.'

She took a sip of her tea before she said, 'Don't expect me to contradict you and make things easier for you,' and he laughed, and his crippled hand shook so much he had to put his cup and saucer onto the side table. Then, looking at her again, he said, 'We've strayed. Where were we in the beginning? We were talking about our Joe, weren't we?'

'Yes, we were talking about Joe.'

'Do you think he's got a woman back there' – he motioned towards the window – 'in the town?'

She wetted her lips and stared at him for a few seconds before she said, 'Why ask me? You can't imagine he confides in me on such matters.'

'Well, he talks to you, doesn't he? He talks to you more than he talks to me now.'

'Well, I can assure you that the subject hasn't come up.'

'There's no need to get on your high horse about it; it was only a question.'

'And what a question.'

'Well, it puzzles me, because I can't think that he's gone without all these years. He's me son, and he's a man, very much a man; he couldn't have put up with being denied his rights all these years . . .'

'Rights?'

'Aye, rights. It's a man's rights to have satisfaction from his wife.'

'And what about the woman's rights? Oh, I'm not just thinking of Elaine. What if a woman can't get . . . satisfaction as you call it and goes off into . . . town?' She imitated him now in nodding towards the window. 'Would people excuse her and say she's done it because she's been deprived of her rights? No, she'd be hounded.'

'Look—' He eased himself slowly towards the edge of the chair and, peering at her, said, 'What's got into you? Don't take it personal; you sound like one of those suffragettes.'

'Perhaps I am one at heart. I know this much; that your dominant male doesn't carry any water with me; most women could buy a man at one end of the street and sell him at the other, in business and otherwise. Did you see that case in the paper the other morning that made front-page headlines? A man was brought up for badly using his wife. And why did he badly use her? To quote his own words, because she was always one up on him. Apparently the woman was highly intelligent and had married beneath her and, like many other men, he couldn't stand a woman, particularly his wife, knowing more than himself. So what does he do? He beats her up. And that's just one case.'

'Well, I never!'

220

Mike was grinning widely now and once more he was lying back in his chair; then, looking at her, he said slowly, 'You are on your high horse the night, aren't you? But talking about that case. Aye, I read it and, strange as it may seem, I agree with you; that is up to a point because' – now the smile left his face – 'it's my opinion, and I think you've heard it afore, that no man, if he's sensible, should marry a woman who's better educated than himself. Let him be the one to be educated and bring her up to his standard; oh aye, that's all right, but a man being a man needs to be looked up to with pride. But if a woman, especially the one he marries, has more up top than him, it thins his pride and he feels less of a man. I know what I'm speaking about because I'm speaking from experience.'

Betty got to her feet and, picking up his cup and saucer from the table, she placed it on the tray before she said, in a low voice, 'I'm sorry.'

'Don't apologise. Don't apologise, lass, just give me me cup back; I haven't finished me tea.'

She did not take the half-empty cup back to him but poured him out a fresh one, and as she placed it in his hand he looked gently up at her and said, 'We've got a week on our own; let's make the best of it, lass.'

She smiled at him now, then went to the fire and using the tongs she banked it up with some coal from the scuttle; then, as she dusted her hands, he said, 'Did Joe tell you where he's taking the boy the morrow?'

'Yes. Yes, he told me.'

'Do you believe in this hypnotism?'

She turned towards him but looked past him thoughtfully for a moment before she replied, 'I don't know. I don't know enough about it; in fact, I don't know anything about it, but I understand that Mr Levey's brother is a very good doctor and has been using this form of treatment on special cases for some time.'

'Yes, that's what I understand an' all. But it's a funny business probing the mind. Still, if the man's able to ease whatever is troubling the lad, then I'm all for it. I'm all for anything that will stop those screaming fits. By! the sound makes me blood curdle every time I hear him. But there's one thing I'm afraid of.' He looked up at her and nodded slowly now.

'That he'll come out worse than he went in: as it is, he can't remember what he did, but what's going to happen if he should remember?'

'I've thought of that and Joe's thought of that, but apparently, as I understand it, hypnosis can quell the memory.'

'Quell the memory?' Mike shook his head. 'It sounds like acting God, and I always suspect anybody who attempts that. Still, we'll see what we shall see . . . I wonder what Madame Elaine will say when she gets back? I can tell you one thing: she wouldn't have allowed any hypnotist to get at her son if she'd been here. What do you say?'

Betty didn't reply, but in her mind she endorsed what Mike had said: No; no hypnotist would have been allowed to tamper with the boy if Elaine had been here.

3

It had snowed steadily throughout the night and Joe, driving the car along the deserted road that passed through the mining village towards the town, glanced at Martin and grinned as he said, 'Well, that's a nice start, betting me half-a-crown that I won't be able to drive the car back; I'll take you on.'

'Well, look at those drifts.' Martin pointed out of the window. 'They must be all of four feet high.'

'You've got your measurements wrong. Anyway, they're not drifts, they're likely just humps of snow thrown up on the bank.'

'You won't say that when you've got to pay me that half-a-crown.'

They smiled at each other now. Then presently the boy said, 'Will Dr Levey be able to stop my nightmares, Father?'

'He'll have a good try.'

'What will he do?'

'Oh, he'll just talk to you.'

'Well, Dr Pearce has talked to me and that hasn't stopped them.'

'But there are all kinds of doctors: you don't go to the

223

optician to have your teeth out, do you? nor to the dentist if you want spectacles; there's doctors for all kinds of things.'

And that was true. Yes, there were doctors for all kinds of things, and he hoped he was doing right in getting this one to probe into the boy's mind. He'd spent a wakeful night going over and over the situation and wondering if he was doing the right thing.

He had explained to Dr Levey that the boy had accidentally killed his baby sister; he did not say his monstrosity of a sister. Now what he was asking him to do was to erase the memory of it from the boy's mind. Hypnotism, as he saw it, was based on suggestion, and if he could suggest that he should forget the whole incident, then the boy could have a normal future before him, even that of a student attending a university, because he was a bright boy; but, as things stood, such a future could not be contemplated for a student who would probably raise someone's household with unearthly screams in the middle of the night.

If the experiment was successful he would blame himself for not having taken Marcus's suggestion earlier, for it was almost four years now since Marcus had suggested taking the boy to his brother for hypnotic treatment. But at the time the very term had smelt of hocus-pocus; whereas now, as he understood it, hypnosis could be induced in all normal persons under suitable conditions, and also in those who weren't normal.

Dr Levey had talked of sub-conscious awareness; a stage which, when reached by the patient, would make him so receptive to suggestion that he could be made to re-enact the particular incident or incidents that were worrying him.

Well, he didn't really want his son to relive that night again, yet if it meant obliterating the memory then the boy would have to endure it.

'He won't keep me in, like a hospital, will he?'

'No, of course not.'

'What will he do?'

'Oh, just talk to you, as I said, and expect you to talk to him.' . . .

And that was exactly what was happening, Joe thought, a short while later, whilst sitting well back in a deep chair in the comfortable room and listening to Dr Levey and Martin talking. Of all things, they were chatting about football and the chances of Newcastle United. It appeared that Dr Levey favoured Sunderland, and Martin laughed as he said, 'That's not right, and you living in Newcastle, doctor.'

'I know it isn't right,' replied the doctor; 'but don't let on.' And at this they both laughed again.

'Now just lie back in the chair. That's it . . . look straight at me . . . you've got a very fine pair of eyes . . . Now when I count up to six you will go to sleep.

'*One . . . two . . . three . . . four . . . five . . . six.*'

Joe watched the boy's eyes close and his body slump further down in the chair; then he listened to the doctor saying, 'Are you afraid of anything, Martin?'

There was a pause before the answer came. 'Yes, about . . . about dreaming of the black lady.'

'The black lady? What does she do to frighten you?'

'I . . . I can't remember; it's a long time ago.'

'How long? When you were a baby?'

Martin did not answer, and the doctor said, 'Go right back, Martin, to the time when you first saw the black lady.'

'*No, no! No. No.*' The boy's head was wagging from side to side; his whole body became agitated; but the doctor's voice went on quietly, 'What is she doing? Tell me, Martin, what is the black lady doing?'

'*Oh no, no! No, no.*' The boy now placed his hand, with fingers spread wide, over his face.

225

'What are you seeing through your fingers, Martin?'

'The . . . the black lady. The black lady.'

'What is she doing?'

'*Oh. O . . . h,* she is . . . she is. *Oh. Oh, no; no, don't!* Tipping up . . . tipping up the mattress. Poor little girl. Poor little girl. *Oh, no. No,* don't, please. Please don't.'

Now the boy's hands were thrashing about in the air and he was crying, 'Wake up! Wake up! little girl. Poor little girl. Wake up! little girl.' Then again he spread his hand across his face, but this time his mouth opened wide and he emitted a long, piercing scream, followed by another, and another.

The doctor's voice cut into the spine-chilling sound, saying quietly, 'It's all over, Martin. It's all over. Lie still.'

When the boy became still the doctor went on. 'The black lady has gone. She's gone away, away, away, and she won't trouble you any more. Never again will you dream of her. The incident will remain like a memory you can't recall . . . Now go to sleep for ten minutes and dream that you are watching Newcastle United play football.'

Joe was on his feet, but instead of looking at the doctor he was staring at his son; yet at the same time not seeing him, for the whole screen of his mind was taken up with the black lady, while a voice deafened his brain, yelling, 'My God! My God!'

The black lady. Elaine! And that black negligée!

It had been a puzzling mystery to everyone how the heavy iron side of the cot had been lowered. He could hear Betty's voice saying, 'It's impossible, it's impossible. Nellie must have left it down by mistake.' And he could hear Nellie almost going into hysterics as she denied this. 'Martin could have rattled it down,' she had said; 'he could have rattled it down.'

Secretly Joe had gone into the nursery, lain on the floor,

put his hands up and rattled the side of the cot to see if it would jump its sockets, but it hadn't.

Why hadn't he probed the mystery further? Why? Had he known in his mind all the time that she had done this? No, no. But why had he let the matter drop? Was it because, like everybody else, he had thought it was the best thing that could have happened to the child? Again, no, no!

'Do you understand about the black lady?'

Joe blinked his eyes as if he were emerging from a trance, and he stared at the doctor, but gave him no answer; and the doctor stared back at him and after a moment he said, 'Well, I hope it's done the trick; but only time will tell if the memory has been buried deep enough not to trouble him again.'

He turned about now and as he re-crossed the room he asked casually, 'Have you seen Marcus lately?'

'Yes. Yes, I . . . I saw him on Monday. He was in the club.'

'How is your wife keeping? Is she quite recovered?'

Joe swallowed deeply, and it was with some effort that he replied, 'Yes, she's . . . she's quite recovered. She's in London, shopping at the moment.'

No more small talk passed between them. The doctor remained standing, looking at his watch; then sat down facing Martin and said quietly, 'When I count to six, Martin, you will wake up and you won't remember anything that has happened, but you will say you are thirsty and ask for a drink.

'One . . . two . . . three . . . four . . . five . . . six.'

'Oh!' The boy opened his eyes, passed one lip over the other then said, 'I feel very thirsty. May . . . may I have a drink, please?'

'Yes, yes, of course. What would you like? Lemonade? Ginger beer?'

'Oh, ginger beer, please.'

While Martin drank his ginger beer and Joe a cup of coffee, the doctor chatted amiably. Then a short while later, when he was bidding them goodbye, he looked straight at Joe and said under his breath, 'A doctor's surgery is like a confessional.'

Joe gave no reply to this statement, but just stared back into the deep brown eyes for a moment before, his head drooping forward, he turned about and followed Martin into the street.

4

'Where the hell has he got to?' asked Mike.

'How should I know?' Betty's voice had just as strong a note of impatience in it. 'I told you what he said on the phone.'

'He didn't say where he was going?'

'No; he only said that David was taking Martin to see Elizabeth in the school concert.'

'And he rang from Fellburn?'

'Yes.'

'Well' – Mike shook his head slowly – 'if it was four o'clock in the afternoon when he rang and he had passed the boy over to David, that would mean David taking him on to the Egans', because the school concert wouldn't start before six, if then. My God! if she was to hear that she'd go hairless . . . mad! Not that I'd mind.' He lifted up his hand and wagged his bent forefinger at Betty. 'That's what the lad wants, to get around and see how the other half lives. But what I'm saying is, he's never gone against her this far before . . . do you think something happened at the doctor's? Didn't he say anything about it?'

'No, he didn't.' Betty sat down across from Mike and,

229

leaning towards him, she said, 'I've told you, Mike, exactly what he said. He was very brief. He had brought Martin back to Fellburn, he said, and David was taking him to see Elizabeth in the concert, and when I asked him if he himself was on his way home, he said he was going back to Newcastle.'

'Did he sound drunk?'

'Drunk? At four o'clock in the afternoon! Of course not, but . . .'

'Aye, go on. "But", you said.'

'He didn't sound himself; he was very abrupt.'

'How do you mean abrupt? Offhand or short or . . .?'

'Oh, Mike!' She got to her feet. 'Look, I've told you all I know. And for goodness' sake stop worrying, or the next thing you know you'll be in bed again. And let me tell you' – she wagged her finger at him now – 'if that happens I'm bringing you down to the first floor; our legs are worn off to the knees running up and down these stairs.'

'Oh! Oh!' His head began to bob as if it were on springs. 'That's it, that's it, I'm a trouble and I'm to be treated like some doddery old bugger.'

'Yes, exactly.' She turned now and went hastily to the door, and as she went out he yelled after her, 'Well, you take it from me, when you get me down to the first floor it'll be in me box, and I don't care if all the bloody legs in the house are worn down to the hips!'

Betty stood on the landing, her lips tights as she tried to stop herself from laughing. Mike was a stimulant. You could say that for him.

She went down the stairs, crossed the first landing but stopped at the head of the main staircase and looked down into the hall.

The telephone was on a table to the right of the door, and as she stood there she recalled Joe's voice. There *had*

230

been something about it that she couldn't make out: offhand didn't fit it, tense didn't fit it. She had been about to ask him what had transpired at the doctor's when he had rung off. Yet Martin must be all right, else he wouldn't have allowed David to take him, and, as Mike had said, with understandable surprise, to the Egans'.

She now continued her way down the stairs, across the hall and into the kitchen. Mary was sitting by the table cleaning fruit, and she looked up and said, 'You after your supper, miss?'

'No, no.' Betty shook her head. 'And I'll see to it myself. Can I help you with that?'

'No.' Mary emptied the currants into a large, brown, earthenware bowl, saying again, 'No, thanks, miss. I'm just gettin' them ready for the morrow. Eeh!' She shook her head slowly. 'Other years I've had the Christmas cakes and puddings made weeks afore this. But I've only one pair of hands.'

'Yes, yes, I know you have, Mary. And don't worry.' Betty leaned across the table towards her. 'Anyway, what does it matter when they're made so long as they're there for Christmas?'

''Tisn't the same, miss; they should be made well in advance and tinned; it helps to richen them.' She puckered up her lips now as she ended, 'Duffy used to do all the fruit for me. Sit here he would, hour after hour, cleaning pound after pound. Since he died, I miss him, miss.'

'Of course you do, Mary.'

'The house isn't the same; it's not the same in any way, miss, like it used to be. Do you think it is?'

Betty didn't give her a straight answer, but replied, 'Well, I haven't been here as long as you, Mary.'

'No, that's true, miss. You know, when the first mistress was alive we had seven in the house and four outside. Yes,

231

we did. We had one maid alone for doing the washing, and now what have we? Meself and Ella . . . I mean, Jane. She's a good girl, is Jane. Her tongue's the worst part about her, but she's a good worker. Yet she can't make up for Duffy and Nellie. And them stairs up to that attic could kill a horse. They're takin' their toll on you.' She nodded now at Betty, and Betty replied quietly, 'We'll never get him to come down to the first floor. It's the view, and his workshop.'

'Aye, I know, I know. And I wouldn't do anything to disturb what peace is left for him. But . . . but I do think Mr Joe could engage another lass; a young 'un whose legs would take the stairs.'

'He would like to, Mary.' Betty's voice was low now. 'I know he would like to very much, but things are not going well at the works; he's having to cut down all round.'

'All round, did you say, miss?' Mary now slanted her gaze up at Betty, and Betty looked down towards the table. She would have liked to reply to the implication in Mary's tone by saying, 'I know, Mary. I feel the same about it as you do.' But you just didn't say things like that to a servant about the mistress of the house who was also your sister.

There had been times of late when she found it difficult not to tell Elaine that the money she spent on cosmetics alone would pay for another housemaid; and that for just half the money she spent on clothes she could have a kitchen maid and an outside boy to help David. But on consideration she knew she wouldn't have mentioned David's name, for Elaine's hate of him seemed to increase with the years.

'I'll have a talk with Mr Joe, Mary,' she said, 'and see what we can do about getting you some help in the kitchen. By the way, how is Jane going to get back tonight?'

'Oh, she'll get back all right, miss; she's used to snow. And, anyway, Bill Laidler will be only too glad of the chance to carry her over his shoulder.' She laughed now, a deep chuckling laugh; and Betty laughed with her; then she asked, 'When do you think they'll be married?'

'Oh, God only knows that, miss. Things were looking up this time last year, but since this Hitler business they've stopped building; they can't get the stuff. He's been on the dole again now for five weeks. As Ella said, come the war there'll be work for everybody, and the sooner the better. She's got a tongue, has that Ella, but she's right, come a war men will become men then, not just corner-end props.'

'Yes, I'm afraid you're right, Mary. But I wouldn't want to see a . . .'

Her voice was cut off by the distant sound of Mike's bell ringing furiously, and they looked at each other across the table as Betty said, 'I've just come down.'

'I'd let him ring. He takes advantage of you, miss, he does. We all say that. He does. You know what Duffy used to say? He used to say that if miss was his wife himself couldn't expect more from her. And he said, an' it's true, that with one an' another of them they'd make you old afore your time.'

Dear God, people rubbed it in, even the kindest of them. She turned from the table, saying, 'Well, I'd better see what the trouble is; he doesn't usually ring for nothing,' which elicited a grunt from Mary.

The bell was still ringing furiously as she mounted the main staircase, but she didn't hurry. Old before her time. Did she look that old at forty? Her mirror showed her no change in her face: her features looked the same as they always had, large and plain. What had altered over the years was her figure; she was slim now, as slim as her frame would allow.

At the foot of the attic stairs she paused and looked up and was amazed to see Mike standing on the landing; and when he cried at her, 'Where've you been, lass? Come on!' she began to run up the stairs, but on her reaching the landing he had already turned and was shuffling towards his sitting-room door.

'What is it? What's wrong?'

'Our Joe.'

'Joe?'

'Aye, Joe, in the car.'

He was now leaning on the window-sill. 'I saw his car coming along there a few minutes ago,' he said, nodding his head as though indicating the road that passed by the gate. 'It went over, head over heels down the gully into Robson's field.'

Betty now peered at him through narrowed lids and said slowly, 'Mike! Mike! you could never have seen his car . . .'

'Look, lass' – he turned on her furiously – 'I've sat at this window for years; I know every turn of the wheel of that car. What's more, there's no other cars come along this way unless it's the doctor's or tradesmen's vans and such, and nobody would be taking that road the night with the snow up to the axles. Our Joe's car's down there in the gully, I tell you, lass.' His voice ended in a yell, and hers was almost on the same key as she cried back at him and pointing to the window, 'But you can't see a thing out there, Mike.'

'Look.' He brought his body full round to face her and he gritted his teeth for a moment. 'I was sitting here in the dark. I was on the look-out for him comin', and if you look into the dark long enough you're able to see. And I saw its shape in the distance against the snow. Anyway, I know those headlights. I should.' And now there was an imploring note in his voice as he ended, 'Believe me, Betty, I haven't gone round the bend; I tell you the car's gone down the little gully. Put out the light and look for yourself. You won't see the car, but after a minute or so you'll be able to see into the distance.'

She didn't follow his command, for now she believed him

234

and she put her hand to her lips as she said, 'There's nobody in The Cottage, and even Jane's out for the night.'

'You go, lass; go down and see. If I've been wrong, well, you've had your journey for nowt, but if I haven't . . .' His head drooped. 'Go on. Go on, lass, for my sake. Ease me.'

She turned now and ran from the room, down the attic stairs and across the landing to her room. There she pulled on a pair of ankle-length boots, then snatched a hooded coat from the wardrobe and struggled into it as she ran across the landing and down the main staircase. In the hall she grabbed up a large torch from the drawer of the side table; then she paused a moment and looked towards the kitchen, wondering if she should tell Mary, but decided against it.

The journey to the gates was comparatively easy, for David had cleared a path earlier in the day, but once on the main road the going was difficult, and the snow came over her boot tops. It was still snowing, but it was thin and was being blown about like curtains of mist.

Within a matter of minutes she had reached the part of the road where the ground sloped quite steeply away down to a field. It was the boundary field of farmland, and the drop from the road to it, always referred to as Robson's Gully, was about fifteen feet deep, and towards the bottom and seeming to separate it from the field fence was a border of trees.

As she left the road and turned towards the top of the bank her feet gave way beneath her and she found herself part-way down the slope and up to her waist in snow. Gasping, she pulled herself up the bank again, and all her bemused mind could think of at the moment was that she still had her grip on the torch. Flashing it now along the ditch, her petrified gaze took in the car, lying with its rear wedged cornerwise between two trees and its bonnet facing diagonally up the bank.

'Oh my God!' Mike had been right. 'Oh Joe! Joe!' Yet even

as she cried out aloud she cautioned herself against her rising panic.

Again she flashed the torch. The only immediate impression she could gather from the tracks was that the car, having gone into a spin and its back wheels having slithered first over the bank, was thankfully brought to a stop and prevented from overturning by the trees.

She slid down the bank now towards the car, and as she slithered with a bump into the front wheel she shouted, 'Joe! Joe!'

She couldn't see into the car because of the snow on the windscreen and so edged her way to the door and directed the flashlight through the dropped weather curtain. And then she saw him. He was lying slumped in the seat behind the wheel; his head hanging to the right. He looked as if he were asleep.

'Joe! Joe!' As she yelled his name a swirl of drifting snow almost choked and blinded her, and she leaned against the car, gasping. After a moment she gazed about her frantically. What was she to do? She needed help; she could never get him out of there alone. Or could she? Not from this side maybe, but if she could open the door from the other side, she might.

As if obeying a sharp order she suddenly reached over and grabbed the figurehead on top of the radiator cap, and slowly dragged herself up and over the still-warm engine casing. Then she was standing on the sloping running board and clinging with one hand to the side of the windscreen.

She loosened the side curtain and then opened the door with remarkable ease; but before she could get at Joe she had to close the door again and move further along the running board beyond the door. This time when she opened the door, Joe almost fell on top of her, and his dead weight made it difficult for her to maintain her position. When she heard the groan she thought it was from herself, until it came again. Now she was shaking him gently, crying in an agonised tone, 'Joe! Joe! Are you hurt? Say something. Oh, Joe! Wake up! Wake up!'

Her face was hanging over his. She sniffed loudly and shook her head; he stank of whisky. 'Oh Joe! Joe!'

'Wh . . . where? Wha . . . t?'

Thank God! He was alive . . . 'Are you hurt?'

He groaned; then very slowly he said, 'Oooh! My . . . Go . . . od!'

'Joe! Joe! Listen to me. Are you hurt?'

'Betty.' He opened his eyes and blinked in the light of the torch, then said again, 'Betty.'

'Can you sit up?'

When he made the attempt she helped with one hand while steadying herself against the back of the seat with the other. Then as the car rocked slightly she cried, 'Careful! Oh, be careful, Joe.'

'Where? . . . What happened?'

'The car. You ran off the road.'

He blinked his eyes slowly, then stretched them, and in a voice that was almost a croak he asked, 'Where is it?'

'Robson's Gully. You've dropped down into Robson's Gully.'

'God in heaven!' He groaned and lifted his hand to his head, and she asked, 'Are you hurt anywhere?'

'I . . . I don't know. My head's spinning.'

'Your legs? Your arms?'

Slowly one after the other he moved his limbs, then shook his head; and she did not say, 'Thank God!' but, 'Do you think you can get out? The car's tilted; you'll . . . you'll have to be careful in case it slips further. Look—' She shook him gently by the arm now. 'Open your eyes, Joe.'

'What? Oh yes, yes, Betty. Yes, I'll . . . I'll get out.'

237

He pulled himself upwards.

'Careful!' The word erupted on a yell as the front of the car moved a little.

'Look.' She was gulping her words now. 'You'll have to move over and get out of the other door, in case your weight makes the car tip if you get out this way. I'll get back the way I came.'

'Right. Right, Betty.' He made an effort to open his eyes wide. He followed the direction of the torch as Betty pulled herself upwards and on to the running board, and then back over the bonnet. And then he edged himself slowly across the seat to the door, which she had already opened. But when, getting out, he went to stand on the running board he almost toppled backwards into the snow. Only her cry made him instinctively grab at the panel by the side of the door, and then gingerly he let himself down into the snow.

Now half supporting and half dragging him, she tried to get him up the slope; but he fell onto his face into the deep snow and lay there inert.

Grabbing at him, she cried harshly, 'Joe! Joe! For God's sake, make an effort. Come on! Now, come on!'

She managed to turn him on to his back and he lay gasping. His eyes were closed but he spoke to her, quite plainly now, saying, 'I'm tired. I'm tired, Betty, very tired.'

'Joe! listen to me. We must get out of this.' And, taking hold of his shoulders, she dragged him into a sitting position and tried to shake him whilst crying at him, 'You can't stay here! You'll freeze. Look, hang on to me. Grip my arm.'

'No; you . . . you go on, Betty. Go on. I'm . . . I'm all right.'

As he went to lie down again, she took his wet, snow-covered head in her hands and she yelled into his face, 'I can't go on. If you don't make a move we'll both freeze to death; so come on! Damn it! you've got to try.'

238

She never recalled the effort of the next ten minutes, during which she hauled him to the top of the bank, without wondering from where she had got the strength. Physically she wasn't weak, by any means, but Joe was a big man and he was almost insensible now with shock and drink. When she finally pulled him over the edge of the bank and on to the road she lay by his side, her face in the crook of his arm, her own arms outstretched as if on a rack, and the sweat of her body melted the snow that had gathered on her head and neck. Unaware that she was soaked up to the waist, all she could think about at that moment was that once she got her breath back she must get him home as quickly as possible.

Within a few minutes she was shaking him again, and when she had managed to get him to his feet she pulled his arm around her shoulders and hung onto it with one hand while with the other she gripped him around the waist. Half dragging him, she talked to him constantly to keep him awake, and they both stumbled their way towards the gates, and from there it seemed a comparatively easy walk up the drive to the house.

Before she kicked at the front door she was yelling at the top of her voice, 'Mary! Mary!' She made no attempt to ring the bell, for she knew that once she let go of him he would drop to the ground, and she knew that she wouldn't have enough strength to lift him yet again.

'Oh my God above! What is it? What is it?' Mary was on the other side of him now. Her support, however, was more moral than practical, and as they dragged him into the hall Betty gasped, 'The drawing-room.'

Going at a wobbling run towards the double doors, Mary thrust them open, then rushed towards the couch and pushed it towards the fire.

When Joe slipped slowly from her grasp in a limp heap

239

on to the couch, Betty dropped onto her knees on the hearthrug, then fell onto her side and lay gasping; and when Mary's agitated voice came to her, crying, 'Oh my God! miss,' she put up her hand and muttered, 'It's all right, Mary. Give me a minute.'

The minute became two before she managed to drag herself on to her knees; and then she looked at Joe where he was lying stretched out now, Mary having lifted his feet up and put a pillow under his head, and she silenced the old woman's spate of questioning, saying slowly, 'In a minute, Mary, in a minute; we . . . we must get him undressed; and bring some water-bottles. And I must phone the doctor. I doubt if he'll get through. But . . . but first, I'd better tell himself.'

It took her all her time to make the two flights of stairs, and Mike, having heard her coming, met her on the landing.

'Oh God! lass, what's happened to you . . . and him?' he asked.

'It's all right; he's in the drawing-room.' She put out her hand and leaned against the landing wall, and when he asked, 'Is he badly hurt?' she gave a short laugh.

'What's up with you, lass? I said, is he badly hurt?'

'I . . . I know, Mike, what you said. Well, there are no bones broken. There might be concussion, but . . . but his main trouble is, he's drunk.'

'Loaded? What do you mean?'

There was silence for a moment before he said, 'The bloody fool!' Then he made to turn towards the room, but looked back at her again, saying flatly now, 'If that's the case, come and have a drop of the dog that bit him.'

'No, no; he's . . . he's got to be seen to, I must go down.'

As she made for the stairs he turned round to her again, asking, 'You got him up there on your own?'

She was half-way down the stairs when she answered, 'We didn't happen to meet Father Christmas with his sleigh.'

Another time he would have laughed, and so would she, but the tone in which she had made the remark didn't signify amusement.

In the hall she got through to Dr Pearce, and when she explained what had happened he said, 'I doubt if I can get through; in fact, I'm sure I can't. They're having a job to keep even the main roads clear. You say there are no bones broken?'

'There doesn't appear to be.'

'Does he appear sleepy?'

'Yes.'

'He's likely concussed then; but if he walked from the car then I don't think it can be anything serious.'

At this she dropped her head back on to her shoulders, and closed her eyes tight.

'Are you there?'

When she answered he went on, 'The main thing is to keep him warm, give him plenty to drink, such as weak tea; no stimulants, and if things aren't improved by tomorrow morning I'll try to get over. In any case, give me a ring then.'

'Thank you, doctor.' She put down the phone but remained standing with her hand on it for some time, her body leaning over it; then she looked down at her feet.

A short while ago she had been sweating, now she was cold, shivering. She told herself that she should get out of these boots and change her stockings; then she would start on him. Now that she knew he wasn't physically hurt in any way, she did not feel concern for him, only irritation that if he hadn't been stinking drunk this would never have happened. It was just as well that Elaine wasn't here, and that Martin was still at the Egans'.

It was about four o'clock in the morning when Joe awoke.

241

He opened his eyes and found that the shaded light in the room pierced his brain like rapier points. When he put his hand to his head it was beating as if a drum and fife band were inside it, and his body ached from head to foot. Oh, how it ached! Where was he? What had happened? After a few minutes he squinted through narrowed lids and with a painful effort turned his neck to the side. The drawing-room. What was he doing in the drawing-room? And who was that sitting huddled in the chair? He blinked and the slits opened wider. Betty. What was Betty doing there? What had happened? He closed his eyes again. He had taken Martin to see Dr Levey. Yes, yes. Oh! Yes. Yes.

His memory was stirring. Yes, indeed, he had taken Martin to Dr Levey. Oh my God! He would have to go through that again. But Betty; where did Betty come in? He'd had a drink. A drink? He'd had two, three, four, five; he'd lost count after a time. He didn't go to the club. No; to bars, three bars. And then he got into the car. He was nearly home; he had seen the lights in the house.

'Lie still. How are you feeling?'

He looked up into Betty's face. 'Oh Betty.'

'You're all right; you're not hurt in any way.'

'What happened?'

'You took a short cut down Robson's Gully.'

'No! Oh God!' He tried to nod his head; then put his hand up and gripped his brow as he said, 'Yes, Robson's Gully. How . . . how did you find me?'

'Mike saw the car going over; I . . . I went down.'

'You?'

'Yes, me. Now go to sleep.'

'No, no. Aw, Betty, I'm sorry. I'm sorry.'

'It's all right. Now go to sleep.'

'Can . . . can I have a drink?'

'Tea?'

242

'Yes, anything.'

She went to the tray standing on a side table and poured two cups of tea from the thermos; and when he had drunk his he asked, 'The car, is . . . is it smashed?'

'Well, it's almost hung up between two trees.'

'Hung up between . . .' He made a small motion with his head. 'How . . . then how did you get me . . .'

'Oh, it's a long story. I wish you didn't eat so much; you're a dead weight.'

Again he said, 'Oh, Betty;' and now he bowed his head deeply on to his chest as he muttered, 'I was drunk, stoned.'

'Yes, I should say you were.'

'There was a good reason, Betty.'

'Yes?'

'I . . . I found out how the little girl died.'

When Betty didn't speak he raised his head slightly and looked at her. She had taken a seat by the side of the couch and she stared at him wide-eyed as he said, 'Elaine. You remember the black negligée? Well, the . . . the boy saw her come into the room. He . . . he had his fingers splayed across his face like this.' He demonstrated. 'He couldn't have realised who she was: the nightlight was low and . . . and, as you know, she always bade him good-night in her room; I don't remember her ever going into that nursery after that first time. He . . . he couldn't have recognised her, what with the light and the black clothes, and likely she had the collar turned up; but he saw her lift the side down, tip up the mattress, and throw the child on to the floor.'

Betty didn't cry, 'No! No!' in loud denial at the voice of truth she had stilled since the time when she herself had lifted the railed side of the cot down and asked herself how the boy could ever have managed to move it out of its sockets; yet even so, against the voice of truth, part of her mind had cried, 'Oh no! No! Elaine? No! No!' It was unthinkable.

243

'What am I to do, Betty?'

She gave him no answer, because whatever she might suggest she knew he would take his own line with regard to his wife. And so she asked quietly, 'Martin . . . will . . . will the treatment do him any good?'

'I think so. Under hypnosis the doctor told him he would never have any more nightmares.'

'It was as simple as that?'

'Yes. But at the same time it was . . . well, something inexplicable, something beyond reason.'

Joe bowed his head again now and he muttered as if to himself, 'It isn't only the fact that she could do it, Betty, but . . . but that she put the burden on the boy, knowing that some day someone who had heard Nellie McIntyre's version of the affair – but then, not only hers; there was Ella's and Duffy's and Mary's too – someone somewhere would throw it at him, saying, you killed your little sister when you were four. I could kill her myself for that. If she was here now, I just don't know what I would do to her. I remember I thanked God yesterday she was away, for I would have been straight home, and God only knows what I would have done to her.'

She was now looking at her hands, the fingers picking at each other on her lap as she said, 'Well, if you rid him of the stigma by telling him the truth, what is he going to think of his mother? I should imagine his next state would be worse than his first, because he's very fond of her. Naturally he's very fond of her.'

'He's not, not really.' His words were clipped, his voice harsh and, her eyes widening in surprise, she said, 'How can you say that?'

'Because I know. I'm not the only one she's frustrated. Anything he's really wanted to do she's put a stop to: he's very fond of Elizabeth but he mustn't speak to her; he's also

244

very fond of David and Hazel but he mustn't go into their house. Well, from now on, all that is going to be changed. No matter what I do about this, all that is going to be changed.' Of a sudden now he covered his face with his hands as he groaned, 'God! God! I just can't believe it. She's so delicate, so frail-looking, yet she can tip a child out of its cot.'

Betty took one long deep breath before she said, 'You mustn't forget that it wasn't an ordinary child and . . . and that she gave birth to it.'

'That makes it worse.' He was looking at her now. 'Don't you see that makes it all the worse? I was its father, but I didn't want it to die.'

'But you wished it hadn't been born. You wished it wasn't there. Now, now, Joe' – she lifted her hand – 'don't deny it, please, because I myself wished it time and time again, I wished it wasn't there. And I think you will agree I had more to do with it than either you or she. In its helplessness I should have grown to love it. That's what you're supposed to do, but I couldn't. I did what I had to do for it, but when I knew it was dead I felt nothing but relief. And if you were to speak the truth you would say the same . . . At the time it didn't matter to me how she had gone; she was gone.'

He stared at her, his mouth slightly open, and said, 'I . . . I thought you cared for her . . .'

'Oh, Joe' – she moved her head slowly at him – 'I had compassion for her and pity, and I cared for her needs, but if you mean loving, let me ask you something: did you love her? You were her father.'

Again he had his head bowed, and he lifted it sharply as she sneezed, and when he saw her shudder, he said, 'You're cold.'

She didn't answer, but turned to the fire and poked it into a blaze, then added some logs.

Yes, she was cold. She was cold and sick to the heart of

her. At this moment she longed with a deep longing to be out of this house and in the room that was always kept ready for her at Lady Mary's. She was tired of everything and everyone here. What was there in life here for her, after all? Nothing but work and frustration. And now every time she looked at her sister she would see her letting down the side of the cot, tipping up the mattress, and hurling her helpless child to the floor.

5

'You mean to say you condone it?' Joe said.

'Agree with it, condone it, use whatever term you like' –
Mike nodded at Joe – 'if you want my opinion, it's the only
good thing she's ever done in her life.'

'You must be joking.'

'I'm not joking, lad. That thing she gave birth to was a
monstrosity. Just think, it could be alive now, this very day;
its body would have grown, and just imagine what it would
have looked like: a thing with no mind, 'cos it had no mind.
That's what you've got to remember, its mind was blank. No'
– Mike moved his head wildly from shoulder to shoulder –
'you haven't staggered me, lad, with your news. And if you
take my advice you'll let sleeping dogs lie. If, as you say, the
boy's going to be all right, you should be thankful.'

'Be thankful?' Joe's voice was grim. 'Be thankful that my
wife could do a thing like that?'

Mike now leaned forward in his chair and said quietly,
'I've never liked her, you know that well enough, not from
the day I clapped eyes on her. When I saw her coming
in that door there, I thought, oh my God! not the same
type as bewitched me. But aye, she was. As I've told you

afore, she was the double of your mother. And you know it's been proved, lad, right up to this very minute, because she doesn't only take after her in looks but in character, too. Just think, lad, if your mother could have lifted a cot rail down and flung somebody we both know onto the floor, my God! she would have done it. Now I'm not going to say that what Elaine's done is going to make me like her, because I never could, yet I'm going to give her credit for courage. And don't you forget, lad, when you're condemning her, that she had to pay for her courage, for as I see it, a breakdown is something to contend with. And that's what caused the first lot. Why she should go off the rails again because you brought young Elizabeth into the nursery, God alone knows. But I suppose when you're in that state any frustration will knock you back. Anyway, there it is. If you want my advice you'll let things go on as they've been going on for years. The only other course of action is divorce, and that's a mucky word to me. And anyway, you've got nothing on her to bring that about.'

'I wouldn't be too sure of that.'

Now Mike screwed up his eyes as he stared at Joe and said quietly, 'No?'

'No. Can you see her traipsing regularly to London merely to do the shopping and stay with her uncle? She wouldn't put herself out to stay with that old fellow unless it was for her own purpose, and I know what that purpose is.'

'Aye?'

'It's over two years ago now that Marcus saw her in a restaurant with a man . . .'

'Well, that isn't much to go on.'

'Wait a minute. He was up there for a week's conference, Marcus, I mean. The third time he came across them he made himself known and she had to introduce the fellow.

Marcus mightn't have thought too much about it even then if she hadn't said that the man was an old friend and they had just met that day.'

Mike let out a long breath as he said, 'Friends are always helpful, I'll say that for them.'

'I don't blame Marcus for telling me, and it didn't upset me. Well' – he turned his head to the side – 'the fact that I was being gulled did, but where my feelings were concerned, no. You once said I would have a slow awakening; you were right; but now my eyes are wide open, having been finally unglued some time back when I came across letters from him.'

'Came across?'

'Yes, I said, came across, after I had looked. She keeps the desk in the sitting-room locked these days, but I have a number of keys. Those letters alone would give me a divorce.'

'Who is the fella? Do you know of him?'

'Oh, I know of him; she threw him up at me once or twice in the beginning. From what I pieced together they should have been married. I think she came to me on the rebound. Anyway, now he is married and has a family.'

'My God! the things that happen in this house. You know' – Mike turned his face towards the window – 'this has never been a happy house, and yet, in a way, I've always loved it, sort of wanted to look after it. I was wondering the other day just how much longer we'll be able to hang on to it.' He turned now and looked at Joe. 'It worries me that, among other things, lad, the fact that it might have to go.'

'Oh, it won't come to that.'

'How can you be sure, if Baxter's out-box us, so to speak, and with orders fading away?'

'We've still got our capital.'

'The capital will soon vanish, lad, if it's got to boost a dying firm.'

'Don't worry; I won't let it get that far; we'll sell out first.'

'My God!' – Mike wiped the spittle from the corner of his mouth – 'what things have come to after a lifetime of striving. It's unbelievable. But anyway, to get back to where we were. What are you goin' to say to her when she gets back?'

'I'll have to think about it.'

'Aye, you do that, and try and think on it calmly. But what we both have to think about in the meantime is, how is Betty? She's got a cold on her. And is it any wonder? How in the name of God she got you up that bank and home, I don't know.'

'Neither do I.'

'Is she in bed?'

'No; she's lying on the couch in the drawing-room.'

'Well, if she gets no better I should ring the doctor.'

'Yes, I had thought about doing that.'

Mike turned in his chair and watched Joe walking towards the door and he said, quietly, 'The next time you decide to get bloody drunk, lock yourself in your room.' And Joe answered, 'Yes, I'll do that an' all, and it could be tonight.'

The doctor was called in to Betty on the Tuesday morning. Her temperature was a hundred and three, and he pronounced that she had a bad dose of bronchitis. During the day, her condition became worse, and Mary, meeting Joe as he entered the house, said to him, 'Miss is real bad. I'm worried; I think the doctor should come again. That's not just bronchitis, it's pneumonia, if ever I've seen it.'

When Dr Pearce arrived through slush and rain at eight o'clock that evening he confirmed Mary's diagnosis; Betty had pneumonia, but he said they were not to worry; if Joe

250

would send his man down he would give him some medication for her and some linctus to ease her breathing and cough, and he would look in again first thing next morning.

By Friday everybody in the house knew that Betty was seriously ill. Her fever was still raging and her breathing was still very laboured. Joe went to the factory for an hour in the morning, then returned straight home. Twice during the day he phoned London, but there was no reply from the Hughes-Burton house.

After putting the phone down for the third time he went into the dining-room and poured himself out a stiff measure of whisky, and as he sipped at it he told himself that if Elaine didn't come home that night he'd have to engage a nurse, because they couldn't go on like this much longer. Everybody in the house was tired: Mary and Ella were worn out; even his father had struggled down from his attic abode to sit by Betty's side, his face grim, his eyes wide with anxiety.

Joe walked to the window with the glass in his hand and looked up into the sky. It was low and leaden-coloured. The garden was leaden-coloured, the house was leaden-coloured, his life was leaden-coloured.

What if she died?

He turned abruptly and sat down, pushing his glass along a table; then, dropping his elbows on to his knees, he gripped his hands together and leaned his body over them and said to himself, 'No, no, she won't. She's strong, is Betty, she's strong.' But contradicting this statement, his father's voice yelled in his head as it had done to his face yesterday: 'It would have taken the strength of a horse to haul a man up that slope, then half carry or drag him along the road to the house. But Betty's no horse: inside that big frame of hers is a woman, a sensitive, wonderful woman, and if anything happens to her I'll never forgive you, lad.'

And if anything happened to her he'd never forgive himself. Life was pretty grey now, but without Betty about the house he knew he would experience a feeling of desolation such as he had not known before; not even Elaine's going, by desertion or death, would affect him in the same way as would Betty's. And this was odd, hardly understandable.

The door opened and he lifted his head to see Martin standing there. The boy came hurriedly towards him now, saying, 'Mary wouldn't let me go in to see Aunty Bett, Father. I would have been quiet, I would have just sat . . . I . . .'

Joe got to his feet and put his hand on the boy's head, saying, 'Your Aunt Betty's ill, very ill; she mustn't be disturbed in any way.'

'Is . . . is she going to die?'

'Oh. Oh, no! No.' Joe's tone ridiculed the question.

'Then why was Ella . . . I mean Jane . . . Oh, anyway, why was she crying in the hall just now?'

'Oh.' Joe turned away, picked up his glass from the table, and drained it before he said, 'You know Ella: she cries at weddings, and when she goes to the pictures . . . and when she's tired, and she's very tired now. And so is Mary.' He again put his hand onto his son's head, adding, 'So don't trouble them. But' – he nodded at his son now – 'I tell you what you could do: you could help in the kitchen; I'm sure Mary will give you something to do; or you could go down to David; he's always glad of a hand.'

The boy looked up at his father for a moment, then said slowly, 'I'll . . . I'll stay in the house, Father.'

'Very well. Go and tell Mary you'll be her second pair of legs.' He smiled wanly. But the boy didn't return his smile, he simply turned and walked slowly out of the room . . .

The doctor called again at four o'clock, and when he came out of the room he stood on the landing, shaking his head at Joe as he said, 'She's in a very low state; but she's got a strong constitution. Let's hope it's strong enough.' Then he added, 'She mustn't be left, you understand that? I . . . I think you should have a night nurse.'

'I was thinking about that too. But I'm expecting my wife back tonight, and we should be able to manage then. But if for some reason she doesn't return, I'll see about a nurse first thing in the morning. In the meantime, I'll stay with her all tonight.'

The doctor looked at him closely for a moment. 'She needs a woman there,' he said; 'she mustn't be left lying in the wet bedclothes.'

'Well' – he hesitated – 'there's Mary and Ella; one or the other will be with me. And . . . and I'm not helpless; I've helped to see to her over the last few days.'

As Dr Pearce went down the stairs he asked over his shoulder, 'Can't you get in touch with your wife? They're sisters, aren't they? She should be here.'

'I've tried numerous times today, but I couldn't get a reply, which makes me think she's on her way back. She's been staying with her uncle in London.'

The doctor made no further comment, but simply made a small nodding motion with his head, continuing even as he went out of the front door, which Joe interpreted as disapproval, whether of him not engaging a nurse before now, or of the fact that Elaine wasn't here when she was needed, he didn't know.

It was three o'clock in the morning. The room was hot, airless, and the only sound was of Betty's painful breathing. The bedclothes rose and fell into a half circle about her neck; her face, right up to the roots of her hair, was flushed a deep pink, and over it, from out of her hair, ran thin rivulets of water.

Joe alternated wiping her face down with a soft towel with stroking her hair back from her forehead and spreading it

253

over the pillow; occasionally he would put his hand inside the bedclothes and lay it across her breastbone, for this gave him an indication of how much her body was still sweating. He had already changed the sheets twice since eleven o'clock, from which time he had been alone with her, having made Mary and Ella go to bed, promising them he would call if he should need them. As for his father, he knew that he was still up, for from time to time he could hear the thump of his stick on the floor above.

'J . . . oe.'

'Yes, dear?' He brought his face above hers.

'J . . . oe.'

Her voice was a mere croak, and it was evident that it was painful for her to speak.

'Do you want a drink?' He went to move from the bed and she made a slight motion with her hand, then lay staring at him as her breast heaved painfully.

When a few minutes later he put his hand inside the clothes again the sweat of her body felt cold and when he said softly, 'I'll have to change you,' she made no sign one way or the other.

Going to the clothes-horse that stood to the side of the fireplace, he took from it a nightdress and two sheets; and now, keeping the eiderdown and blankets over her, he slowly and gently manipulated the wet sheets from under and above her; then, following Mary's method of starting from the bottom of the bed and unrolling the clean sheet upwards, he eased her legs over it, then her buttocks, then, putting his arm about her shoulders, he brought her upwards before pulling the sheet into place. The placing of the top sheet was much easier to accomplish. But now he had to change her nightdress.

As with the sheets he had already changed it twice before, and now, as then, she made no protest whatever. He could,

254

as it were, have been performing the duty every night of her life, so seemingly indifferent was she to his hands on her bare flesh.

Decorously he had to pull her nightdress up from her body underneath the bedclothes, and it was only her breasts that he looked upon. They were firm and rounded, and a section of his mind made him wonder if he were the only man who had seen them.

The pillowcases changed, he laid her gently back, saying, 'There now. Is that better?'

She did not try to answer, but just continued to look at him. After bundling the sodden bedclothes into the clothes basket he washed his hands and rolled down his shirt sleeves; then returned to the bed and, taking her hand, he stroked it gently, and when the fingers gripped his he looked at her enquiringly. And again she gasped, 'J . . . oe.'

'Yes, dear?'

'J . . . oe. I'm . . . I'm going to die.'

He gulped in his throat, moved his chin slowly down into the open neck of his shirt before he said, 'No, no, Betty.'

'Yes . . . Joe.'

His throat was too tight for speech. There was a burning sting at the back of his eyes.

'J . . . oe. I . . . I want to tell you something.' The bedclothes heaved, even higher now. 'I can . . . I can tell you now.' Her eyes were fixed tight on him. 'I . . . I love you . . . Joe. I've . . . I've loved, I've always lo . . . ved you. I can tell you now, because it doesn't matter . . . any more . . . hurting no-one.'

His mouth was open, his face stretched and he was silent; it was as if everything within him had stopped. He saw her face swollen red and sweaty, her long hair like a dark halo, a foreboding halo, a foreboding halo around her.

The stillness within him was gradually being probed. What had she said? She had said she loved him, she had always

255

loved him. Betty had loved him. There flashed into his mind that particular night years ago when thought of her had presented a way of easing his starved body. Then, even then, he had known something, felt something. All these years she had been in this house with him and not a sign. Oh dear God! Oh, Betty. Betty.

He was bending over her. Her hand held between his was pressed into his chest. His head was moving slowly. Words were pouring from his mind but he couldn't get them into his mouth for the blockage in his throat was choking him.

Slowly he bent forward until his face was half buried in the pillow, his cheek touching hers, and when, after a moment, he turned his head his lips traced her burning brow, then moved downwards towards her mouth, and he kissed her. Now raising himself above her, he slipped his arm under her shoulders; then turning her heavy body towards him, he pleaded, 'Stay with me, Betty. I . . . I need you. I . . . I want you.'

When she moved her hand the slightest amount, as if in denial, his voice coming deep now and strong, he said, 'Believe me. Believe me, Betty, I do want you. Not as before, for the house and everybody in it, but for me. I . . . I want you at this moment as I've never wanted anything in my life before. Do you hear me? You've got to believe me, Betty. You're the one, you're the real one, you're the one I need. It's as if I've been blind for years. Yet not so blind. Listen . . . Listen.' He made a small movement with his arm, then drew her nearer to him, 'Seven, eight years ago I was for asking you, I was, I was.'

Her breathing became agitated, but her face moved into the semblance of a smile and she lifted her hand and touched his cheek; and, when his tears splashed over her fingers, she gasped 'Oh, J . . . oe! J . . . oe!'

Now laying her head back on the pillow, he swallowed deeply before he said brokenly, 'Fight, Betty, fight. I'll be with you every step of the way. Only fight! Don't go . . . You can't go now, you can't!'

She lay looking at him for a moment before she gasped, 'I can't, can I? I can't . . . go now.'

6

It was not until early April 1939 that Betty went out of the house for the first time. The drugs that she had taken to quell the pneumonia had left side-effects: her bowels would not retain the food and she became the victim of constant diarrhoea. Only now, during the third week since she had been out of bed, was she able to travel: and Joe was about to take her to stay with Lady Ambers.

She had said goodbye to Mary and Ella, and to Martin before he went to school; she had made a slow journey up the attic stairs to Mike, and he had held her hands and said, 'Promise me you'll come back, lass.' And she had replied with quiet emphasis, 'Oh, I'll come back, Mike. Never fear, I'll come back.' She could have added, 'Where else would I stay but where my heart is?'

She had never known such happiness in her life before. From that night when he had stopped her from going over the border into what she thought of as release and peace at last, Joe had come no closer to her than to hold her hand, because Elaine had come back on the Saturday and the nurse had taken over the night duty. After that there was never a time when they were alone together.

258

But it didn't matter; her heart was full of him and she knew with amazing certainty that a miracle had happened and that his heart was full of her.

She didn't know how it had come about, she didn't even bother to question, she was still so very weak. She was content . . . yet content wasn't the right word to fit the thankfulness in her for life as it looked to her now.

In the hall, when Elaine kissed her and said, 'Come back strong,' she knew that Elaine didn't care whether she came back or not. Elaine had no more use for her; in fact, she hadn't had any use for her for a long time, not since she had challenged her with the fact that her frequent visits to London were to meet Lionel Harris. She had come upon Elaine's secret on one of her rare visits to town. Another cousin, Turnbull Hughes-Burton's only son, had died, and she and Elaine had gone up to attend the funeral, and it was during this short stay in London that she saw Elaine and Lionel Harris together; and, as she'd said to Elaine, a blind man could see their meeting wasn't merely that of friends, even friends who weren't supposed to have seen each other for years.

Anyway, now she was leaving them all behind, at least for a time; and for the next few hours she would be alone with Joe.

When Joe had seated her in the back of the car, tucked the rug around her and had taken his position behind the wheel, he did not turn and wave to Elaine, where she stood at the top of the steps, but as he passed the corner of the house he put his hand out of the car and raised it upwards knowing that his father would be watching.

He knew that they would hardly have got out of the drive before Elaine would be packing for her journey to London. These past weeks must have been a terrible trial to her, and at times he had been human enough to enjoy her agony; he had even wanted to confront her with his knowledge, so as to let her see she wasn't as clever as she thought, nor he as gullible as she imagined; and no doubt he would have done this long before now if it wasn't for what had taken place between Betty and himself.

They were well out of the town and on a deserted road when Betty leaned forward and said, 'Let me sit in front, Joe.'

He slowly pulled the car to a stop and, turning and looking back at her, he said, 'You won't be able to stretch your legs here.'

This statement was followed by a silence while they stared at each other; then with a swift movement, he was out of his seat and had opened the back door of the car and was sitting beside her. With their hands gripping, they gazed at each other; then his arms were about her and hers about him, and, their mouths pressed close, they held each other tightly for what seemed an endless time.

'Oh! Betty. Betty. I can't tell you, I simply can't tell you how I feel. You . . . you believe me, don't you?'

'Yes, Joe.'

'It's . . . it's as if I was starting a new life. I . . . I never believed I'd get a second chance at happiness . . . not that.' He screwed up his face and turned his head aside for a moment. 'My marriage has never spelt happiness. Madness, yes, insanity, anything, but not happiness. And . . . and you, you really care for me, Betty?'

'Oh, Joe, I haven't words; I've worn them out over the years by burying them. The only comfort I had were dreams. Not daydreams; I wouldn't allow myself those, but I dreamt of you most every night. And always you loved me, and . . . and I was beautiful.'

'You are, you are beautiful.'

260

'Oh! Joe. Joe' – she now closed her eyes and bent her head – 'don't scoff.'

Her chin was jerked upwards, his fist tight under it, and his voice was tender as he said, 'Look at me. Look at me, Betty. I'd never really seen you until the night you nearly died. And, you know, that night you had a beauty that was all your own, and you haven't lost it since. It's in your eyes. I never really thought you plain, but now, since . . . well, since we know how we both feel, you've taken on a beauty that will grow with the years.'

As her eyelids blinked rapidly he traced his fingers around the outline of her mouth as he said, 'What are we going to do, Betty? Things can't go on as they are.'

'Oh, my dear, we'll have to think, think carefully. There are so many people who can be hurt.'

'It won't hurt Elaine.'

'Oh, there you are mistaken. If you'd picked anyone else she might forgive you, but not when it's me. As for what she will say about me . . . Oh!'

'She can't say anything about you, she's meeting another fellow in London and has been for some time now.'

When she said nothing to this, he narrowed his eyes at her and said, 'You knew?'

'Yes.'

'And you said nothing?'

'How could I?'

'Yes, how could you? But you see it makes things easier; she can't throw any stones.'

'I wish I could think so.'

'Betty, we must come together; I need you. Do you need me?'

Her hand tightened on his and he looked deep into her eyes and said softly, 'Where? When?'

With gaze averted, she said, 'I've thought about it. In her

261

last letter Lady Mary said that she's got to have her teeth out; four back ones, and that she must stay in hospital overnight. She . . . she goes in next Friday.'

He turned her face towards him and they looked into each other's eyes for a long moment before he kissed her gently on the lips; then, giving her his hand, he helped her out and into the front seat of the car.

Lady Mary's greeting of Betty was characteristic. 'Well! You've arrived at last,' she said. 'And my! you look like a scarecrow. What have they done to you? But need I ask, they have worked you to death.' She now turned to Joe and said, 'And let me tell you, you can phone or whistle or send smoke-signals, but she's not going back there for at least a month, and not at all if I have my way.'

A short while later, when they were all in the sitting-room, and when she could get a word in, Betty asked, 'And how are you?'

'Me? Oh, I'm as fit as a fiddle except for these accursed teeth. I would let them stay there, even when the aching nearly drives me mad, but they are causing my breath to smell like a cesspool. I just noticed it recently. Why don't people tell you your breath is offensive? Why don't they give some sign, wrinkle their nose or something? I would.'

Betty smiled quietly as she thought, Yes, indeed, you would. But oh, how nice it was to be here. It was like coming home. This room wasn't half the size of Elaine's drawing-room, nor yet as big as her own sitting-room, but it was more comfortable, and more gracious.

'Did I tell you that Nancy got married? Fool of a girl. Living down in the village now. I bet that Mrs Bailey put her up to it. "Get married," she would have said to her, "so you'll have an excuse to live out." I could never stand that Mrs Bailey; an upstart, a real upstart. Sending her son

262

to Oxford, indeed! Mrs Pollard is much better, knows her place . . . I've been here a fortnight on my own.'

'What about Dobson and his wife; have they gone?'

'No, no, they haven't gone. Why should they go? They know when they are well off. Do you know what I have done? I've had a bathroom put in their cottage. Yes, a bathroom. But they are three hundred yards away along the road; what if I needed them in an emergency?'

'You must put the phone in, so you can ring them whenever you want them.'

'Yes, yes' – Lady Mary nodded now – 'of course. That's what I'll do. She won't like it, his wife. You know why?'

She now turned to Joe, and he, his lips in a twisted smile, replied briefly, 'No.'

''Cos she's afraid of me, scared stiff of me. And I play on it.' She grinned wickedly. 'I stare at her without speaking and then I let out a bawl. The creature jumps. Stupid woman! I want to say to her: You're a fool. Do you know that? You're a fool. You shouldn't be afraid of anyone. If you are, you should have the sense not to show it. I nearly took her hand the other day and pulled her in here and said, "Sit down, woman, and look at me. What do you see? A bundle of old-fashioned clothes on an eighty-plus emaciated body. But what does the body matter? what do the clothes matter? it's the mind that matters, and you've got a mind, woman. Use it and make it tell you that you're as good as the next."'

Betty bent her head and bit on her lip. Contradiction on top of contradiction. She still held it against Mrs Bailey for having sent her son to a grammar school in the first place; and yet here she was, the old autocrat of autocrats, preaching equality. What would have happened if poor Mrs Dobson had stood up to her in the way she was advocating? But she hadn't time to give herself the answer before Lady Mary

263

supplied it by crying, 'And what would have happened to the poor individual had she stood up for herself, eh?' She now put her head back and laughed, a high trilling laugh. 'I would have thrown her out of the door. And what does that go to prove, Mr Remington?' She was now confronting Joe.

'That you are very much of a woman, Lady Ambers.'

'Huh! Well—' Her old head wagged, her lips pursed themselves, her eyes twinkled, and she answered him, 'Neatly put,' but it was a superficial answer. 'Now if I'd asked the question of Betty here, what would she have said?' She now turned and looked at Betty: 'What would you have said, eh? Come on, tell me.'

Betty glanced at Joe before she looked back at Lady Mary and said, 'Much the same, that your attitude would have been characteristic of you.'

'No, you wouldn't. You're just saying that so that his remark' – she nodded towards Joe – 'won't be considered trite. Had we been on our own you would, in your own particular way, have let me have it.' She now turned to Joe again, saying, 'That's the difference between her and other people: she's not afraid of me! she never has been. And why? Because she's herself, and she's got a mind, and she uses it; I don't think she has much chance for intelligent conversation in your home.'

Joe's face was unsmiling now. His jaw moved from one side to the other before he said slowly, 'We're not a lot of morons, Lady Ambers.'

'Oh, you surprise me.'

A quick signal from Betty's eyes quelled the sharp retort that he was about to make, but as quick as it was it didn't escape the old lady's scrutiny, and her head went back and she laughed again as she cried, 'Oh my! Oh my! the male ego must not be affronted. Don't worry, Mr Remington' – she now leaned towards him – 'I'll behave myself from now on and play the hostess. Lunch should be ready any time now. Let's have a drink. Ring the bell.' She motioned with a bob of her head towards a hand bell on the table to the side of Joe's chair, and after he had rung it and no-one appeared in the room, she commanded, 'Again!'

His eyes were downcast and his head was slightly to the side as he again picked up the bell. After a few moments, during which she had asked Joe what he would prefer to drink, and there was still no answer to the summons, Betty, making an attempt to rise, said, 'I'll go and see.'

'You'll do no such thing!' The old lady was on her feet. 'She'll be outside sunning herself in the garden; taking a mouthful of air, she calls it.'

A minute later, when they were left alone, they looked at each other, Betty smiling, Joe, lips compressed, his head shaking.

'You mustn't mind her,' Betty said softly.

'Mind her?' He moved his chair closer to hers so that he could touch her hand. 'She's a tartar. And yet you're so fond of her?'

'Yes.' She nodded slowly at him. 'I could say I love her; next to you I love her best in the world.'

'Next to me? Oh! Betty. Betty.'

The following Friday Betty accompanied Lady Mary to the hospital; and when she was about to leave her she felt overcome with guilt for a moment when the old lady patted her hand and said with genuine concern, 'You needn't be afraid to stay in the house alone, we never get prowlers, not at night, anyway.' The old lady's further words of explanation and suggestion were heard but hardly registered: 'The men who are still on the road come begging at the gate during the day but I've never been disturbed at night. Anyway, should you be alarmed, go to my bedroom window and shout. Mrs Dobson will likely hear you; from her own account she never sleeps.'

And now Betty was back in the house. Both Mrs Pollard and Nancy had gone to their homes over an hour ago. It had turned eight o'clock and he hadn't yet arrived. He had said he would be here around half-past seven.

At nine o'clock he still hadn't arrived. She was tired of walking from the drawing-room to the kitchen, the window of which looked out on to the yard and the narrow drive leading to the side road. She had purposely not switched on the kitchen light so that she could see the road.

Had there been an accident? Had something happened at the house, something that would prevent his coming? But surely he would have phoned her.

She rolled her hands in the collar of her dressing-gown and pulled it tight around her throat. She had known it was too much to ask, too much to expect that this thing should happen to her. She was forty-one years old, she was in the time, or nearing the time, when the cycle of life would change, a time of life when women who'd had a succession of children thanked God that nature had let up on them. But she had never tasted such nature. What was more, she had never discussed the subject with anyone, not even with Elaine. Oh no, not with Elaine, who looked upon nature, at least where it concerned Joe, as something to cause the lips to draw back from the teeth.

By ten o'clock she was no longer standing by the kitchen window. Sitting on the couch in the sitting-room, staring into the fire, she questioned the whole experience of the last few months. Perhaps she had dreamt it. After all, what had actually happened? When she had thought she was dying she had told him that she loved him, and he had held her in his arms and kissed her. But that memory was hazy, as were the days that followed, days when she couldn't hold any food in

266

her stomach, when diarrhoea and sickness made her at times wish she had died. What had transpired between them then? The touch of the hand, an exchange of glances. They had never been alone together until they made the journey in the car. But that had been real. Yes, that had been real; that was no dream. Yet she did not know for certain if he loved her; what she did know was that he needed her as much as she needed him, and that if it had been possible he would be here now. Yes, she was certain of that. Something had happened. So what must she do? She must phone the house.

She had already risen from the couch when she heard the knock on the front door, and she seemed to leap from where she was to the actual door itself, and when she flung it open to see Joe they each remained still, gazing at each other before, their arms going out, they pressed close and stood silent for a moment.

On a deep intake of breath, she said, 'I . . . I never heard the car; I . . . I thought something had happened. Did . . . did you have a puncture?'

'No, no.' He took off his coat and, putting his arm around her shoulders, walked her into the sitting-room; then, sitting close together on the couch, he rested his eyes on her for a moment before taking her face between his hands and kissing her gently on the lips. 'There were ructions on at home,' he said.

'What about?'

'Martin let it slip that he had been to the Christmas concert with David.'

'After all this time?'

'After all this time. And not only that, but that he had been in the Egans' house more than once. Elaine went on like someone insane; I'd never heard anything like it. I thought she was in for another spasm of hysteria. But no, this was a bout of sheer virulent temper. Oh, how she hates David and

Hazel. It's beyond all reason. If either of them had ever done anything to her you could understand it, but right from the first time she set eyes on David she's loathed him.'

Betty shook her head and glanced towards the fire. Yes, she knew Elaine loathed David; she knew that in many people there was a natural bias to colour; but she, too, had never been able to understand Elaine's antipathy towards the young man, for no-one could be nicer or more pleasant than David. She looked at Joe again and asked, 'What was the outcome?'

'Well,' he sighed, 'I was supposed to be off tonight to York for a conference, as, of course, I shall do tomorrow. But at one time, Betty, I really did think it would have to be tomorrow before I could leave there, because I became so blindly furious with her, I . . . I don't know how I prevented myself from telling her what I'd learned. But I knew if I had, the session would have gone on all night.'

'Oh my dear.'

'How did the old lady fare at the hospital?' Joe now asked.

She smiled as she replied, 'You should ask how the staff will fare,' and at this they both laughed; then, her face becoming straight, she said, 'I feel a little guilty at deceiving her.'

'Don't. You know, somehow I think she'd understand.'

'Yes, perhaps she would. Being who she is perhaps she would . . . I made something to eat. It just needs warming up. You must be hungry.'

'I couldn't eat a bite. Honestly. I'm sorry if you've gone to any trouble, but just a cup of coffee.' They again stared at each other in silence; then, their hands still clasped, they rose and went into the kitchen . . .

*   *   *

268

It was midnight. Joe lay with his head on her breast, his arm about her bare waist. He had never felt so content in his life before. He loved this woman. He knew, as in the moment when pure truth is revealed, that he loved her, and not just because her body had satisfied him as no other had done, but because she was who she was; Betty: a woman he had lived in the same house with for years without once touching her; a woman whose mind was broad and whose heart was big and whose compassion was boundless.

He now moved his lips against the firm flesh of her breast, and she made no response in any way. She had not spoken a word since his first gentle loving, nor through his not so gentle taking, when his mind became subordinate to his senses, nor since he had lain in the deep valley of contentment against her warm flesh. He now took his hand from her waist and turned her face towards him and saw in her eyes an emotion that was impossible for him to translate into words. Winding his fingers now in her loose hair, he brought his face slowly down to her and, placing his lips on her mouth, he lay still.

PART FIVE

I

They had sung, 'We'll hang out the washing on the Siegfried Line', but they hadn't been able to do it.

When, on 3 September 1939, Chamberlain's appeasement of fear had failed and England declared war on Germany, the sirens went for real for the first time and people scuttled to the air-raid shelters and waited for the bombs to rain down. But nothing happened that day, nor the next, nor the next, and as days moved into weeks the whole thing became a bit of an anti-climax. Except for what was happening in France.

But then there was the Maginot Line, wasn't there?

Poland, of course, had got it hot and heavy, but Poland was a long way away. As long as the Germans didn't bomb here, that's all that mattered. Of course, there were irritations, such as blackouts and having to carry gas masks in those horrible little boxes. And then you weren't allowed to use the headlights on your car.

And, of course, there had been the business of evacuating schoolchildren and teachers, together with mothers with children under five, from what were known as danger areas.

Re-shuffling the population, in those first months, had been as big a headache as organising rationing. And by early

1940 many of the evacuees had returned home. Yet, later in the year, after Dunkirk, when Hitler's bombing sent them scattering from the industrial towns, doors that had been shut were now opened to them. There was a broadening of understanding of how the other half lived, at least among certain sections of society, for there were still those who strenuously refused to give shelter to evacuees; and Elaine was one of them. 'Where,' she asked Betty, and not for the first time, 'would we put them?'

'We still have one spare room, and the morning-room could be turned into a bedroom.'

'Why not suggest taking over my sitting-room?'

'Well, it didn't happen, anyway, and it certainly won't now.'

'Look!' Elaine peered through narrowed eyelids at Betty before she went on slowly, 'what's come over you recently? You're different: you've turned into a different being during this last year; you have no concern for me now at all.'

'Perhaps you're right.' Betty nodded slowly now. 'Looking back, I'd say I've wasted years of concern on you.'

'Well!' Elaine took a step back and she narrowed her eyes as she said, 'Now we're coming into the open, aren't we? Now we know where we stand. Are you looking for an excuse to leave? Because if you are, it's a dirty way to go about it. And it would be just like you to walk out and go to that old horror when you're most needed here.'

'And what am I needed for? Tell me what I am needed for. Not to see to Mike, because you don't give a damn what happens to Mike. What you need me for, Elaine, is to enable you to continue your jaunts to London; you couldn't go off so frequently and leave Martin to his own devices if I weren't here, because Martin might take to visiting The Cottage, or some other infectious place. And don't tell me that it is concern for Uncle that takes you up

274

there, because I'd laugh in your face. You haven't fooled anyone . . . anyone. You understand?'

Her mouth agape, Elaine was now standing with her back to the couch. Her face was red with temper and she stammered as she said, 'I . . . I wou . . . would never have believed it . . . And what do you mean, I haven't fooled anyone? What do you mean?'

'I'll leave you to work that out, Elaine. And also, I think you'd better spend the afternoon writing a long letter to Lionel and explaining how it will be impossible for you to come up this week-end, as Betty has walked out.'

Elaine slowly eased herself to the front of the couch and, gripping the edge of it, she said, 'You're not! You wouldn't.'

'I am, and I will. In any case I'd have to leave shortly. You've just said you've noticed a difference in me during the last year. Well, I've been wondering that you didn't also notice a greater difference recently, for I am now four and a half months pregnant and my baby will be born in October.'

Elaine fell back against the couch and, bringing her hands up, she placed them one after the other across the lower part of her face; and then, her hands leaving her face, she flapped them as if throwing off something unclean as slowly, her lips spreading away from her teeth, she hissed, 'You! and that dirty old man up there? You're disgusting, filthy.'

'*Shut up!*'

'I won't shut up. I could go up there and spit on him, and you too.'

Then she shrank back as Betty took two quick steps forward and, bending towards her, said with deep bitterness, 'How often I've wanted to take my hand and slap you across the face, and never more than at this moment.

275

You dare to call anyone filthy or dirty when you've been carrying on with a married man for years under Joe's nose, while depriving him of his rights under the pretext of nerves. Your first breakdown might have had some reality about it, but you've used it since to have your way and deprive him of his rights as a husband. And now you dare turn your lip up at me. Well, for your information I'll tell you that the father of my child doesn't happen to be Mike. If I'd known years ago what I know now he would have been, and I would have had a family running around me in this house. And I would have been its mistress; I wouldn't have had to say thank you to you for the pittance you gave me; that is, until Joe found you out.'

The colour drained from Elaine's face now, the skin looking as taut as a piece of alabaster. Her eyes were wide and almost spitting fire as she cried, 'You wouldn't have been here at all if it hadn't been for me. You would have been pushed from dog to devil, going the rounds as an unpaid companion. You've had the run of the house, you've done what you liked, and I still say it's dirty and indecent that you, at your age, should go with a man. I suppose the old witch arranged it. Was it her chauffeur?'

Betty's hand came out and up, but just as Joe's had done years previously it halted in mid-air. She closed her eyes and as her hand dropped to her side so did her head bow on to her chest, and she turned slowly about and went from the room. But before she closed the door Elaine's voice hit her, as she shouted, 'You're pathetic! That's what you are, pathetic!'

Blindly now, Betty made her way across the landing but, hearing Martin's voice in the hall below and knowing he would come to her room, she began to mount the stairs to Mike's quarters. But half-way up she stood and leant her head against the wall and repeated to herself,

'Pathetic. Pathetic.' Was that how she would appear to others, pathetic? She hadn't felt pathetic, at least not until now. For weeks she had felt wonderful, warm, alive, and everyone had said how well she looked. She hadn't meant it to end like this. They'd had it all planned: she was going to make the excuse that she must go and look after Lady Mary, who was ill. She had thought to be away by next week. The hardest part, she had considered, would be telling Mike; and now that hard part lay immediately before her and she didn't know how she would begin the telling of it.

As if the child was already bearing her down, she walked heavily up the rest of the stairs and into Mike's sitting-room.

He greeted her straightaway. Shambling from the work-shop, he said, 'That was you and her at it, wasn't it? I thought the bloody Germans had arrived without knocking. What's the matter, lass?' He came slowly towards her, and for answer she said immediately and simply, 'I'm leaving, Mike.'

He stared at her but didn't answer, then moved towards his chair near the window; and he looked out and up into the bright blue sky before he said, 'I've never heard you say it like that afore. You mean it this time. For good, is it?'

'Yes, Mike.'

He was looking at her again. 'What brought it about?'

She went slowly towards him and took the seat facing him, the seat she had sat in for years whenever he had wanted a bit of a crack, as he called it. Then, her head bowed slightly but her eyes still looking into his, she said quietly, 'I'm going to have a baby, Mike. I'm pregnant.'

It was a good thirty seconds before he made any response whatever; and then he hitched himself in the leather chair and took in a deep breath and emitted one word: 'Aye.'

She nodded slowly.

'Huh! Huh!' It was a derogatory sound. Then, looking at her from under his eyebrows, he said, 'You've nearly left it too late. I could have put you in the family way years ago if that's all you wanted. I told you at the time.'

'I know you did, Mike, and . . . and I wish now I'd taken you at your word. At least, no, that isn't true; what I mean to say is, I should have taken your offer at the time, then there would have been no need for this to happen as it has. But now that it has, I'm glad. I'm more than glad. I'm overwhelmed with the happiness of it.'

'May I ask who it is?'

Her head was well down now. That was one thing she wouldn't and couldn't tell him: after refusing him, to have taken his son would be too great a blow to his ego; crippled as he was, Mike was still very much a man inside.

The next moment she almost fell off the chair, so quickly did her head jerk up as he asked quietly, 'Would our Joe have anything to do with it?'

She stared at him silently, her body still now, except for her lips, which were trembling. She watched him pull himself to his feet and stand by the broad window-sill, and, leaning on it for support, he looked down into the garden as he said, 'It doesn't surprise me, but . . . but it's bloody hurtful, nevertheless. Still, like father like son, I suppose . . . What's that? Who's she at now?'

As he turned from the window Betty rose sharply to her feet and they both looked down towards the floor as Elaine's voice, raised to the pitch of a scream, came to them. The words were unintelligible but that they were flowing on a wave of rage was only too evident.

'He isn't in? Our Joe isn't in?'

'No; only Martin.'

278

'Go on down. See what she's up to. By the way, does she know?'

'She knows I am pregnant but . . . but not who the father is.'

'Well, look out for squalls when she does' – his voice was quiet, his words coming slowly – 'because although she has no use for him herself she would do her damnedest to put a spoke in your wheel.'

She had no doubt but what Mike said was true: Yes, she'd put a spoke in her wheel if she could, but one thing she couldn't prevent was the life that was already inside her. No; that was hers, and nothing and no-one could take it away from her.

She had just stepped from the attic stairs onto the landing when she saw Elaine's sitting-room door burst open and Martin dash out and fly down the stairs.

Before she reached the door it was banged shut. She paused for a moment to stare at it, then hurried after the boy.

When she reached the front door she saw him disappearing beyond the tennis court and she stood for a moment gazing in that direction, before she turned and looked back up the stairs. What had she said to him? Likely thrown at him that she, Betty, was leaving, and the reason too, and in such a way that it would appear dirty.

She knew Martin liked her, even loved her. Hadn't he once said he wished she was his mother? Over the years she had allowed the thought of this to give her a secret satisfaction, which she would justify by telling herself: And why shouldn't he, because she had brought him up and loved him unselfishly. And that was the point: unselfishly.

She now ran down the steps and in the direction the boy had taken. He wasn't near the greenhouses, and he wasn't with David, because she could see David working over near the strawberry bed. Eventually she espied him sitting amid

279

the roots of the big oak in the copse near the boundary.

She called softly as she approached him, saying, 'Martin. Martin. What is it?' When she reached his side he didn't look up at her but, taking a bit of broken branch, he stubbed at the hard ground between the roots; and when she knelt beside him and took his hand he turned his head away from her.

'What . . . what was your mother saying to you?'

He shook his head, and when she pulled his face around towards her he muttered, 'Oh, Aunty Bett,' and she said softly, 'Tell me what she said. I . . . I can explain.'

Now his head jerked up towards her as he said, 'How can you? You don't know.'

'Don't know what?'

'About Father.'

Her eyes narrowed slightly, and now she asked very quietly, 'What about your father?'

He shook his head wildly and, pulling himself from her, he turned on to his side and, picking up the stick again, he once more jabbed at the earth.

Now she gripped him firmly by the shoulders and pulled him around to face her, demanding, 'Tell me! Martin! Everything. Now come along, tell me what she said about your father.'

The boy swallowed, blinked his eyelids rapidly, very much as she herself did when she was agitated, then he muttered, 'He's bad.'

'Your father bad? Your father's a good man. What did she say?'

'She . . . she said I must never speak to Elizabeth again or . . . or go out with her because . . .'

'Elizabeth?' Betty almost shrieked, then drew in a deep breath of relief and flopped down beside the boy as she released it, and said, 'What about Elizabeth? And . . . and what's it got to do with your father?'

280

His head drooped on to his chest, as he muttered, 'I . . . I told her that I thought our school was going to be evacuated and she said it was nonsense. And I said it wasn't, because Elizabeth's was being evacuated too, and . . . and she almost sprang on me, Aunty Bett.' He looked at her in bewilderment before going on, 'She said I'd been seeing Elizabeth again after she'd told me I hadn't to, and I answered her back, saying, Well, it was impossible to come in the gate with Elizabeth and not speak to her. Anyway, I . . . well, Aunty Bett, I . . . I told her that I liked Elizabeth. And then I said something silly.' His head drooped lower now, and she waited until he muttered, 'I . . . I said I'd always liked Elizabeth and . . . and she was my girl. Lots of fellows have girls, Aunty Bett, and Elizabeth's pretty, and she likes me and . . . and I like her. But . . . but I shouldn't have said it. Anyway I did. And then . . . well, she went mad, Aunty Bett. She pushed me on to the couch and held me down and . . . and then she yelled something at me.'

She had her arms about him and was staring at the top of his head as she asked quietly, 'What did she yell at you?'

'She said Elizabeth could . . . could never be my girl that way; never anything like that, she said. She . . . she was gabbling. Then she took me by the shoulders and shook me and said that Elizabeth was my sister or my half-sister, and that Father was her father, and that Elizabeth's mother was a bad woman.'

'Oh, my God!'

Betty now pulled herself to her feet and dragged up the boy with her, and she took him by the shoulders and shook him as she said, 'Now listen to me, Martin. They're lies. Lies. Do you hear? Elizabeth's mother and father love each other, and Elizabeth is their daughter. Your father and David were brought up together when they were boys like you.

He would never, never—' Now she was gulping in her throat and shaking her head, and again she said, 'Oh my God!'

Grabbing his hand now, she cried, 'Come on back to the house; your father will be in shortly; he'll straighten all this out. And it wants straightening out.'

'No, no.' He resisted her tugging. 'I don't want to see him, Aunty Bett.'

'You've got to, boy. I'm telling you that your mother doesn't know what she's saying; she's ill. Listen!' She turned her head to the side. 'There's the car going up the drive. Come along.'

'No, no, Aunty Bett.'

She looked at him helplessly for a moment, then said, 'Well, promise me one thing: that you'll stay here till I come back. Now promise me that.'

He hesitated for a moment, then said, 'All right.'

She ran from him and between the trees, past the greenhouses, over the tennis court and she reached the side of the drive as Joe was going in by the front door.

When she called to him he turned towards her, and she was gasping as she said, 'Come here a minute; there's something I must tell you.' And, turning from him, she hurried into the courtyard and towards the garage.

Once inside, he asked anxiously, 'What is it? What is it?'

'There's . . . there's been ructions here this morning.'

'Oh.' He nodded. 'She's found out?'

'About us? No; not everything. I . . . I had a row with her. I told her I was leaving and . . . and about my condition. I also told Mike. Then I heard her going for Martin. I've just come from him. He's over in the wood; he's in a dreadful state. Joe—' She put her hands out to him now and as he gripped them she said, 'Now . . . now

282

you must try to keep your temper at least until you explain to the boy. Apparently he told Elaine that Elizabeth was his girl; you know, as a boy would, and she screamed at him. She told him it was impossible.' She now closed her own eyes and screwed them tight for a moment before opening them again and finishing in a rush, 'She says you are Elizabeth's father and that they are half-brother and sister.'

He continued to look at her as if he wasn't seeing her; then he said slowly, 'You mean she . . .?'

When it seemed impossible for him to state the matter in words she nodded slowly, then said, 'Yes. And he's in the wood. He's in a dreadful state; you'd better go to him. He promised me he would stay there until I went back.'

He looked out of the garage door now, then turned his head to the side and said below his breath, 'No, no;' then again, 'No, no; you bring him, Betty; I'm going in.'

'Joe! Joe! Please be careful.'

'I've been careful too long. Yes, that's been my trouble; I've been careful too long.'

'Joe, don't do anything you'll be sorry for. Think . . . think what it might mean.'

As he looked at her now his expression softened as he said, 'I'll think what it'll mean, dear. Don't worry. Don't worry. Fetch him.'

While she hurried across the yard he walked quickly towards the front door, his stride covering the ground as if he were flying over it, so that he was through the hall and up the stairs within seconds.

When he thrust open the sitting-room door Elaine was standing in the middle of the room. The sun was glinting on her hair, taking the colour out of it; her face, her dress, all of her appeared like a pale flame, a delicate, fragile flame that could be extinguished by the slight stir of a summer wind. But Joe didn't see the outer casing, he was looking at the woman underneath.

After closing the door he took a step forward, then stopped, and his Adam's apple jerked spasmodically in his throat before he said, 'So I'm Elizabeth's father, am I?'

'You should know.' Her voice was high, yet it sounded like a thin whisper.

'You dirty-minded slut.' He moved another step towards her; and now she backed away from him but, her voice even higher now, she cried at him, 'Don't you dare call me dirty; you, above all people! You had the nerve to bring that child into this house. Anybody who wanted proof had just to see your faces together. As for dirty; huh! Dirty you say. The blackie went and married her. That upset you, didn't it? You couldn't have him so you took his wife. Or did you share her?'

The cry that escaped her as he grabbed her throat rang through the house, and when the door burst open he had her pinned against the wall.

'Joe! Joe! My God! Let go. Let go.'

Of a sudden, he released his hold and stepped so hastily back that he almost knocked Betty to the floor.

Elaine was leaning against the wall, her hands to her throat, her breath coming in painful gasps. Her head was to the side and she was staring at Joe with a mixture of terror and hatred.

Joe now stood by the head of the couch. His body was bent forward, his arms hanging limp, but his gaze was directed straight onto Elaine; yet he spoke to Betty, saying, 'Take her upstairs to Father.'

'To Mike? But why?'

'You'll find out in a minute. Just take her up, because . . . because I don't want to touch her again.'

284

A somewhat bemused Betty went towards Elaine and, gently taking her arm, she drew her from the wall; then, making a wide detour around Joe, she led her from the room.

Left alone, Joe turned towards the head of the couch, and, gripping it, he bent over it for a moment before turning abruptly and going to the window. This he raised, and then he yelled out across the garden, 'David! David!' Then, louder still, 'David! David!'

David came running through the gap in the hedge that bordered part of the drive, then stopped and, looking up at the window, called, 'What is it? Do you want me?'

'Come indoors.'

Over the distance they looked at each other; then David said slowly, 'What do you mean, come indoors?'

'You heard me. I said, come indoors, come upstairs.'

'Why?'

'You'll know soon enough. Do as I tell you.'

David glanced about him; then, rubbing his hands tight across his mouth, he moved slowly towards the front door; and, for the first time in his life he entered the house.

In the hall, he paused, looking about him, before making for the stairs and mounting them to where Joe was standing at the top. And when they were face to face he said, 'What is it? Why am I here?'

Joe made no answer, but, turning about, he said, 'Come on.' And David followed him along the landing, up the steep stairs to the top floor and into the sitting-room, where Mike was standing with his back to the window-sill.

Elaine was sitting half crouched forward on a chair, and Betty was standing behind it.

They all turned towards the door and the two men standing within it; Joe, his face grim and almost purple with anger,

285

David, standing very straight, his lips set tight, his eyes directed straight across the room to where Mike stood.

And now Mike spoke. 'What's brought this about, eh? Have . . . have you all gone mad?'

Joe didn't move from David's side, but he looked straight at his father as he said, 'Tell them what relation David, here, is to you and to me.'

When Mike brought himself from the support of the window-sill, his stick wobbled under his hand before he straightened himself as much as he could and growled, 'What's this? A showdown you're wantin'?'

'That's it; it's a showdown I'm wanting. And not afore time.'

All their eyes turned on Mike now, but his were focused on the dark face that was staring at him from across the room, and he spoke to it, saying, 'It's rather late in the day, isn't it, to make a claim?'

'I'm making no claim.' The deep resonance in David's voice at that moment seemed to speak of his coloured forebears.

'Father.' Joe moved hastily forward now until he was standing between his father and Elaine, and he stared at his father as he pointed to Elaine, 'Make it plain to her, will you, because her cute mind has pointed out to her the resemblance between Elizabeth and me, so she accuses me of being her father.'

Mike now looked straight back into Joe's eyes. Then, after a moment, he turned his gaze on to Elaine's tight pallid face and he said slowly, 'David is my son.'

Elaine, staring up at Mike, made a small movement with her head, and her nose twitched just the slightest. She went to open her mouth, then closed it again . . . Rising from the chair, she glared at Joe, then back to his father, then turned her bitter gaze on David, and it would seem that her eyes had dragged a cloak of disdain over the three of them before she stalked from the room.

'Well! Well!' The words seemed to break the embarrassed silence, and as Mike lowered himself down into his chair he looked to where David was standing near the door and he said quietly, 'Come on in, lad, and sit down.'

'No, thank you.' The words still came slow and deep. 'I've stood on the sidelines all this time and that's where I choose to stay. As you said yourself, it's too late in the day.' And on this, David too turned about and left the room.

But Joe was immediately after him, calling, 'Wait a minute, David. Hang on a minute. Please!'

Mike now turned his head towards Betty, saying, 'Don't you walk out on me an' all, at least not at the moment. Shut the door, lass; then pour me a drink.'

Betty closed the door, and she poured out two drinks, and after handing a glass to Mike she sat down facing him and stared at him for a moment before she asked quietly, 'Why have you kept silent all this time?'

He threw off the measure of whisky in one gulp, wiped his mouth on the back of his hand and said, 'I might have kept silent, lass, but it was well known in most quarters; at least, it was guessed at.'

'But you never openly acknowledged him?'

'No, no; I couldn't, not while his so-called father was alive. And then there seemed no point afterwards. And I was in the thick of this.' He tapped his knees. 'I think I might have done at one time, but then our Joe brought his lady-wife home. I took one look at her and said to meself, she wouldn't stand for that. And it is strange, but she hated David from the minute she saw him. And from the minute I saw her I predicted in me own mind the life our Joe was going to have 'cos I had the same meself. That's why David came into being.'

287

Mike looked out of the window now and said quietly, 'She was a beautiful woman, his mother. Mary engaged her in the kitchen. She had the muckiest jobs to do, yet she always carried herself like a queen. I used to watch her from the window. I took to watching her, and when I spoke to her, and I did at every opportunity, her smile was warm. She was seventeen when she came but she was already a woman: she was a full-blooded negress and she could sing. She had a beautiful voice. But she could neither read nor write, but she could talk. Oh, how she could talk.'

He turned to Betty now and, nodding his head slowly, he said, 'She was wiser than Solomon in some of the things she said. And I wasn't the only one that liked to look at her and hear her talk or sing. Brooks, he did the garden then – he used to come out from Fellburn – he lived with his widowed mother, a quiet fellow, church-going, no drink, that kind of a bloke. Well . . .'

He now leaned back in the chair and gazed at the ceiling as he went on, 'I'll leave the rest to your imagination. I'll only say this: it would never have happened if me wife had been anything like a wife to me; but from the time she fell with Joe she wouldn't let me near her; that kind of thing was only for—' He now brought his head down and his gaze slanted towards Betty and, his smile twisted, he said, 'The word was procreation. A mouthful, that, isn't it? But oh, I remember that word, I heard it often enough.' He laughed out aloud as he said now, 'There might have been another after Joe, when she felt the need to procreate again, but she found out about Nessy, and God! didn't she give me hell! Unlike Elaine, she didn't shout or bawl – I could have met that kind of attack from her – but no, she smiled at you while cutting your throat. She talked at me, showing up me ignorance. Did I ever tell you that's why I started reading so much, because I was ashamed of being so ignorant? Anyway' – he brought his hand tightly down over his face – 'Nessy got pregnant. And I was at me wits' end: I didn't want her to leave, yet she couldn't stay. Then one night Mary came and said Frank Brooks wanted to see me, and in a most formal way that fellow asked if I would object to his marrying Nessy. He knew all about what was going on. He was a good man, and he was a brave one an' all, because I knew he would have to fight his mother and the chapelites, not forgetting how the ordinary folk looked upon a fellow marrying a black woman and vice versa. I can see him now, standing looking me straight in the eye, yet never hinting at the truth. I can hear meself saying that I saw no reason why he shouldn't marry Nessy, while at the same time I felt like opening a vein and letting me blood run out, because me heart ached. You see, I loved her as I've never loved anybody afore or since. Anyway, I said he could have The Cottage, I'd have it done up, but . . . but he was to understand that Nessy couldn't work in the house any more. I can hear him saying in an ordinary tone, "Yes, I understand that, sir."'

He stopped speaking; then he wetted his lips a number of times before saying, 'Pour me another drink, lass, will you?'

Betty poured out a single drink and gave it to him, and he sipped at it, then looked up at her. 'It's been a day of revelations, hasn't it?' he said.

'Yes, it would seem so, Mike.' Her voice was soft.

'Do you blame me for not recognising him?'

She considered for a moment before she said, 'Yes; yes I do, Mike. I . . . I think you could have done it, at least to him personally after his father died; I mean, the man.'

'Aye, lass, I suppose I could. But when you're confronted with decisions like these they're never simple. You look back on them and you think you should have done this or that, but at the time there are so many pressures around you. Yet I suppose I could and I should have done it, because me wife was dead by then.'

'When . . . when did . . . David's mother die?'

'Four years after he was born. You know what I believe, lass? You can make yourself die, you can will yourself to die. Aw, yes, you can.' He nodded his head as she shook hers as if in denial; and then he went on, 'Once she married she hardly spoke to me. The only time she talked was in the depths of the garden there, and she said to me, "I used to love life, but I'm going to leave it early." I never forgot those words. You see she cared for me as much as I did for her.' He drew in a deep sigh now before he ended, 'When she went, I expected Frank's attitude to change towards the lad, but it never did. As I said afore, he was a good man. David was lucky to have him: anybody else might have given him hell. Well, now.' He drained his glass. 'Where do we go from here? Oh, oh, I know where you're going, to the old girl's. What do you think she'll say . . . if she doesn't already know?'

'No; as yet she doesn't know. And I haven't the slightest idea what she'll say. I can't for the moment imagine she'll want me to have the child there, but she might want me to stay with her until, as she might put it in her own words, it was time I was making other arrangements.'

'Things will never be the same again in this house, lass, once you're gone. What's he going to do about it? Our Joe.'

'There's no need for him to do anything.'

'That's very magnanimous of you, but what about the bairn? They don't call them bastards so often now but, nevertheless, there's still the stigma.'

'Well, that will be for me to deal with.'

'Oh no, no, it won't; it'll be for the bairn to deal with when he grows up. That amuses me, that viewpoint, that it doesn't matter now if you have a bairn on the side. No, it doesn't matter so much to the mother; she's not pushed into the workhouse any more; but, let me tell you, it'll still matter to the child.'

'Well, what's the remedy? Have you got one?'

'Aye; you could take my name.'

'Oh, Mike. No! No!' She turned quickly away from him and made for the door, and he called after her, 'Am I so objectionable to you?'

Swinging round, she looked towards him, saying, 'No; nor have you ever been objectionable to me; but, you know yourself, I couldn't do such a thing.'

'Aye. Aye, I suppose you're right. Aw, lass, I'm sorry. I'm sorry.' He shook his head slowly. 'I'm gonna miss you like hell . . . Will you look in afore you go?'

'Yes, I'll look in, Mike.'

She went out and closed the door quietly behind her.

A day of revelations, he had said. Indeed, indeed, it was a day of revelations.

2

Lady Ambers had just been listening to the six o'clock news on the wireless and she was now looking around the room as if in search of someone on whom she could pour out her feelings against . . . that man! All those poor men on the beaches of Dunkirk. Why couldn't they send the Navy in? What was the Navy for? All those little boats paddling backwards and forwards. It was all very heroic, but they were being sunk by the dozen. What was needed was big guns to blast those Germans to hell, then ships to gather up all those poor men. She was glad she hadn't a son. Yet in those far-off days she had longed . . . oh, how she had longed to bear a child. And she was sure it wasn't her fault that she hadn't succeeded. Yet, as she had told herself many times before, she must stop hoodwinking herself on this point: she'd had three registered husbands and quite a number of unregistered ones; it was very unlikely that they had all failed to implant a child in her. She hated the word barren. She never uttered it or thought about it, except when it crossed her mind in dreams, for who would ever dare to associate barrenness with her vivacity.

But now she was genuinely glad she'd had no son, for there would have been a grandson, and he, inheriting her own spirit, would more than likely be on that beach now; and it was such a beautiful evening, a real first day of June.

She rose from her chair and walked very slowly to the french window and gazed out over the lawn and down to the river. It was all very beautiful and peaceful. The war was not touching her; but oh, she wished it would in some way, for she was so lonely. It being Saturday, Mrs Pollard left at twelve o'clock, and Nancy at five, and she wouldn't see either of them until tomorrow at nine. They came later on a Sunday.

'Hello!'

Lady Ambers put her hands tightly to her heart before she turned round. Then, her mouth dropping into a gape, she cried, 'Betty! Oh Betty! Oh, how you startled me!'

'I'm sorry. I . . . I came in the back way.'

'I didn't expect you. Why didn't you ring? What's the matter? How did you get here anyway?'

'I came by train and took a bus to the crossroads and walked the rest of the way.'

'My goodness! And you had a case?'

'Oh, it wasn't very heavy. The rest of my things are at the station.'

'The rest?'

The old lady's mouth fell into an even wider gape and, grasping hold of Betty's hands now, she said, 'Sit down. Sit down.'

'No; you sit down.'

'Well . . . well, we'll both sit down. Now tell me; what's happened? What's brought you here, without my phoning, or begging, or praying?'

'Do you think I might have a cup of tea first?'

Lady Ambers stared at her, then said quietly, 'Yes, my dear. Come along; we'll go into the kitchen; Nancy left a tray set.' . . .

It was almost fifteen minutes later, back in the sitting-room, when, unable to contain herself any longer, she straightened her back, joined her hands on her lap and demanded, 'Well, out with it! You've left them, haven't you?' There was a note of triumph in her voice.

'Yes. Yes, you could say I've left them.'

'Years too late. Years too late. How did it happen? Tell me . . . Why didn't you bring all your things along with you? You could have got a taxi from the village or phoned Dobson to come and fetch you. Of course, as always, he'd have an excuse about a local defence volunteers' meeting or some such.'

'I . . . I don't know whether I'm going to stay or not, Lady Mary.'

There was a moment's silence while the old lady screwed up her face, and when she did speak there was a slight tremor in her voice as she said, 'What do you mean, not going to stay? You haven't gone and joined the Army?'

'No, no.'

'Then what do you mean? Out with it.'

'What I'm going to say will come as a surprise to you and no doubt a shock.'

'Well! Well! I'm waiting and I'm used to shocks. Out with it! I say.'

'I'm . . . I'm pregnant. My baby is due in October.'

Betty now watched the old lady lean back in her chair. She watched her eyes stretch, her nose stretch, her mouth stretch. For the moment she seemed utterly lost for words. But only for the moment; and then she said, 'Well! Well! So you're pregnant. I suppose at your age you look upon it as a sort of miracle. And I'm not going to ask you who

294

the father is; I'm going to tell you. It's him, isn't it? Mr Joe Remington. Oh! Oh! I've seen it coming.'

'You haven't, Lady Mary!'

'Don't contradict me, girl. Yes, I have. He hasn't come here year after year and dragged you away just to look after his wife and his father, it was because he missed you. Well, what do you want me to say? What a clever girl you are, eh?'

'No; all I want you to say is that you don't think too badly of me.'

'Oh!' Lady Mary looked as if she were endeavouring to throw herself about but was being impeded by the arms of the chair. 'Think too badly of you? You should have done that years ago; but properly and after you were married. Yet—' Her restless thrashing movement stopped and she put out her hands and gripped those of Betty, saying, 'If you had, what would I have done all these years without you? You know, you've been like a daughter to me. But mind' – her voice had taken on its strident note again – 'a very neglectful daughter, giving me only smatterings of your time, the rest to that ungrateful lot. But now' – her voice dropped again – 'you've come home and you'll be my daughter in truth and I'll have a grandchild.' She thumped her chest now with the flat of her hand. 'Yes! I'll be a grandmama. Oh! my dear. Now, now. Don't. Don't.'

Betty had slid from the chair on to her knees and, her face now buried in the old lady's lap, she gave way to a storm of pent-up weeping; and Lady Mary held her but remained quiet, staring ahead while she prayed in her own way, giving thanks to God for easing her loneliness and, moreover, for ensuring that she wouldn't die alone.

3

To Joe, the house seemed starkly empty. There was no activity in it. There was activity everywhere else, in the towns, in the whole country, in the whole world, but the house seemed to have died. For most of the day only his father and Mary were in it; he himself went out in the morning and didn't return until six o'clock, when he would call at The Cottage and pick up Martin and they would go back to the house together and have a scratch meal. And the meals *were* scratch these days.

Elaine had gone to London later on that day when so much had been revealed: she had left the house without speaking to anyone except Martin, and to him she had said, 'I'm going up to town to make arrangements. I shall come back for you.' And that was a fortnight ago.

The boy now knew that David was his uncle and that his grandfather was also David's father. It had also come to him during the past two weeks that, although he liked his Aunty Bett better than he did his mother, he was very sorry for his mother. Yet he had never felt sorry for her before. He couldn't understand these feelings, only that nobody seemed to like her, and it was a pity, because she was beautiful to look at, and she could be so nice when she liked. And too, she had always been nice to him, except when he disobeyed her about seeing Elizabeth.

He knew that when she returned it would be to take him away with her and that he should tell his father what she intended to do, yet at the same time he considered it unnecessary to do this because, as much as he would like to please her, he couldn't possibly leave his father and his grandfather and Elizabeth. And he must tell her so, but in such a way that she wouldn't be upset.

The boy now looked towards the door, and as Joe entered he greeted him: 'Hello, Father,' he said, and Joe walked over to him and ruffled his head as he said, 'Hello, son,' and again, 'Hello, there,' as he now ruffled Elizabeth's head. Then turning to Hazel and David who were seated at the other side of the tea-table, he said, 'Well, that's the end of that: Goodbye, Remington Wood Works.'

David rose slowly to his feet and went to the hob, from which he brought the teapot and poured out a cup of tea. He pushed it towards Joe, who was now sitting at the table, saying quietly, 'When this is all over you'll likely start again.'

'On what?'

David didn't answer, and Hazel asked, 'Are you going to take Baxter's offer of manager?'

Joe looked at her, then nodded his head for a moment before replying, 'Well, it goes very much against the grain, but it's either that or munitions.'

'Have they made up their mind what they are doing about the factory? Renting or buying?' asked David now.

'Renting. They're going to use it just as a storage place, but they're buying the equipment.' He lowered his head and his voice was a mutter as he said, 'I never thought it would come to this.'

'How is it they can keep going and you can't?

Again Joe looked towards Hazel. 'Big government contracts,' he said, 'and Baxter's got his fingers in so many pies. Well' – he smiled weakly – 'I suppose I'll have to swallow my pride and take it. Some would say I'm lucky to get the chance of running a similar business only twenty times bigger than my own was.' He sighed, drank the rest of his tea, then rose to his feet, saying, 'Come on, young man. Mary will be fuming at the mouth because the meal will be getting cold . . . or shrivelling up in the oven. Either way.' He looked at the table. 'You haven't been eating here, have you?'

'He just had a bite,' put in Hazel, laughing.

'I don't know where you put it.' Joe now smiled at his son, and Martin answered, 'I'm always hungry, Father. Mary says I'm a growing lad.'

They were all laughing together when the sound of a car coming in through the gates checked them, and David, moving quickly to the window, looked through the curtains, then back at Joe, and after their glance had held for a moment Joe said, 'Elaine?'

David nodded briefly, and Joe, now turning quickly to Martin, commanded, 'Stay here! Don't come up for a while.' Then he looked over his shoulder towards David, adding, 'Send him back in about an hour.'

'Father . . .'

'Look, Martin, don't argue.'

'I . . . I wasn't going to, Father, I was only going to say . . .' The boy shook his head and looked down.

'What?'

Martin glanced from one to the other; then, again shaking his head, he said, 'It doesn't matter. It doesn't matter.'

Joe went swiftly out and up the drive. A taxi was turning about. In the hall he turned towards the stairs, then went swiftly to the drawing-room and opened the door. She wasn't there. A few minutes later he unceremoniously thrust open

298

her bedroom door and saw her sitting at the dressing-table. Her coat and hat were lying on a chair to the side of her and she was dabbing her face with a pad of cotton wool.

'So you've come back.'

There was a moment's pause before she answered very calmly, 'For a short while.'

'Long or short, we've got to talk.'

He moved slowly now to the middle of the room where he could see her reflection through the mirror, and she nodded at him, saying, 'Yes, as you say, we've got to talk. But what we've both got to say to each other won't take long. I came back for one purpose, to fetch Martin.'

'The hell you did!' He laughed mirthlessly, and the sound brought her swinging round on the stool; but her voice was still calm as she repeated, 'Yes, the hell I did. If you think that I'm going to let him be brought up under the influence of your father and his half-caste son, not to mention you, you're mistaken.'

'And what grounds would you put forward for taking him away from me?'

'Adultery. Oh, I know all about your trips to Newcastle.'

His eyebrows moved up slightly before he said, 'As I do about your trips to London.'

'You can't prove anything about my trips to London; I stay with my uncle.'

'Who is stone-deaf and almost blind and whose only servant is a daily.'

She shook her head. 'You can prove nothing.'

'I can and I'm determined to do so, because I want a divorce.'

The muscles of her face under the wrinkled skin tightened; then she laughed as she exclaimed, 'You've got some hope. Let me tell you here and now I'll never divorce you, or let you divorce me. What I will do, though, is grant you a separation if I'm amply compensated for my trouble and have custody of our boy.'

'I want a divorce, Elaine, and I mean to have it.' He was spacing each word now. 'I'm about to become the father of a child and I want to give it my name.'

Her brows puckered into a frown.

'It's a wonder,' he went on, 'that with your astute little brain for digging into things, you didn't guess when Betty told you she was going to have a child.'

Slowly her entire body arched, the upper half leaning backwards as if from a blow. Her mouth, which was still beautiful, opened to its widest extent, then slowly closed, and with it her eyes narrowed almost to slits as she spat out at him, 'You . . . you and *her*? My God! The sneaking, two-faced sanctimonious bitch!'

'You could be speaking of yourself, Elaine; at least, two-faced and sneaking bitch describes you to a T; but you've never been sanctimonious, I'll grant you that.'

Her shoulders, from being pressed back, now hunched themselves forward and she thrust out her head towards him as she said, 'I hate you. Do you know that? I hate and loathe you. And this has clinched it: I'll never give you a divorce as long as you live; she can have your bastard, and good luck to her, but she'll never have your name.'

'No? I think she will. If you want to save yourself from going to court and facing a charge of murder then I think you'll see eye to eye with me over this matter, Elaine.'

Her body was still bent forward, but now she was looking at him in amazement as he said slowly, 'You shouldn't look so surprised, for you know what I'm referring to; you killed the child, didn't you?'

She stepped back against the dressing-table stool and almost overbalanced: then putting her hand out, she gripped the edge of it and lowered herself down on to the seat before saying, 'You're mad.'

'No, no, I'm not mad, and you know it. But it wouldn't be my word against yours, it would be Dr Levey's.'

Again her face was screwed up and she mouthed, 'Dr Levey?'

'Yes, Dr Levey. Perhaps you've noticed Martin hasn't screamed in his sleep for some time now. Dr Levey put him under hypnosis, and the boy relived the scene when he saw you; the black lady, he calls you. You remember the negligée? Strange; you never wore it after that night, did you? What became of it?'

She was now gripping the front neckline of her silk dress and she gave a silly laugh as she said, 'Who would believe that? Hypnotism. They can make you say anything.'

He ignored her remark, but said, 'Remember Nellie? She stated flatly that the boy would never have been able to unhook the side of the cot. And we're forgetting Betty, of course.'

The name seemed to banish her fear for the moment and she brought her teeth grinding together as she cried, 'Betty! Betty! I don't know who I hate the more, you or her.'

'And that's odd, because we're the two people who have done most for you in your life. You used her and you used me; in fact, you made use of her long before you met me.'

'And in compensation you've given her a baby, is that it? Well, I suppose she needs compensation. Did you look at her face when you were at it?'

His jaws were tight. For a moment he couldn't answer her, but when he did what he said was, 'Yes, all the while, and I found it more beautiful that I ever found yours.'

Her hand, now groping backwards, gripped the heavy-silver hand-mirror and the next minute it was flying through the air; and when it struck the mirror above the mantelpiece

301

the glass splattered about him. He didn't move, but stood perfectly still for a moment; his breath had caught in his throat and he seemed to be holding it endlessly. Then he moved slowly towards the door, all the time keeping his eyes on her where she stood supporting herself against the side of the dressing-table, and when he reached it, he said, 'Get out, and now. You'll be hearing from me through my solicitors.'

He opened the door, then closed it quickly behind him, so preventing the matching silver brush from coming in contact with his head.

He walked slowly up to the second floor. His father would have heard the commotion and would want to know the reason for it. When he opened the door he found the sitting-room empty, and when he stood in the doorway of the workshop he was amazed to see that the shelves along the side wall that had held dozens of miniature models of all descriptions were bare. Some of the models were on the long wooden carpenter's bench that ran down the centre of the room; others, he noticed, were in boxes.

His father was sitting on a high stool towards the end of the bench, and he turned and looked towards him, saying brusquely, 'Getting rid of some of these. They can raffle them; bring a little in for something or other.'

'But why?' Joe approached him slowly. 'Why now?'

'Do you need to ask? But I bear you no hard feelings, lad, not about Betty.'

'Thanks, Father.'

They stared at each other for a moment longer; then Joe hurried out and down the stairs.

It was as he crossed the hall towards the front door that he heard Elaine speaking on the telephone in the study, and as he went through the door he heard the click of the receiver.

When he was half-way down the drive he saw David hurrying towards him.

302

'I'm sorry, Joe.' David said, 'I'm on duty at half-past seven, so I've got to go. I've been looking round for Martin. He was out in the back with Elizabeth; she's just come in and said he ran off. He must have gone back to the house.'

'I've just left it; he wasn't there. Anyway, you go on; I'll look for him.'

They parted, and Joe hurried behind The Cottage and through the vegetable garden, past the greenhouses and into the woodland, calling now, 'Martin! Martin!' But he got no reply. He then spent almost ten minutes searching the grounds, and as he was nearing The Cottage again he saw a taxi entering the drive and thought to himself: That's what she was phoning for.

He entered the cottage by the back door calling, 'Is he there, Hazel?' And both Hazel and Elizabeth came hurrying from the sitting-room.

'No. No, Joe.'

He was on the point of asking Elizabeth if Martin had said anything out of the ordinary to her before he had left, when the wail of a siren brought their eyes upward, and Hazel cried fearfully, 'Oh, dear. It can't be an air-raid, surely; not in daylight.'

'Get into the shelter!'

Joe was reaching out to bustle them through the room when the back door was thrust open, and they turned to look at Martin standing there, panting.

'It's . . . it's the siren, Father.'

'Where do you think you've been?'

Joe almost sprang on him and gripping him by the shoulders he shook him, demanding, 'Why did you run off like that?'

'I . . . I . . .'

'Well?'

303

'If . . . if you'll stop shaking me I'll . . . I'll tell you.' The answer was so unexpected that Joe took his hands from his son's shoulders and stared at him, while the boy stared hard back at him before answering defiantly, 'I . . . I wanted to see mother . . . just to see her.'

'Well, did you?'

'No. I mean yes. She . . . she saw me from her bedroom window when I was crossing the drive. She shouted to me to stay there, that she was coming down immediately.'

'Well?' Joe now watched the boy shake his head before allowing it to droop on to his chest.

'I didn't stay; I ran into the garden.'

'Why did you do that?' It was a gentle question and Martin answered quietly, 'I . . . I didn't want to go with her – she was making arrangements to take me with her – but . . . but I thought I'd just like to see her.'

Joe's hand went slowly out and cupped the boy's head, and now he asked quietly, 'But where have you been? I've searched the whole place, shouting for you.'

Martin's head remained down while he answered, 'I know; I . . . I heard you. But . . . but she came after me into the garden. I hid behind the thicket near the fence. And I saw her going up the wood path. She . . . she was dressed for going away.'

The wail of the siren had died, but now the sound of the car on the drive outside caused Martin to lift his head and the eyes of the others to look towards the sitting-room.

It was Elizabeth who ran through the room, to return after a moment and say, 'It's a taxi. It's gone.'

At this point Joe heaved a deep sigh of relief, then said briskly, 'Come on; let's get into the shelter.'

As he again went to hustle them from the room there came the sound of nearby anti-aircraft fire, which was followed almost immediately by a distant but nevertheless ominous thud.

'My God! they're at the town.'

Soon they were all scampering down the back garden and into the air-raid shelter; at least, all but Joe, who stopped at the top of the steps and looked down at the three faces staring up at him and said, 'Now stay put. Don't worry about David; he'll be all right. I must go up to the house to see to Father. Even though there's no hope of getting the old fool to leave that floor, nevertheless . . .'

His words were cut off by another earth-shattering thud, this time closer by.

Joe looked up into the sky and as he heard the unmistakable drone of planes he exclaimed, 'God! they're almost overhead.'

'Come in, Joe!' Hazel screamed, at the same time grabbing hold of Joe's trouser leg. But before he could move either one way or the other the earth gave a mighty shudder and he almost fell backwards on top of them. A second later they were all huddled together in a heap in the narrow space of the shelter, with both he and Hazel lying on top of Elizabeth and Martin.

After what seemed an eternity they slowly raised themselves. Joe didn't speak: he was filled with a great fear, the fear of going up the three steps and of what he would see when he emerged from the shelter.

It was Hazel who said, 'Those last two were near. Why would they want to drop bombs out here, three miles or more from the docks?'

Joe made no reply, but slowly he went up the steps and into the open.

He had hardly straightened up before he cried aloud, 'The house! Hazel. The house!' and then he was tearing over the vegetable garden, through the gap in the hedge and on to the drive. But before he rounded the bend he knew what he would find, for he couldn't see the sky for the cloud of dust. When he reached the rubble that had been his house he folded his arms tightly around his waist and hugged himself in an agony of despair as he whimpered, 'Oh! Father. Father. Oh no! No! Father. Father. Oh my God! No, no.'

The house had taken a direct hit and the blast had spread the rubble to three times its area. He looked down at the block of masonry at his feet, the clematis leaves still clinging to it. The spire of the observatory was wedged downwards like an ice-cream cone in the forks of an oak tree. Part of the wall of the drawing-room was standing, the mantelshelf protruding above the rubble, and above it, hanging at an angle, the picture of a Dutch interior. He could only make out the frame, but in his mind's eye he saw the housewife and the child and the wonderful perspective of the tiled floor.

A burst of flame to his right brought his head slowly round to where the kitchen had stood . . . Mary would be at that end.

He wasn't aware that anyone had joined him until he heard Martin whimper, 'Oh! Grandpa. Grandpa.'

Joe turned slowly and looked speechlessly at Hazel and Elizabeth. The girl was crying and for a moment he envied her: he wanted to cry, he wanted to fling himself down on the ground and beat his fists into the earth. Oh! Father. Father.

Why hadn't he insisted on his father's living downstairs? But would that have made any difference now? Why hadn't he stayed with him a little longer this evening and helped him pack away the efforts of a lifetime? Well, there had been Elaine. *Elaine. Elaine.* Always Elaine. Blast her! Blast her to hell! He recalled the look on Mike's face: it was as if he had known what was coming.

They all turned slowly away from the smoking rubble and looked down the drive from where was coming the sound of a heavy vehicle and also the ringing of an ambulance bell.

The twilight was deepening when they lifted the last piece of timber from across Mike. The beams supporting the tower must have struck him immediately. He was all grey from the hair on his head to his slippers. Even the blood from his neck, which had soaked his clothes, was dusted with grey.

It was Joe and David, with the assistance of two Local Defence Volunteers, who carried him over the tangle of debris and laid him on the grass verge.

As if in respect, the men walked away towards the ambulance, to leave the father and son together for a short time. What they didn't know was that there were two sons looking down on their father, and it was David who spoke. His voice deep, yet scarcely above a whisper, he said, 'It's the first time I've touched him in my life.'

Joe said nothing. He was weighed down with sadness, yet David's words pierced it with a thread of condemnation: 'It's the first time I've touched him in my life.' How would he have felt if his father hadn't acknowledged him? David hadn't known that he was the son of the boss until after his supposed father had died, when Frank Brooks had left him the truth in a letter.

He himself had come to the truth through his mother. He was eight years old when he knew that David was his half-brother.

A voice behind them said now, 'If you don't mind, sir,' and both he and David stood aside to allow the two men to lift the twisted body on to a stretcher; and they had reached the ambulance with it before Joe, seeming to come to himself, hurried to them and asked, 'Where are you taking him?'

'To the hospital mortuary, sir, at St Margaret's.'

He nodded at them, then watched them close the doors on the man he had loved . . . and pitied.

307

As the ambulance drove away he turned to where David was still standing and he said quietly, 'Don't hold any bitterness against him, David. He thought of you. Most of the time he thought of you. It lay heavy on his conscience. He watched you; he had pride in you. You know he would have done things for you years ago if you would have let him. Don't be bitter.'

'How would you feel in my shoes?'

'Much the same as you are feeling now, but the past is something that can't be relived. What we can do, though, in the future is to let it be known what we are to each other.'

David made no reply; he simply turned to look towards where the kitchen had been and muttered, 'We'd better find Mary.'

4

Four days later they buried Mike. There had been quite a number of people waiting in the cemetery, and the little chapel had been full. Joe and David stood side by side at the open grave; Martin stood on Joe's right, and next to him was Betty.

When the first clods of earth were thrown on the coffin, slowly, one after the other, they turned away. But instead of returning to the cortège, they followed the minister down the centre drive of the cemetery to where Mary was now being borne to her place of rest . . .

Then it was over and they were in the car again being driven back to The Cottage.

For the last four nights Joe and Martin had slept in the tiny spare room in The Cottage, and for the past three nights Betty had put up at an hotel in Fellburn.

They were all silent until they entered the sitting-room, and then in a burst of activity Hazel set about making the tea and talking rapidly as she did so.

'Get your things off and sit up; it's ready.' She pointed to the table that was set for a cold meal. 'The kettle won't be a minute. Elizabeth, take Miss Betty's things. David, fill that scuttle, will you? The fire's getting low. What a change in the weather this last two days.'

When there came a knock on the door Hazel stopped her prattling and looked towards it, and then at David, saying, 'See who that is, will you?'

David opened the door to a uniformed boy, who offered him a buff-coloured envelope.

'It's . . . it's for a Mrs Remington. The house is down but I thought . . .'

David turned and handed the telegram to Joe and he, after staring at it for a moment, opened it and read it. 'Tried to ring you. No reply. Uncle T worried. L.'

'Is there any reply?'

Joe looked at the boy, then said, 'No. No.' He now handed the telegram to David; then, after a moment, he said, 'What does it mean?' and for answer David said quietly, 'But she returned to London, didn't she?'

'Yes, yes.' Joe nodded slowly. 'She took a taxi.' He looked at the telegram again. 'Uncle T worried. L.' He knew who L. was. And it wouldn't be Uncle Turnbull who was worried; no doubt he had gone to the uncle's and found she wasn't there . . .

When he raised his eyes and met David's questioning stare, he shook his head and said, 'No, no; she definitely took a taxi.' He now turned swiftly towards Martin. 'Did you see your mother get into the taxi?'

'No, Father.'

'When did you last see her?'

'When . . . well, I told you, when she was going back towards the house dressed for out.'

'Dear God!' Joe turned his head to the side and looked down towards the floor. What if she hadn't got into the taxi and gone into the house again! They had only looked for two people, his father and Mary. Ella had

310

escaped, for it was her day off.

'Whose taxi would it be? Fowler's?'

Joe lifted his head and looked at David, who nodded at once, saying, 'Either him or Rowland's, whichever was available. Well, we'd better get on to them and see. You can ring from the call-box at the junction.'

'Yes, yes.' Joe now looked at Betty. She was standing with her fingers across her lips. He did not speak to her but they exchanged a look, and then he went out, followed by David.

In answer to Joe's enquiries, Fowler's said they'd had no call from Mrs Remington. But Rowland's said they'd had a call, but the driver hadn't been able to get an answer and then the siren had gone and he thought it better to make tracks for home.

'So he didn't pick up Mrs Remington?' Joe cast a glance back to where David was standing holding open the door, and when the answer came, 'No; I've told you,' he slowly replaced the receiver. And stepping out of the box he gripped a handful of his hair as he said, 'She must be in there.'

Three hours later they brought her out. She must have been in the hall when the bomb struck. But for the dust that covered her she appeared to be unharmed. She still had her handbag over one arm and her hands were encased in grey silk gloves. A beam lay across her legs but the upper part of her body had been protected by the section of the stairs that had acted as a lean-to over her, and this had prevented the masonry from crushing her altogether. It was strange that a matter of a few yards away Mary's body had been unmercifully blasted, yet Elaine looked apparently untouched . . .

The following day when Joe stood by the coffin in the chapel of rest and looked down on the face that had once enthralled him, he was glad that her beauty hadn't been marred; she would have hated that. All his thoughts concerning her now were guilt-ridden, and he resented this feeling, yet could do nothing about it. And he said so as he and Betty walked away from the undertaker's chapel.

'If I had divorced her I'd have gone on loathing her and felt justified inside, for, one way and another, she had led me a hell of a life; but here I am all the time asking myself, was I to blame in the first place for bringing her here, which to her was a foreign environment. I'm even viewing her killing of the child now as compassionate; I'm seeing her action from Father's point of view. And although I know that she would likely be here now if she hadn't tried to take Martin from me, I can't help but see her point of view. It's unreasonable, it's hypocritical, for death doesn't wipe away people's meanness, cruelty or physical torture, and I know this, yet here I am swamped with remorse.'

'You're not the only one,' replied Betty. 'She was my sister; I knew her longer than you did, Joe. From when she could first walk she showed selfish traits. As a child, everything had to go her way or else life for those around her became trying, to say the least; and even then, she could make you feel that you were in the wrong. She made use of me all my life, and there were times out of number when she was cruel to me, mentally cruel. The scars of a physical beating heal but never those of the mind. There were times when I hated her, and now I've got to confess that there was no time when I ever loved her. Other women couldn't love her, either: she was a threat to them, and she enjoyed hurting them through their men. Yet, knowing all this I, like you, am consumed at this moment with guilt, more so because of my deception this last year. Until now I had thought I wasn't doing anybody any harm, that she didn't want you and I did. Now I don't know what to think.'

At this point Joe caught hold of her arm and pulled it

312

tightly against his side as he said, 'That's one thing you need have no regrets about. And we have to face up to the fact that we're in an emotional stage; but it will pass, please God. Dr Pearce said something to me this morning to that effect. He knew the situation between us, has done for years. "You're going to feel hellish about this," he said. "For weeks it will appear as though she was an angel; but then reality will take over again."'

'He said that?'

He nodded: 'Yes, he did. I didn't take much heed of it at the time, but now I feel he was speaking from experience. He said it happens frequently with women who have looked after parents, given their life to them, then when the old people die they are eaten up with remorse and guilt for the thoughts they have harboured against them. He said it's a most natural reaction.'

'I only hope so.'

They were walking by the river now and, gazing down at the path, he said quietly, 'You told me that you promised to stay with the old lady. Does that still hold good?'

It was some seconds before she answered, 'Yes, Joe; I'm afraid it must. She . . . she welcomed me with open arms when, under the circumstances, she could have shown me the door, being of a generation that didn't hold with looseness.'

'Looseness!' His look was accusing.

'Yes, that's what she could have termed it, looseness, although she didn't. I promised to stay with her until she dies. And . . . and what I'm about to tell you now makes no difference, but I just want you to know how she considers me: she made a will, you know, some months ago, leaving me the cottage and' – her voice dropped to a whisper – 'the bulk of her money, which is a considerable amount.'

When he made no comment she turned and looked at him, and he said, slowly, 'I'm glad for you.'

'Oh, Joe! I'm in a cleft stick, but . . . but you can get me out of it.'

'I don't see how.'

They walked on, and it was some seconds before she said, 'I was on the phone to her this morning. She . . . she wants you and Martin to come there, too, and to make it your home.'

He stopped dead and confronted her.

'Live out there with her? Oh' – he tossed his head – 'she wouldn't tolerate that; and I don't know whether I could, either.'

'She would not only tolerate it, she would love it. I understand her, and I'm telling you, Joe, she would love to have you in the house. And Martin too.'

'But what about my work?'

'You didn't want to manage Baxter's place anyway, did you? And the town's quite near, you'd find something else; in fact, as things are you're likely to get something more important that managing a box factory.'

They walked on again, and then he said quietly, 'I'd have to see, Betty. I'd have to see about that. At the moment I only know one thing: I love you and I need you. Oh, how I need you. And I want to marry you.'

5

⟫

The sun was glinting on the river. Martin was sitting on the river bank, his feet dangling an inch above the water, and glancing to the side of him where Betty lay resting on her elbow in the grass, he said, 'Would it be possible to have a sculler on here, Aunty Bett?'

'A sculler? I don't see why not, though I don't know how far you could go without bumping into a rock. Still, this part's clear.'

'I like it here, Aunty Bett.' The boy's voice was quiet.

'I'm glad of that, Martin.'

'I miss Grandpa, Aunty Bett.'

'I do, too, Martin.'

'And . . . I've been lonely since Elizabeth was evacuated. It was only last week, but it seems years ago.'

'She'll write.'

'It won't be the same.'

'Do you like Lady Mary?'

'Oh yes.' The boy laughed now. 'I think she's fun. She punched me in the chest this morning and told me I'd have to take boxing lessons.'

'Boxing lessons!' Betty laughed. 'Why boxing lessons?'

'She said because she always admired boxers.'

Their laughter joined now, and Betty turned her head to see the lady in question sitting in her chair, with Joe to the side of her, and she sent up a silent prayer that Lady Mary's acidity would be watered down this afternoon.

And undoubtedly it was, but questionably, for she was saying now, 'If I'd had a daughter I'd have wished her to be like Betty: plain, so that she wouldn't have outshone me even in middle age, and sensible, no damn nonsense. But, of course, she wouldn't have been: she'd have been beautiful and selfish and spoilt and I would be sitting here now bemoaning her neglect of me, and she'd be waiting for me to die in order to get my money. Oh! Oh! don't look so disapproving, for the world is full of mercenary people, and what we won't own up to is they are part of ourselves, our offspring.' She became still for a moment, plucking at a lace ruffle on the front of her gown, then she smoothed the long skirt down over her knees before she went on, 'It would appear that there is going to be a tug-of-war between us, Mr Remington, and I'm sure neither you nor I want that. Yet you are bent on marrying Betty and making her your wife, and rightly so, yes, rightly so, because she is carrying your child. For myself, I want her, at least partly, for a number of selfish reasons; I want her company, but more so I . . . I don't want to die alone. However, there is another side to it: I want to give her security; I want to see her with a place of her own. And mind' – she now wagged her finger at him – 'I saw to this before I had any real suspicion of what was between you both, because I didn't want her to go on being a slave to stuffy old women. I'm not a stuffy old woman. No, I'm not. So what are we going to do about it . . .? No, wait; I haven't finished yet.' She now pressed her buttocks back on the wicker chair, straightened her back, turned her head away from his and looked down towards the river bank to where Betty and Martin were sitting, and she said quietly, 'It would give me the greatest pleasure to have you live in this house, permanently, because a home is not really a home unless there's a man at the head of it . . . When I lost my third husband I began to wander from hotel room to hotel room, and when I finally settled in this cottage, with the hope that it would be an inducement to Betty to join me, I pictured our life going along happily together. And undoubtedly it would have done, but without the zest that the presence of a male gives to a house. It is the male that makes the family in more ways than one, and so, Mr Remington, if you would care to come and be the head of this house I would welcome you, for then in my dotage I could imagine that I have not only a daughter but a son, and . . . and grandchildren.'

A short period of time followed before she turned and looked at him; and now, his face breaking into a slow smile, he said gently, 'What can I say but thank you, Lady Mary?'

'Well, that's settled then. Huh! Huh! After all the worry, fuss and bother it's as simple as that. Well! well!' Her voice rose. 'So what you sitting there for, with Betty worrying her guts out? Get yourself away!'

As he rose to his feet he nipped at his lip, but his eyes were bright as he looked down on her, until she said, 'I understand you have a coloured half-brother. Well, he'll be welcome here too. I don't believe in the sins of the father, et cetera.'

His face was straight but his eyes held a tender light as he again said, 'Thank you,' then added, 'so very much, and I hope you will live to . . . to find me a good son.'

She made no reply, only champed her lips until he was walking away, when she stopped him with her strident call: 'Is there any chance of your getting any petrol on the side? I like a trip out now and then!'

317

He turned fully round to face her, and as his body shook with laughter her own face crinkled and, her mouth wide, she cried, 'Well, they're all at it, so why not us? See about it!'

Betty was waiting for him; and Martin, too, was on his feet, and he put his arms around them both and hugged them to him, and Betty asked softly, 'It's all right?'

'Yes, yes, it's all right, except that . . . that I'm expected to join the black market. There's a price to be paid for everything.'

Joe now pushed Martin gently from him, saying, 'Go up and sit with Lady Mary,' and when the boy ran off he took Betty's hand and led her along the river bank until they were hidden from the house by a group of trees; and there, taking her in his arms, he held her tightly and, looking into her eyes, he said softly, 'It's all too good to be true. At the moment I can't see an obstacle on the horizon; but if one should appear in the future, and I'm serious about this, promise me one thing.'

'Anything. Anything, Joe.'

'Promise me you'll never lock your door on me.'

'Oh! Joe. Joe.'

'Stop laughing.'

'I can't. Don't lock my door on you . . . oh! Joe.'

As her laughter died away she saw revealed in his face, perhaps for the first time, the true depth of his feeling for her. And there rose in her a new estimation of herself: she had the power of someone who was beloved. An ingredient of love is the fear of loss, and it was this fear that was making her man say, don't lock your door on me. She was now a woman who had the power to lock her door on a man . . . if she wanted to . . .

Men were strange. Life was strange, for she felt in this moment she was holding both Mike and him to her. Both had suffered from women locking their doors on them, and in Joe's case it must have been a threat to his manhood, a

318

blow to his ego. But the very fact that he had now voiced his fear made her feel . . . what? Desirable?

Yes, desirable.

She put her mouth on his and held him tightly until lack of breath and the uncomfortable mound of her abdomen made her draw away.

And now, holding each other at arms' length, they both laughed; and when their laughter grew louder, Martin and Lady Mary looked at each other. Then the boy impulsively caught the old lady's hand and as she wagged it their laughter joined, but was quickly smothered, as if they were sharing a secret joke.

THE END